# PANDAEMONIUM

# PANDAEMONIUM

## Ben Macallan

SOLARIS

First published 2012 by Solaris
an imprint of Rebellion Publishing Ltd,
Riverside House, Osney Mead,
Oxford, OX2 0ES, UK

*www.solarisbooks.com*

ISBN: 978 1 78108 052 8

10 9 8 7 6 5 4 3 2 1

A CIP catalogue record for this book is available from the
British Library.

Designed & typeset by Rebellion Publishing

Printed in the US

*For Karen.*

*This second half of a still unfinished story.*

# CHAPTER ONE

THEY WERE GOING to hang my boyfriend up by his heels and bleed all the life out of him, and they thought I'd want to *watch*.

No. Almost all of that is true, but none of it is right.

No. Almost all of that is right, but none of it is true. He was not my boyfriend, and it wasn't his life they were taking, not really. Just his blood. And they just assumed that I'd stay, because – well, it was a privilege they granted me. I should be grateful, apparently.

They were his parents, and they thought I should be grateful.

No.

\*   \*   \*

ACTUALLY, THEY WERE feeling grateful to me, in so far as they could. In that cool, distancing way that people do when they're that much older and wealthier and socially significant, superior in every way including manners. The way a lord might be grateful to his groom, *here's a sovereign for your trouble*, or a billionaire to her secretary, *take the day off, dear, you deserve it*: graciously, generously, affordably.

*Stay and watch.*


NO.


THEY OWED ME, and they knew it. I had a strange, wayward love for their strange, wayward son, and they knew that too. To them, that didn't matter. They would have made the same offer if I'd been a traitor bought and paid for, or a servant, or a bystander. *We sought him so long, and could not find him; you brought us to him. Thank you. Stay and watch.*

And Jordan was terrified, trapped at last, and alone except for me – and even so.

"No," I said, trying to make it sound flat and final, determined, strong. Trying not to sound terrified myself, saying no to this man.

Even *man* is wrong there – this figure, this Power, this god I should say, perhaps – but he looked human enough, at the moment, in this world. And very male, he did look very male. And middle-aged but well-kept, no hint of grey at the temples. Well, you wouldn't expect that, would you? *Mature* might be a better way to say it. Not quite untouched by time. Experienced, familiar with loss; a little sad, a little solemn.

Not mortal. Never that. Even in this skin, and even if you were mortal yourself and had no inkling that there was any other kind of person out there: even then, you couldn't possibly convince yourself that this was somebody acquainted with the possibility of old age, decay and death.

His son was dead, his younger son, recently and appallingly, and even so.

His older son was upstairs. With his mother, this man's wife. Because I'd called them, given them directions, kept Jordan here till they came.

I was glad to be dealing with the father, although he scared me so. The mother would be harder. Harder to say no to.

"No," I said, "I won't stay. I-I can't. I'm sorry..."

"He'd want to see you here."

"No. I don't think he ever wants to see me again, after what I just –"

"Afterwards. He'll want to see you, afterwards. It'll be different, then."

That would be then. This was now. Right now he was upstairs with his mother. He must be terrified; he must be hating me. I was sure of that, at least.


THIS WAS MY cottage, my hideaway, place of greatest safety. No good to me now.

I'd said everything I could to the guy, everything that mattered. *No*, I'd said. Time and again I'd said it.

That was enough to be getting on with, enough for him to think about. Besides, he was going to be busy any minute now.

So I got on. I turned on my heel and walked away from him.

I don't suppose that happens very often. Who says no to Pluto, to Dis, Lord of the Underworld? Who walks away from Death himself?

He isn't Death, of course, in the greater scheme of things, but he might as well be. It's a distinction without a difference.

Except for the breeding, the fertility that was another of his aspects. The sons.

Son, now. It used to be a joke, almost, that Death had two boys to inherit when the time came. An heir and a spare. It wasn't ever funny; now it wasn't even true.

He was master of Hell, one of the senior Powers, one of the immortal greats; and I turned my back and refused what he was asking. What he was offering.

Walked out of my cottage, out of my home, away from my last best hope. Because I couldn't bear to stay, to see the consequences of what I'd done.

I'm not proud of it. There's a lot I've done that I'm none too proud of, but that moment went at the top of the list, right then.

Right by the door there, where there should have been roses growing? Was an old sack, dumped and hanging open. Inside were ropes and shackles, hooks and blades.

The sack was probably traditional. They weren't sack people, by and large. The rest, the contents – well.

I glanced up at my precious balcony, and shuddered.

And kept walking. Out onto the towpath, where my boat should have been moored and wasn't.

Past the end of the lane, where my bike should have been parked up and wasn't.

And on upriver, because that was the way I was facing and it felt technically harder, moving against the stream, and I deserved it. I'd done a great and a terrible thing, and nothing should come easy after that.

Nothing about this was easy already. I was crying, I realised, after a bit. People were staring. Not that many people, this time on a workday morning, but still. People enough to take note of a mad girl plunging down the path, hands in pockets, scowling, shoulders hunched, not stopping. Not for anyone. Weeping as she went.

One or two of them did stop on their own account, did try to stop me: "Excuse me, are you – ? Can I – ?"

Yes I was, and no they couldn't. I just ploughed onward, ignored them utterly, brushed them off if they dared to touch.

I didn't even need to reach for my Aspect. This much I could do just as myself: there's not much that's easier than self-pity, but self-contempt can crown it every time.

I couldn't scrub his face out of my mind. Just after I'd cut away his amulet, his only protection; just as he realised what I'd done, just before I left him sitting stunned in the bath there and went downstairs to let his parents in.

That moment. Trust betrayed. He was naked and defenceless, I was booted and spurred and should have been his wall, his rock, his knight and guardian. It was what he expected of me, what he depended on.

Instead I opened the door to what he feared most. He knew it figuratively, he could see it, his amulet in my hand; he understood that I was about to do it literally.

I was still hoping that he would understand why, that too. But hope doesn't cut it, can't stand against guilt. There's a hierarchy of emotions, like a periodic table, where some weigh heavier than others. Well, hell, of course there is. We build our interior lives to match the world we know, the way we know it works.

Well, hell. Hell needed its young prince. I'd just delivered him, and now I was running away.


No.


IT WASN'T A decision that I made, it was a state that overtook me. Took me a while even to realise that I was walking slower. That I'd stopped crying.

That I'd stopped moving, that it was only the river that ran by me now. Not the scenery, not the trees and the moored boats. I stood there in the path and stared at the water for a while, maybe hoping for a naiad to erupt and attack me; I could just use a good fight, a good excuse. It didn't happen and didn't happen, and in the end, inevitably, I turned and went back.

It was my house, best approximation of my home. He was... well, he was Jordan. Best approximation of my boyfriend. His parents were my guests, come at my invitation. Whichever way you slice that, I should be there.

And the worst should be over by now, so I could go on lashing myself for not being there. Guilt doesn't like to let up.

Back I went, then. My boots had never felt so heavy, my skin had never crept so cold, but I did go back.


THERE WAS NO body hanging from the balcony, head down and bleeding out. I'd gone far enough, been slow enough, missed the main event.

No sodden spot beneath the balcony, no mud of blood, no spillage. Perhaps they caught it all in a bucket, perhaps they kept it. Perhaps it had a use. I didn't know.

I could ask, I supposed. If I could speak.

If he could.

I found his parents in my little sitting-room. Sitting. It all seemed almost normal, almost human, until you remembered who they were. You don't think of Pluto and Penelope doing normal human things. Sitting down. Waiting. Things like that.

Contentment sat on them both like a layer of light. She almost smiled at me; he cocked a wry eyebrow.

"He's upstairs," he said. "Getting dressed."

Keeping them waiting. It really was very nearly human, the whole scene. If you didn't know quite how long they'd been waiting for this, quite what they'd paid for the moment.

Quite what he'd paid, what they'd taken from

him, what they'd given in return. The Overworld can be like that: wealth and power and immortality, sure, but it all comes at a price. Even if you're born to it, as Jordan was. Me, I was just as glad to be human yet, albeit human-with-benefits. And Jordan of course had clung and clung to the last precious moment of his humanity, stepping out of normal time to do it, holding himself that one day short of eighteen for years uncounted, only to avoid his birthright. This.

"I'm glad you came back," his father said. "Go on up, I expect he'll be glad of the company. It's not his parents that he needs right now."

That was... unexpectedly insightful. I nodded – well, actually, I almost bowed. It was hard not to; they held such authority, just sitting there on my sofa side by side. Paisley fabric and white plaster under a low beamed ceiling, and they still looked enthroned.

The stairs creaked beneath my boots. Never mind what my skin was doing, there was no point in creeping now.

The bedroom was empty. I found him where I'd left him, in the bathroom with the door wide open. Not in the bath, not now. Not conspicuously getting dressed, either, or not in any hurry about it. He'd pulled on a pair of jeans, but was still bare-chested and barefoot, standing with his back to the landing, looking into the mirror on the cabinet door.

It's a small cabinet; I don't need much in the way of medicines. Or mirrors. I know what I look like. It's a side-effect of what I am, that we have a better idea of ourselves. Or you could say that the other way round, that we're not so good at self-deception.

Whichever. Small mirror, in a dark corner; I couldn't see what he was seeing. Only the lean back and the smooth shaved skull, and...

"Jay?"

My voice had a shiver in it, that I heard and hated. He'd need me to be strong now if ever, confident, certain of the right. It was a new world now, for both of us. Hand in hand, we could face it down and find the joy in it. There did have to be joy. Yes.

If he hesitated a fraction before he turned, it was only for effect. He knew I was there. But then, if he was looking in the mirror it was only habit, unless it was vanity. He knew what he looked like, better than I did; how could he help it, now? It's a hierarchy, and he'd just overleaped me by a long, long way.

He turned, and now I knew what he looked like too.

He'd always been pale, it was the only reason his white eyebrows didn't stand out more startling than they were. Now he was – well, bloodless. Colour would come back, I knew; his brother had gone this same route before him, and he'd been golden. Suntan? Did they tan, could they, in the mere sun? Helltan, I guess you could call it else.

The gash in his throat gaped red and hot and dry. I wanted to offer him a safety-pin, to stitch it all together. A whole pincushion of safety-pins.

I had no idea what they had put into his body, in lieu of blood. Hellsand, or something like it. Perhaps that would come to account for the golden glow; perhaps he'd be tanned from the inside out, no need for sunshine here.

He looked at me, and for a moment I thought he had nothing to say. Then I realised that his lips were moving lightly, only that there was no sound. Like a TV with the mute on.

I saw him realise it himself, and figure out the problem; and lift a hand to cover the wide hole in his throat, like a stoner covering the choke-hole in a bong to channel the flow of smoke.

He said, "Desi. Why are you still here?"

It wasn't his voice. I wouldn't have recognised it on the phone, this rough grating difficult sound, picking its cold, careful way from one word to the next; I didn't recognise it even face to face. It was like he was lipsynching, live and close-up.

"I came back," I said, which was really a confession: *I went away*. "Of course I came back." Defensively. "I couldn't leave you to go through all of this alone, everything that's coming now. You've been alone too long already." *You've got me now* – that's what I wanted him to hear and remember and think about. Not the way I'd left him to go through the worst bit on his own.

Especially not the way I'd forced him into it.

Sometimes? You just don't get what you want. Sometimes you don't stand a chance.

He drew air in, pushed it out again; you couldn't call it breathing. Then he shaped the air into sounds again, and you could hardly call it talking, but the words came out savagely clear. "You're not safe here."

I said, "Your parents won't harm me. I think I offended them, a bit, maybe, but..." But I was still the girl who had handed their precious remaining son back into their care. They owed me for that, and they knew it. They'd still be grateful. Gratefulish.

*Noblesse oblige*: they'd enjoy that, being the obligated nobles. Patronising the peasantry.

"Not my parents," he said. "You should run. Seriously."

"What? Why? Jordan, whatever comes at me now, your parents are downstairs. We don't need to run anywhere." *Not any more.*

"My parents," he said, "won't lift a finger. However grateful you think they ought to be."

Oh. Finally, I was beginning to understand him. I said, "Jordan..."

"If you run, right *now*," he said, "they might stop me coming after you. No promises, but I'm guessing they won't let me out of their sight for a while. For a *little* while."

"Jay, no. Don't..."

"Did they pay you?" he asked, almost conversationally, if a raw vicious flaying can be conversational. "Thirty pieces of silver? Like that, is it? Were they the ones you were working for all this time, your secret employer?"

"No. Not that. Not any of that." I felt sorry for them, though I couldn't conceivably say so. "They'd had enough heartache, don't you think, losing Ash that way? And you couldn't run for ever, it wasn't doing you any good..."

I wasn't doing myself any good, I knew that; this wasn't an argument you could win by arguing. Only, I wasn't prepared. I hadn't expected to find us arguing at all. I'd come back to hold his hand, to stand by him, to see him through.

"You think this has been good for me, do you? *This?*"

His hand would be as hot and dry as his voice, wind over sand. If I reached to touch him now, I realised, he would tear me apart. Very literally, and very quickly.

On the thought, I was reaching for my Aspect – and then deliberately not doing that. Letting it go again, letting it fray out of my grip; facing him as I was, human and nakedly guilty.

It was only a moment, but he'd seen. He said, "You'll need that. It won't do you any good, but you'll need it anyway."

Of course it wouldn't do me any good. I was a human with a gift, but he was a true immortal, a prince of Hell newly come into his power. Tinfoil armour would be about as much use against a crossbow bolt.

That wasn't why I'd set my Aspect aside, though. I just didn't want anything between us except the truth: the core of him and the core of me. Only one of us was truly human now, with all the limits that implies. All the fears and weaknesses and loss. The part of him that was raging and betrayed, the Jay I'd known and slept with, the Jay who'd maybe loved me, that boy was human too – but that was only an echo now, a memory, a false step off an inevitable path.

Right now, that boy wanted to kill me for making a man of him – but he was torn, still half in love and half himself, not a boy who went around killing people. The other half, the man, the prince of Hell, oh, he would without a second thought – but he had no reason to. He had power in his fingertips and fire in his bones, all thanks to me.

Between them they were giving me the chance to run, while they both knew full well that they'd chase me. Chase me and catch me, that too. Not in a cat-and-mouse way, they weren't playing games here; he was at war with himself, my all-too-human boy, while the ascended immortal was barely more than an audience and a vehicle for now. That wouldn't last. My Jay would be subsumed, swallowed up, assimilated – and then, if I'd run far enough and fast enough, if I'd been clever, I'd be all right. Maybe. Jay loved me and wanted to kill me for what I'd done to him, both at once; if I was lucky, Jordan wouldn't care.

But I really did need to go now, while Jay could still hang on to enough of himself to let me, before the cold rage got the better of him.

"We need to talk," I said; and then, "Keep your phone charged. I'll text you."

And then I turned on my heel and was out of there, down the stairs and into the day with not a moment wasted, not a word of farewell to his waiting parents, nothing.

# CHAPTER TWO

ONTO THE TOWPATH and turn downstream as though that would be easier, as though it would carry me along. No boat, no bike; so one foot in front of the other and just run, all too literally. I wasn't sure if that was what he'd meant – Jay himself had used buses mostly, when he was being a teenage runaway, until I caught up with him – but this was my thing. I always was a runner. Even when I was a kid, when I was Fay: cross-country champion, school and county.

Now? I could run all day. I could probably run for ever.

That day, it felt like I might need to.

I was shrugging on my Aspect as I went, like a girl shrugs on a coat: something well-worn and familiar, shaped to her body by time and use and care. I didn't need to think about it, even. I had hard running ahead of me and a hard threat behind; I needed all the help I could get.

Black denim and boots is not the ideal running kit, but that didn't matter now. I wouldn't be working up a sweat. Not with my Aspect on. Henley to London is forty-odd miles by road; along the river path it's probably fifty. Even so. No sweat.

Having an Aspect is – well, not like anything else. It's not at all like having an old coat, unless that coat is a suit of armour with biofeedback loops and seven-league boots beneath and the aggression of a tank besides. It's really not like shrugging into an enhanced levelled-up version of yourself, or swapping your body for a Terminator's, or having your system flushed with adrenalin on demand, or any of the other shoddy comparisons we come up with, those times we find ourselves trying to explain. We all do it, every daemon comes up with helpless similes; and all of them are honest, and none of them is true.

Just, here I am, a healthy young and human woman, with all the limits that implies – and I reach for my Aspect and not one of those limits applies to me. It is not at all like having godhood as an optional extra, but I can run all day and not break a sweat, I can break steel chains and push my way through walls of brick, I can free-dive for a frighteningly long time without breathing and seduce adolescents just with a glance and...

Well, actually I could probably seduce the adolescents anyway, without a hint of Aspect; that comes free under "healthy young woman." But the rest of it is a bit special, and there is still more besides. This happens every time; you start out trying to describe what an Aspect is and you end up with a list of symptoms rather than a diagnosis.

Mostly what it is, though, is real. And accessible. And earned. We call it a gift, maybe, but that's just the politeness of the mortal to the Overworld. Most times an Aspect isn't even a tip, given in gratitude for service; it's wages, payment in kind.

Wages of sin, as often as not. Never ask a daemon what they did to deserve it.


WHEN I SAY I was running – well. I had a prince of Hell at my heels; this was not a jog. I passed some startled joggers, a giggle of schoolgirls and a string of seriously big young men in training, probably from Leander or one of the other rowing clubs. They had the look of Argonauts, all sun-bleached muscle and magnificence. They'd put you in mind of Greek gods, if you'd never actually met one.

I scudded past them all in jeans and jacket, boot-heels pounding into gravel and mud, and left them no doubt gaping in my wake. I didn't look back. This was all about speed and distance, not being there or anywhere near when Jay eventually got by his parents and came after me. I was taking that to be inevitable. Also that he would pick up my trail readily. I didn't actually know whether he had bloodhound skills, or eagle eyesight; I did know that he'd spent long years living on the streets, learning how to hide and how to run, how to lose pursuit. He'd be just as good playing for the other team, on the hunt. I was heading for London – and following the river – because we'd done that selfsame thing before in my poor abused boat, and just maybe he'd outguess himself and think I wouldn't go the same way twice. More, it was because I knew he'd spent those same long years avoiding London. It wasn't natural territory for him; that might give me an edge. For a while. A little while. It might be long enough.

Besides, I did at least have somewhere to go, that just might be a place of safety. What Robert Frost called home: that place where, when you have to go there, they have to take you in.

It wasn't my home, not now, not for a while now, but it had been once. And I didn't deserve the shelter it might offer, but I was back to Frost again, banking on him: *something you somehow haven't to deserve*.

I didn't waste my time at school, oh, no. Not if I learned to depend on the bitter sentimentality of an American poet long dead.

Not if he was right, at least. If I didn't get Frost-bitten, flung out into the Frost.

RUN, RUN. RUNNING girl. I used to run with earbuds and music, but that was long ago. Recently my running had been more metaphorical, more hiding. Hiding and hunting, trying to find Jordan without getting found myself. Then I did find him, and – well. Things changed.

Now I ran and all my music was internal, old songs going round and around my head in snatches, earworms timed to the pounding of my feet. Songs of betrayal and guilt, songs of loss and heartbreak; if I knew any songs about a strong young woman striking out on her own, I couldn't remember them, or else they just didn't apply.

I might have been crying a little, perhaps, as I ran. Turns out that love and families make a zero-sum game: Jay's change was his parents' gain and my loss, by definition. However it turned out, whether he came after me or caught me or didn't care, I still had to lose.

Whether it was a gain or a loss for *him* – well, he'd have to sort that out for himself. His new self. I'd forced him to grow up, all in a rush, and I had no idea how he'd take to that. The only certainty now was that I wouldn't be there to help. Which had been the only thing I'd counted on. A friend in need, a *girl*friend, a strong right hand and a voice of experience, someone to stand between him and his parents if they tried to ride roughshod over his choices and desires...

Stupid of me, really. However he came out of this, what I'd done had been unforgivable to the old Jay, my Jay; and this new Jordan, whoever he was – recovered, rediscovered, son of his father and his mother's joy – he was not and never could be that boy who was half in love with me. I lost either way, I had to.

One thing about having an Aspect to draw on at will, one drawback to all that strength and endurance is that you can't wear yourself out, run yourself ragged. I used to lose myself utterly in the relentless work and the rhythm of the road, grind myself down to nothing, leave all my troubles behind me for as long as I was hurling one foot in front of the other, on and on, all heat and sweat and breath and effort. Run hard enough and far enough, there was just no room left for words or worries, for any thought at all. *I run, therefore I am*: that was all, and it was enough.

Not any longer. If I couldn't exhaust myself physically, if I couldn't even sweat, running offered no kind of escape beyond the obvious. Everything I was, I carried with me; everything I'd done was still right there in my head, in my memory, accusing. All the damage: Jay's raw open wound, and my own where he had ripped himself away from me.

I ran, and bled internally, and maybe cried a little; and hated myself for being so strong, for running so easily, for allowing no escape. I had my Aspect dialled right down, just a trickle-charge, just enough – and even so, I was hyper-aware of my own body and still cruelly tuned in to the world around me.

Which is how come I noticed, how come I knew immediately when the crows moved in.

I guess it was a blessing, then.

It saved my life, at least. One more time.

Which might not have felt like it was worth much right then, even to me, but, y'know. It's the only one I've got. I'm not a cat. Or an immortal.

Or a crow.

*You see one rook on its own, it's a crow. See a whole lot of crows together, they're rooks.*

See two crows? See them in parallel, in consort, tracking you? They're the Twa Corbies, and now you're in trouble.

Or rather, you've been in trouble for a while, with somebody else, and now you know it. Now it's caught up with you.

Stupid of me, really. Stupid *more*. This was clearly my day for it. I'd been so taken up with this new grief, I'd forgotten that I had old enemies of my own; so focused on forcing Jay to stop running, it had slipped my mind completely that I might still be hunted myself. Still be chased by others, still carry a bounty on my head. Jacey had promised to call off the dogs, stop his family coming after me – but it would take time for that to bite, and longer for the word to filter out to all the freelances who would still be keeping one eye cocked for any glimpse of my shadow.

Like the Twa Corbies, for example. True freelances, mercenaries, they might be working for anyone, but the impulse and the money would be coming from the Cathars. From Jacey's parents, ultimately.

I should have been scared, but no. Really not. Was I weird, that I felt a sudden fierce joy in me? This was an enemy I could understand, and better: an enemy I could fight, if it came to fighting. I might not win, but that was another matter. I couldn't fight Jay. All I could do for him was run.

For these two? I almost stopped running.

Almost.

It was thoughts of Jay that kept me going. The most best gift I could give him now was not to let him catch me, until he didn't want to do it any more.

If that gave them a gift too, if it let them think I was scared of them – well, that did me no harm.

It should have been true, anyway. I ought to be scared of them. The Twa Corbies were lethal. Folk wouldn't hire them else.

So I ran, and they did formation flying ahead and behind and around me, wingtip to wingtip, swoop and rise, circle and glide, barely a twitch of a feather to guide and lift them as they soared on unlikely thermals, black birds of ill omen, ominous to me. Ominous and welcome, just because they were very bad indeed but everything else was worse.

These two? Couldn't make me cry. That was a step up.

Muninn and Huginn they like to call themselves sometimes, *Thought* and *Memory*, but they're not. Odin's ravens are birds of class. I should know; I've met them. These two were just crows.

Crows who came swooping down one more time and divided, to fly one on either side of me as I ran. I just ran on, still intent on distance. I couldn't outrun birds, I couldn't lose them so long as I was out in open country. One thing at a time, then. Make sure Jay stayed behind me, before I started worrying about the Cathars up ahead. They must be somewhere ahead, so long as the Corbies were happy just to escort me, like two fighters shadowing a jumbo jet.

That was how I felt, big and lumbering and solid next to them. Crows aren't the most graceful of birds ordinarily, but these two had a sleek guided-missile determination to them and more, a tight and pretty way of flight, a sense of lightness in the air that spoke of time and practice more than nature. Cultivated crows. If you listened to Jay – if you caught him off-guard or drunk, those rare times he allowed himself to be either one of those – he'd tell you that I embody all the feminine physical virtues, even with my Aspect off. You wouldn't want to believe him, but I did sometimes like to listen. Light-footed as a dancer, he liked to call me. Even in my boots. There may be some justice to that; I do have good feet – and good boots – and I always did like to dance. Beside the Corbies, though, that day? My feet stamped into the ground like piles driving deep, my bones felt like iron bars inside the roughcast walls of my flesh, I'd never been so aware of my body as a crude made thing.

I dropped my head and watched my feet pound the pathway, sooner than watch my two black companions where they hung in either corner of my sight, head-high and keeping place as effortlessly as they kept pace. Lord only knows what other people thought, the dog-walkers and holiday-makers, the boatfolk heading to and from the shops or pubs along the river way, the kids drooping over the parapets of a bridge or fishing hopefully at the river's edge. Lord only knows what they saw. A girl not dressed for running, sure, running hard and easy, but did they see the birds? The Corbies might have a gift to hide themselves. Or they might not care, and people might not see them anyway. Too weird: human brains can blank out what they can't encompass.

I didn't lift my head to look. I watched my feet.

And then suddenly there were two pairs of feet, then there were three.

This, now. This I could deal with.

They still had that crow-look about them, even man-size, man-shape: tall and ageless, bulky, long black coats flapping about them as they ran.

"You guys are even less properly dressed than I am," I said cheerfully.

They just smiled at me in unison and matched me step for step, speed for speed.

Sooner or later, no doubt they'd want to steer me away from the river. Probably sooner, if they were shifting already into human form. Bird was easier for hunting or for keeping track, human for enforcing.

I... didn't intend to let myself be forced. Not anywhere, not into anything.

Not again.

I didn't wait, then.

The really cool thing about my Aspect is that it's just there, whenever I want it. Nothing like a coat, that you have to carry about or go and fetch, that you hang up or leave behind or lose. Really, nothing like a coat at all.

Not like anything, really.

I'd had it dialled low, but now I didn't. I felt the surge of it in blood and bone – like water in a mill-race, a seething flood, irresistible – as my arms lashed out, slamming into the Corbies on either side of me.

Perhaps they thought I'd given up. Perhaps they thought they could do this by threat and terror, those alone; or that the Cathars' name alone would overmaster me. Whatever they were thinking, they weren't ready for this. In bird form, they could have ridden the gust of air I made, risen above my flailing arm or skimmed below. As men, though, even these rough sketches of men, shaped by movement more than skin and bone –

WELL. AS MEN, they couldn't duck or dodge. I hit out, and they went tumbling.

There must be some law of the conservation of mass, that I don't know about. I do know that a fifteen-stone man makes a huge werewolf, way heavier than nature makes a dog; I guess all that weight has to go somewhere.

But the Twa Corbies? They're birds at heart. Hollow-boned, light-bodied even in their native form. Stretched to man size, they were hollow all through, no weight to them at all; those bodies were half illusion and all shadow. It felt like overkill, to use my Aspect against them. A baseball bat against a feather ball.

They did shed feathers suddenly, as they fell. One went into the river, overwhelmed, washed away; the other was crumpled, doubled over, hurled across a hedge.

I didn't follow. I didn't even pause, not even to wonder how they'd acquired their reputation if they were such featherweights. Hell, Jay could have dealt with those two even before this morning's change, before his inheritance caught up with him. He'd made a scrawny teenager, and even so.

They must just have relied on threat and bluster, the Twa Corbies. And the names of their employers. Gangsters don't always need to be physically strong...

No matter. I shrugged them off, brushed a glossy black feather from my arm, went running on. More urgently now, more Aspect in my legs and lungs. The Cathars wouldn't stop, any more than Jay would. Not till Jacey stopped them, at any rate. Till then, I needed to get safe; and there was only one way to do that, that I could think of.

Head down, legs pumping. I ran.

# CHAPTER THREE

SOME PEOPLE LEAVE their key-codes unchanged, and it's just complacency.

Some leave them unchanged, and it's a trap.

Some do it for a hopeless romantic gesture.

329 spells Fay; it always has. I punched in the numbers, and the door unlocked itself. No surprise.


NO SWEAT, BUT I did still feel grubby. Fifty hard miles will do that to a girl. Multiply distance by fear – which an Aspect can't touch – and I felt grubby on the inside too. I wanted to shuck my skin along with my clothes, scrub down to my bones.

But. This had only ever been my home for a little, a very little while, and I hadn't called ahead. I might find anything up there. Anyone. I might have run from Scylla to Charybdis; I might have been mad to come here.

An Aspect can't touch fear, but it can kind of bolster courage. If you feel strong, it's easier to be brave. I cranked it up full force, stepped over the threshold and started up the stairs.

I may be light-footed by nature and by training; when I'm really trying, when I've got everything full-on, my tread won't raise a whisper. Even in boots. I climbed that staircase with no more noise than a drifting zephyr might leave behind in falling dust: a sort of mental tiptoe, an attitude of sidling through sunbeams.

And came up onto the landing, and crossed to the living-room door. It was only open six inches; I nudged it wider with a finger's tip, took a breath, slipped through. Might as well know the worst, all at once. If trouble waited, here was where it would lurk.

IT DOESN'T MATTER how silent you are, coming in; someone is always going to hear you. I stood there in the doorway, exposed and helpless; trouble opened his eyes.

I shrieked.

"TYBALT!"

He lifted his chin in that they-call-me-Mr-Tybs way that he'd had even as a kitten. That was all the acknowledgement I got for all my years away; it was all the invitation I needed. I was across that room in a heartbeat, less, and down on my knees to scritch him dutifully. Soon enough I was sitting on the floor with my back against his chair and my legs stretched out before me and him sprawled in that makeshift lap, a purring dribbling molten lump of shaggy bliss, and my clothes were all over cat-hair and I seemed to be crying again.

When I looked up at last, Jacey was in the doorway.

HE SAID, "FAY."

I said, "Don't."

I said, "Call me Desdaemona. Desi. Please?"

He said, "I'll try."

Then he didn't say anything for a while, and neither did I.

Eventually, we fell back on what was obvious and easy. "You were in bed, I guess," I said. "I'm sorry, I should've buzzed up, given you some warning..."

"It doesn't matter," he said, and he was right, it didn't. He had no clothes on, but that was weirdly irrelevant. I knew his body intimately, better than anyone's, or at least I used to; neither one of us was going to be shy with the other. Not about that.

Besides, if he'd been muffled up in sealskin furs with only his nose showing, I would still have felt exactly the same jolt of swift desire. It was nothing to do with his paraded beauty, or at least not much; like it was nothing or not much to do with our history together, or our longer history apart. Thought and memory were a part of it, of course – Odin's ravens again, black birds of ill omen! – and muscle-memory particularly, the way we fitted together, he and I. My own body ached with a hot, familiar longing: that supple skin, those subtle hands, their strength and greed and generosity.

But it wasn't old feelings rewoken, not really. That was just disguise, something in me working to make me feel better about this abrupt surge of lust. It was tacky, inappropriate... and all-consuming. I could feel my own skin flush, hear how my breath was shortening.

It's the Aspect, of course. Or a side-effect, an after-effect. You become so much more aware of your body, of being a physical creature in a physical world; if you flush that awareness through every living cell you own and then just as suddenly drain it away, it's no surprise if something lingers.

For me at least, what lingers is desire. I'm horny as hell, afterwards. And no, it's nothing like wanting a cigarette after sex; nothing ever is like anything else. But I'd run here from Henley tapping Aspect all the way, I'd tangled with the Twa Corbies for that extra adrenalin spurt, I'd come up the stairs wrapped tight in everything I had, then I'd let it all go when I saw Tybs. I was in an absolute definition of 'afterwards.' First sight of Jacey and, well. Yes. A hot flush and a dry mouth, a yearning that ran bone-deep and set my skin all shivering.

He'd know it, too. He had his own burden of memory, and one thing was sure: he knew what I looked like, needy. When we were younger, we used to do this to each other all the time, without benefit of Aspect. Just because we were younger and discovering passion, caught in it, betrayed by it. We used to think we'd be like that for ever: vulnerable, innocently hungry, utterly exposed to each other.

Perhaps we were right. I guess some eternal truths do turn out true after all. We were not so young now and far from innocent, but the rest of it seemed to hold good for me at least. Vulnerable, hungry, utterly exposed.

He was the naked one, but even so. I knew what he was seeing.

He went very suddenly from couldn't-take-his-eyes-off-me to couldn't-look-at-me-at-all. He stood staring at his feet, and I knew that he'd be flushed too, sudden and responsive. Then he made a gesture with his hand that I was clearly meant to interpret as *oh, look, I've got no clothes on, I'd better go and do something about that,* and was gone.

I wanted nothing, nothing on this planet more than to follow him to his bedroom – unseen, achingly familiar – and shed my own clothes as I went, equalise things that way, meet him at the same disadvantage. Which in his bedroom would be no disadvantage at all: there would be all his broad bed to roll around on, the four corners of the room to rediscover if we needed to, my human strength to pit and lose against his immortal, irresistible body. There was my Aspect to tap into if I needed it, new to him and all but irresistible itself to any boy, let alone one primed as he was. The lure of it would pull him in, the power of it would let me meet him on near-equal terms; and still lose in the end but I could make a glorious fight of it and lose gloriously, which would be good for both of us and better after, and...

AND NO. I did find myself suddenly and unexpectedly on my feet, spilling cat heedlessly as I rose – but

Tybalt's squawl of protest was enough, just barely. It held me together just long enough. It was like a call across time, reminding me of the kitten he used to be and the girl I used to be, the girl that Jacey might yet be willing to roll across his duvet with, who was so emphatically not me or anything like me.

I couldn't do it then. I had the ability, the Aspect, sure; and it would make everything easier; and he was suddenly the vulnerable one, and no. I couldn't do that to him. That wasn't why I'd come.

So. I took a breath, deep and steady; I turned my back on the room and the memories both, on any temptation to draw once more on my Aspect. Or to follow Jacey. Instead I went to the window and looked out at what used to be such a familiar view, the balcony and the dark running Thames below.

Jacey's flat was – well, very Jacey. His family would have put him in a penthouse, high over the city in a building they owned and controlled themselves: uniformed guards and a private lift, housekeeping and meals provided, CCTV and valet parking.

Instead he'd found this place for himself, bought it for himself, done it out for himself.

Himself and me. 329 had always been the doorcode.

The building started life as a wharfside warehouse, put up by a Chinese merchant family in the seventeen-hundreds. Two storeys, brick-built, meant to last. Its wooden neighbours were torn down by the Victorians and replaced with grandiose constructions, four and five storeys high. Overshadowed from either side, bullied for its lunch money, our stunted little hero still hung on. Businesses came and went; this one stayed. It survived one war, and then another. Lucky and plucky, sheltered by the high walls of its looming neighbours, it ducked the bombs that obliterated most of the East End, and the fires never found it.

Post-war redevelopment left it untouched; so did the concrete brutality of the 'sixties. In the 'eighties it got new neighbours, all steel and glass, financial corporations and yuppie millionaires. The Fengs just kept on doing what they did, the old respectable kind of market trader.

Except that their trade no longer came up the river. It must have made less and less sense to keep the building and their business here. Finally, along came Jacey, with an offer they couldn't refuse. Maybe his surname had something to do with that, but I always wanted to think not. I didn't like to think that modern Fengs would buckle to bullying, any more than their ancestors did.

However that went down, money or muscle or what, Jacey got what he wanted. He usually did. In this case it was vacant possession of both floors: one big open space below, with access to road and river; upstairs already subdivided, storage space and offices and a high wide loading-door with its own wooden jib-crane jutting out over the water like a gallows-beam, ready to hoist up bales of silk and boxes of tea, direct from the decks of the ships that used to dock below.

Jacey's contractors moved in, and for the next few months he pretty much lived in a hard hat, when he wasn't combing product into his hair and chasing after me. Then they moved out and he moved in. We did. Suddenly I was living with him, which was a whole different kettle of pretty fish, for us and for his family. They scared me stupid, even before I did the stupid thing and had to run away. Jacey was worth it, though; and his house, his home was another kind of compensation. It's hard to feel scared even when you know you should be, where at the same time you feel safe and warm and protected.

I'd been living in one room in a house-share, working in a florist's to boost my student loan. Now I had more space than I could ever fill, even with the ground floor converted into a garage for Jacey's poor-little-rich-kid cliché collection of petrolhead cars and bikes. Our bedroom was the size of a swimming-pool; hell, our *bed* was the size of a swimming-pool. Made to measure, built to fit. The kitchen was a travesty: professional stainless steel and cool black granite, when my culinary expertise barely reached beyond the can-opener and the microwave, and Jacey simply always ordered in, those few nights that he was in at all.

The wetroom was a joy and a revelation; the living-room was big enough to need a map; and the loading-door had disappeared altogether, replaced by floor-to-ceiling sliding glass with a cantilevered balcony beyond.

It was our home, and slowly I learned to live in it. Loving it took no effort, needed no lessons; I never did learn to take it for granted. No wonder I'd picked my own house as I did, a little cottage not so very far away, with its own balcony and the same river though it was younger there, not so big, not so busy. That hadn't been deliberate, maybe – for sure it hadn't been a conscious decision, *why don't I get a place that will always remind me of Jacey?* – but it wasn't a coincidence either. You can hide but you can't really run, you really can't. Whatever you've lost or left behind, you always take it with you when you go.

Downstairs had always smelled like tea to me, despite the new floor and all the renovations, despite the Ferrari and the Mini, the jeep, the array of bikes. I thought two hundred years and more had soaked into the brickwork. Sometimes at night I thought a hidden panel would swing aside and light spill out to show a silhouette, Fu Manchu returned at last, a Limehouse King Arthur only not so well-intentioned, the once and future yellow peril...

Tybalt nudged my leg. I stopped daydreaming, stopped wallowing in nostalgia at least for long enough to bend down and scoop him up. He was almost the only thing that Jacey ever let me pay for, and I only managed that by *fait accompli,* sneaking out while he slept and coming home with a kitten. My contribution to the household; every home should have a cat.

This particular cat was a heavy double-armful now, a fully mature Maine Coon, the weight of a well-grown toddler. I said "Oof!" at him, and asked how much he'd been eating. He settled two enormous paws on my shoulder, licked my ear thoughtfully and purred at me like a chainsaw digging into a telegraph pole.

Only one of us was sincere, and that only if you can trust a cat. Me, I was lying with every bone in my dissembling body. Looking oh-so-relaxed, girl cuddling cat and watching scenery, waiting for boy to manifest. In honesty I was wound up so tight inside – watching the scenery, waiting for the boy – that I could feel my Aspect actually trying to muscle in on me, as if it had a mind and a purpose of its own, as if it sensed my distress and wanted to protect me.

It's really not like that, and I told it so. Gave it a good talking-to, internally: reminded it that it was just a function on a hair-trigger that my subconscious was snatching at, and really not an independent lifeform, so would it please stop nudging me, thanks very much? I was in no danger here, not from Jay and not from –


A CROW CAME flapping into view, to make an ungainly landing on the black tarred arm of the jib.


MY ASPECT SLAMMED into me so hard it was like a body-check from the inside out. I suppose I must have reached for it, touched the hair-trigger, seen the need and made the choice, but it didn't seem like that: instinctive, better than instant, the thing right there before I knew I needed it. That's how it felt, at least, to me. Lord only knows what Tybalt felt, but he squawled and was gone, leaping wildly from my arms onto the sofa-back and away.

Bird stared at me; I stared at the bird, through window-glass that was suddenly frail as clingfilm, soap-bubble thin. I swear, I thought it was going to fly straight in. A shatter and a squawk, and a room abruptly full of black scavenger. I'd fought the Corbies off easily enough before, when they were two together – but somehow birds are always worse indoors, more threatening, something to be afraid of.

This one didn't come in, didn't try. It sat on the jib and cocked its head and looked at me, and I couldn't even tell if it was one Corbie alone or just a common crow. Nothing to worry about, either way – but I didn't like the way its eye glittered, and I really didn't want it spying on me. Nor on Jacey; I was tired of bringing trouble to other people, especially –

No, NOT THAT. Nobody was special, or more deserving. Nobody deserved this. Me. I was sick of myself in virus mode, infecting whoever I touched. Even when I did it deliberately, and with the best of intentions.

Whether that was an innocent crow or a single spy, I went to shut it out. Floor-to-ceiling windows demand floor-to-ceiling curtains, unless you choose to make a drama of your life and act it out for river traffic to observe. Jacey wouldn't do that; nor would I. I'd sewn the curtains, just to show him that I could. He'd fixed up the mechanism that opened and closed them, just to show me that he wasn't an entirely useless, spoiled rich kid with no practical application. So I called him a geek instead, spoiled rich kid playing with electric motors because he had no people-skills worth mentioning. I don't know what he would have called me next, because that was the point where I'd pressed the button that closed the curtains, and kissed him quiet, and offered to teach him all the people-skills he'd ever need, right then and right there, on the carpet.

It was a joke, of course. He knew far more already than a simple human girl could ever learn, about bodies and how to handle them. Even so. It was a joke that took his breath away. He might have immortal confidence when it came to sex, but he knew no more about love than I did. We were discovering it together the way you do, the way you have to, hand in hand and hopeful.

And then – well. Everything came down, as it can when sex and love go sour in the worst way. And now I had to try to rebuild something from the wreckage, and I really didn't want that damn bird watching me. Us. Whatever.

So I jabbed my finger down on Jacey's precious button, wondering if he'd fixed the whine in the motor yet that always slightly spoiled the swish of the curtains as they crossed the glass, and –

Um.

Oops.

Aspect. Full-on. I hadn't exactly forgotten, but I'd been in and out of it, on and off all day, and when it's on I have to go more gently with the world around me, and – yeah. That's the bit that I forgot.

I can push my fingers into solid brick if I need to. Stabbing down on a switch, all hurried and heedless – well.

*Jacey? I fixed that whine for you...*

One thing for sure, the mechanism was never going to whine again.

Never going to do anything again.

I extracted my finger from the junction-box with a lot more care than I'd shown on the way in. Behind me, I heard Jacey coming back. As I turned around, I was already constructing my excuses: *it's not my fault, I didn't reach for my Aspect, it kind of thrust itself upon me; no blame to me for letting that slip my mind...*

No. That was pathetic. I wasn't a kid any more, and grown-ups take responsibility. For their own strength, among other things, and how they handle it.

"Um," I said. "I'm sorry, I just broke your clever curtain thingie."

He shrugged, because it really didn't matter; and came down the length of the room in jeans and T-shirt and barefoot, his absolute definition of dressing in a hurry. But he'd taken time for a shower first, his hair was still spiky with it. Quick and cold, I judged, from the tight skin on his cheeks and the mildly manic alertness in his eyes.

No blame to him for that. I was envious, almost; or I would be, once I'd shrugged the Aspect off again.

*Not yet.* It was easier, just to keep all my defences up. And besides...

He still couldn't look at me; his eyes shifted to the window, to the daylight. "Why were you messing with the curtains, anyway?"

*Oh, just something to do. Occupy my hands. Play with an old favourite toy. You know...*

No. Still no. I had the habit of honesty on me; I said, "That damn bird."

I watched him find the crow, still perched on the jib there. He frowned. "What about it?"

"I'm being silly. Probably. But on my way here, the Twa Corbies came for me. From your parents, I presume."

That frown only deepened. "I told them to lay off you. Of course I did, first thing."

"Well. The message may not have filtered down. It's going to take time, you know? And – well, it's not a worry, the Corbies can't hurt me, but –"

"What do you mean, the Corbies can't hurt you? I mean, yeah, daemon, Aspect, all of that, I get that – but, hell, the Corbies could hurt me. They'd lose in the end, but I'd go a long way out of my way not to give them a chance to prove it. What makes you immune?"

"Nothing, but they're overrated. They tried to muscle in on me while I was running, and I just knocked them away. No bother. I had the Aspect, sure, but I'm not sure I even needed that."

"Wait, what? The *Corbies*? Fay –"

"Desi."

"– Desi, whatever, you don't just..."

His arm waved vaguely at the impossibility of saying what it was that you didn't just, where the Corbies were concerned. I was all set to point out how wrong he was, because here I was and I *did* just; and to elaborate on my new theory about the conservation of mass, which I thought should interest him deeply and might help to see us both over this early difficult bumpy time. Only I didn't quite get the chance to do it, because we were both still looking at that bird.

So we both got to see when it spread its wings out like a cormorant drying in the sun, flapped them *in situ* like a fledgling trying out its feathers, not ready yet to fly.

I was sure then that it was a Corbie, rather than a coincidence. I still wasn't worried.

Only then there was a smudge in the sky above the river, a charcoal sketch of cloud that moved against the wind. And frayed and clumped and came with purpose, came down low and intent and proved to be – of course! – a flock of birds.

Big birds, black birds. Crows.

*See a whole lot of crows together, they're rooks.* But I didn't think so. Not this time.

"How many Corbies make Twa?"

It's always been a question, and never one you want to hear asked. Not in that tone of voice, at least, and not from someone who ought to be a power in the land. Is a power in the landscape of your own mind, someone to run from. Someone to run to.

I drew a shaky breath, and that was almost a first in itself, that something could still shake me even through the solid grip of Aspect. "Well," I said, "half the songs actually say three, but as far as we know there have only ever been two; and whether they started the songs or whether the songs started them, we don't know. Which came first, the Corbies or the legend? Or the eggs? Were they born, or were they hatched? It's all questions, really. But..."

But I was just talking, it was only bravado, and I never do that. Not with my Aspect on. I never need to.

But I didn't think I was humiliating myself, except in my own eyes. I didn't think Jacey was hearing me at all. He certainly wasn't even pretending to listen.

But there are questions and questions, and they mean nothing in the face of what's true, even if it's never an answer.

How many Corbies make Twa? It didn't matter, it hasn't ever mattered. There was only one outside, except that there was a flock swooping and swirling over the water, and neither of us knew whether that counted one or many or at all. Except that then a solitary crow peeled away from the flock and came flapping in to land beside the Corbie on the jib; and now what we didn't know was whether that was the other Corbie reporting for duty or bringing reinforcements, or just a random bird being territorial – his harem, his perch, his patch, his river – or...

His day to disappear. We had neither of us been looking for that, whatever else we expected, but – though we had both been looking – there was still only one bird on the jib there. Looking at us.

"Um..."

Here came another, banking, rising, stalling in an awkward flurry just above the jib, above the perching one.

Dropping down to join it.

One bird.

"What are they...?"

Another bird, and another.

Jacey said, "How many crows make one?"

Now they came thick and fast, forming a queue in the air, shifting and liquid in the wind but binding together and holding like a rope to its one fixed point, that place outside the window where one by one they came to join the one that held still there. On the jib, looking back at us, absorbing every bird that came.

"Jacey..."

It wasn't getting any bigger, just more solid. More weighty, more powerful – just *more*. It was the conservation of mass again, only working the other way. I might need a new theory.

We might not have time to discuss it.

Ordinarily I don't like being hustled, grabbed, shoved around.

Ordinarily, with my Aspect on? You couldn't do it. I'm unshovable, rooted, balanced precisely on that gravitic line that runs from me to the earth's core. And you wouldn't want to grab, you really wouldn't.

Jacey? Grabbed my elbow, tugged me away from the window, shoved me towards the door, hustled me right out of there.

I've never been more glad to be moving.

One glance back, through the doorway; one last glimpse of what was happening out there. One last line of crows, spiralling in – but not a bird now that they fell into like a gravity-well, like a black hole. Big black-clad man, a Corbie in his other guise: standing easily on the eight-inch span of the beam of the jib, where it jutted out above the river. Standing, looking. Watching us go.

We went.

Down the stairs, pell-mell. Before we reached the bottom, we heard shatter-sounds above and behind us, as it might be the sounds of a large man stepping through the glass of a picture window.

Just stepping, through triple-glazed and armoured glass. It was a big window, a little vulnerable; Jacey always did go high-spec, and was happy to deal in redundancy. *I want to keep you safe,* he'd said to Fay.

The man who could step through that glass? Was not the kind of man a girl could knock flying, just with a blow. Even with her Aspect on.

# CHAPTER FOUR

AT THE FOOT of the stairs, Jacey turned automatically to the inner door, through to his garage and his precious motors. My turn to grab, to shove, to hustle.

"Not that way. There's two of them, remember?"

"I know. What makes you think the other one's not out there?" A nod to the street-door, where I already had my other hand on the latch.

"Because they know where I am and who I'm with, and everybody knows you." Poor little rich boy: Jacey had been a petrolhead since he was fourteen, since his parents allowed him his first roadbike. The law didn't, but the law was not an issue for the Cathars. It was Jacey who taught me to ride, and to drive. He never walked, unless he really had to.

Come to think of it, neither did I. Sometimes I ran; but I'd been run to ground here, and everybody knew about Jacey. Nobody would be expecting either one of us to venture out on foot. The second Corbie would be watching the garage door in the side-alley, I'd bet my life on that.

Literally, perhaps.

"We'll still be safer –"

Poor Jacey: I really wasn't listening to him, and he really wasn't used to that. Not from me, historically; not from anyone. If he'd seriously stood against me, *no, we're going this way*, I could never have shifted him, but this was all outside his experience. Stubborn, determined disagreement. Running away. He didn't have the resources for either one. So he let himself be bullied, and more; he let himself be bundled, still protesting, out through his own front door and into the exposure of the street.

I was just pulling the door closed when there was a squawk and a flurry, down about ankle-level; a sudden dark streak on the pavement, there and gone.

I stared after, dismayed.

"Oh! Tybalt...!" A Corbie in the flat must just have been too much for him, too much bird.

"Not to worry." It was Jacey's turn to take the initiative, and he didn't waste it. He took the door from my hand and slammed it, punched numbers into the keypad, talking over his shoulder about something else entirely, our cat. "He'll go down the alley to the Chinese supermarket and be fluffily distressed by their back door, until the Misses Feng have fed him calming giblets. How do you think he got to be so fat? It's not by hunting pigeons."

"He's not fat; he's just big-boned. What are you doing now? Come *on*...!"

Actually, I knew what he was doing now. I could hear strong locks hurling themselves from door to jamb, acting on instruction. He had hundreds of thousands of pounds'-worth of cars and bikes on the garage floor; of course he had protection. With luck, he might have added something more esoteric than magnetic bolts.

Even so, I didn't really think there'd be anything fit to stand against a man who could walk through armoured glass. We could hope, but we couldn't take the time to learn. I snatched his hand and hauled him away.

"So are the Misses Feng any relation to the Fengs you bought the building from?"

"Daughters of. That was the deal. It was a quid pro quo; they gave up their warehouse and I bought them a retail business for the kids. Where they could fatten our cat up, apparently. Don't change the subject. I still say we'd be safer in a car, with a metal lid over us."

He was watching the sky anxiously, and no blame to him for that. Me, I was more caught up with watching behind, waiting for the moment when a Corbie came busting through the door to chase us down the street.

I could talk and hurry, so long as I had hold of his sleeve, so that I knew he was hurrying too.

"You weren't with us in poor Asher's car."

"No," he said. "What happened?"

"That was the time we didn't make it, to meet you in Salomon's club. Harpies happened. A car was no defence at all. Okay, that was a soft-top, but even so. What are you going to back, against both Corbies with that much oomph behind them, all those birds we saw?"

"Well," he said judiciously, "not us out in the open, at any rate. And not me barefoot without a jacket or a wallet."

Oh. Thing is, usually my Aspect makes me hyper-competent, but this time? Apparently not. I hadn't thought; I hadn't even noticed.

I didn't stop moving, but something must have shown. Maybe it was just that I stopped talking. He may have taken that for an OMG-I'm-sorry, I'm-such-a-featherhead moment; at any rate he shrugged easily. "It's okay, I'm not hurting. My feet can take it. But where are we *going*...?"

Initiative: you snatch it when you can. "This way."

Up to the main road, but only for a minute. Dash between the cars, no time for the lights to change; and here on a traffic island, isolated in grandeur, was a tiled building untouched by redevelopment, a gateway, a mystical transition-point from the world above to the world below.

"The Tube?"

"Yes, of course. How many birds do you see down there?"

He grunted, thought about it, said, "Pigeons."

"The occasional pigeon, sure. Hiding from Tybalt, I expect. No wonder the poor boy has to go and beg scraps from the Fengs. But pigeons aside. Crows don't come underground."

"Men do."

"Yes – but are the Corbies men? I think they're crows in man-shape." I thought we'd just seen that proven. Many crows make a man. "I don't think they'd like it down here at all, even if they did manage to see where we've gone..."

All the time I was talking, I was keeping him moving, steering him towards the barrier.

Where he checked, looked around him in that charmingly vague way that privileged people like to pretend is entirely natural, and said, "Aren't we supposed to, oh, buy a ticket or something?"

"Oyster cards," I said. "Remember? You just touch your card to the pad and it lets you through. Jacey, I *taught* you this, years ago..."

"You did. I've probably still got the one you made me buy then." Of course he hadn't used it since; I don't think he'd been down the Tube once before he met me. A lifetime spent in London, and he'd never joined the lifeblood of the city. If he was too drunk to drive himself, he'd take a taxi. The habits of the hyper-rich: I showed him what he was missing, how young people ought to get about town, but he'd have gone straight back to his old ways when I left. I wasn't sure if that was sad or something else. If he was browbeaten by his clan, or seeking comfort in the familiar, or avoiding what he'd discovered with me because, well, he'd discovered it with me.

"But if I do still have it," he went on, almost triumphantly, "and if it's still valid or loaded or whatever, then it's in my wallet. Which is in my jacket, which..." Which was, of course, not on his shrugging shoulders. "So you'll have to treat me. I don't have any cash either."

It was all new to him, being out without money or cards or phone, none of his insulation against the world. Or shoes, but I think they were symbolic. I thought he was enjoying it, even: relaxing a little, now that there didn't appear to be big dangerous bird-men at our backs. Dumping his problems in my lap, waiting to see if I was outfaced. Waiting to be treated, right now. That would be new too, having a girl pay for him.

I flipped out my own purse with one hand, reached the other into my back pocket and said, "No problem. I always carry a spare."

I did, it was true. With two cards you can pick up an ill-prepared stranger, see a stricken friend safe, run in company. Lose your purse or leave your jacket behind and still get home, so long as you've still got your trousers.

So I equipped Jacey and hustled him through, stood him on the escalator – "Moving stairs, remember these? You just stand still, and they take you where you need to go" – and stood myself on the step behind him, my hands on his shoulders and my eyes checking behind us where I knew he couldn't see.

He said, "So where are we going?"

"Down, sweetheart. Then on a train. It's a special kind of train, it runs under the streets, and when we come up we'll be in a different part of London, it's like magic."

"Seriously. Where are we *going*?"

Here was the bottom of the escalator. I left my hands on his shoulders and steered him from behind and found that I was quite enjoying this too. Not least because it meant I could avoid the question, at least until we were on the right platform; and then the train came and I could do more steerage, through the hissing doors and down to an empty pair of seats and squash up together like we used to when we were dating, before the world turned bad.

By then, he'd decided to stop asking and make his own decisions for the pair of us. "Does this train stop at Knightsbridge, or do we need to change? We'll get off there, and I'll take you to my parents' flat. I can be sure you're safe then, no damn bird is going to come after us when there are three Cathars in residence. Well, actually my mother's likely out, but Dad will be around and he's enough. All by himself, he's enough for anyone."

He was way too much for me. He always had been. And, "Jacey, love – you're not concentrating. Your parents are the people I'm running away from. The Corbies are just... messengers. Envoys. Trouble along the way. They're incidental."

"No. No, I told you, you're wrong. Oh, not about the Corbies, but it's not my parents now. Not any more. I called them off. You *know* that."

"I've heard it. I don't believe it. Maybe I can't let myself believe it, after so long being so afraid of what they'd do if they ever caught me. Even if you're right, even if it's only that the word hasn't filtered down yet so everyone still thinks they want me – even then. I couldn't just walk through their door, even with you. I *can't*."

"They're not that bad," he said weakly, helpless in the face of my own weakness. "Honestly, they're not." They were, though, and he knew it; and shrugged at last, and said, "Well. All right, then. I won't take you there. So where, then?"

He wasn't taking me anywhere. I was taking him. If I could trust him. He was still a Cathar, still his father's son; I eyed him warily, and said, "Can you be good?"

"I'm always good."

"I'm serious."

"So am I." And then, on a deep breath, "Fay – no, sorry. Desi. See, at least I'm trying. Also, take a look at me. I'm barefoot and out with nothing, sitting on a Tube train with wet hair, kind of like a crazy person only cleaner and less shouty. And why am I doing this? I am doing this because my ex-girlfriend came busting into my place an hour ago, looking for protection; and whether there's actually someone still after her or not, someone thinks there is, and I've left him smashing my place up and very likely my garage too, all my precious motors. And why have I done that? Because my ex-girlfriend thought she needed to run, and I thought I needed to go with her, rather than staying to defend my home. I'm not looking for praise or congratulations or anything like that, because of course I did it, because that's what you do when you care about someone – but yes, I can be good. I'm *being* good. Okay?"

Just for a moment there, I wanted to cry, and hug him, and make all kinds of tender and dangerous promises for later. There was something about the way he said *ex-girlfriend*, and something about *when you care*, and the way his voice tore a gulf between them.

But I still had my Aspect on, and it helps to keep me focused. Sometimes I can make like it gives me tunnel vision, I can use that.

So I just said, "What, you think you could take the Corbies?"

And he said, "Honey, I *know* I can take the Corbies. Eventually. Whatever they are, they're made men; I was born to this."

He was a Power, he meant, the son of Powers, and for a little bit I wanted to believe him. Then I remembered Asher, and how he'd died. I said, "You're not immortal. Not even you. It might be smart to remember that." *It's smart to run.* And then, "And don't get all high and mighty about crazy people. Not here, not now."

"Why not?"

"Because of where we're going. Where I'm taking you." I'd made the decision, apparently. Perhaps there had never really been a decision to be made, only a foregone conclusion to be recognised. A conversation to be had. "I do know you can be good, so – yeah. You do that, be good, and don't ask too many questions. I don't suppose you can hide who you are, but – well, don't trumpet it about, okay?"

"Oh, great. You mean I get to sit through someone else telling me how my family are barbaric shitheads and should all be done away with? And me too, because of course it's all in the genes and I couldn't be good if I tried?"

"No," I said, "that's not what I meant," though I did think at least half of it was true, and where we were going most people would vote for the other half too, just to be safe. Safer. "It's not about you or even your family, so much as the whole Overworld. You're just a symbol. I'm afraid you'll have to live with that today; but keep your mouth shut and your ears open, maybe you'll learn something that'll make it easier to be good later." Later and for the rest of his life. He could rewrite family traditions and make the Cathar name something to be proud of, rather than something to be feared.

Meantime he didn't look any too happy, and I couldn't blame him. I hadn't really thought before, how much it must grind you down if half the people you know spend half their time talking about how evil your family is. Even if they don't do it to your face. Small wonder if he chose to spend his time with the other half. I might not have noticed when we were together, when I was young enough that everything about him was bright and shiny and immaculate, but the people he hung with weren't the best advertisement for the Powers in their new generation. Playboys and party girls, rich and loud and frivolous and heedless: oh, it was fun while it lasted, but all that superficial glitz and glamour was founded on a grimmer reality that I was too slow to see. Now I thought maybe he'd been deliberately trying not to see it either. If that meant that his own behaviour only bolstered his family's reputation – *Jacey Cathar? He's just like all the rest, he doesn't give a shit* – then so be it. He could at least pretend not to hear the whispers that followed him from restaurant to nightclub to party, not to care what was said openly, just a little lower down the social scale.

Or maybe I only wanted to believe him better than he was, maybe I needed that. If so, it still wouldn't do him any harm to be good for a while. He might even develop a taste for it.

Anyway. I was committed now; I had committed him, and he was willing at least to play along. That was good enough for now.

And here was our stop, and I was up and hauling him to his feet before either one of us was prepared for it. Something to thank the Corbies for, perhaps. An hour ago we could hardly bear to look at each other, and now I was being casually physical with him, making free of his body the way I used to do. Back when I had licence and authority, when I was official: when *Jacey's girlfriend* meant me and defined me entirely.

"Chancery Lane? What's here?"

"Nothing. We're just changing trains," and I was just leaving my arm tucked through his for my comfort, or for better control of him, or...

"No, wait." We were still in the doorway of the train, and he was glancing at the map above, frowning. "There are no connections at this stop. We can't change here, unless we're going back again..."

"Jacey. Trust me." *You said you'd be good. That means don't be too smart, don't think too hard.* I tugged him onto the platform, and he did come, but he still had that not-very-trusting look on his face. The Fay in me wanted to smooth it away with my fingers, or try kisses if that didn't work, if fingers just weren't enough to cut it. Poor Fay. The Desi in me was scowling at her, blaming her for something else entirely that was not her fault at all. If Jacey used one thing to avoid thinking about something else – if he tried to drown the small voice of his conscience with excess and indulgence, if he ran with the fast crowd because he didn't want to sit still and actually think – he wasn't the only one who did that. Right now I was using my own fear of his notorious family to avoid thinking about what

I'd done this morning, what it meant to Jordan, what it meant to me.

Using one boy and his dangerous parents to avoid thinking about another one, and his.

Urgency let me get away with it, if only just. I could almost be grateful to the Corbies. An adrenalin spurt, an Aspect lock-down, that fight-or-flight tunnel vision was just what I needed...

Tunnel vision. Hah. Sharp enough to cut myself, if I only dared to laugh.

He tried to go one way, following the flow of people; I held still until he stopped pulling, then drew him with me in the opposite direction.

"The signs say exit that way," he murmured. Not a protest this time, he was catching on; but he never did like being disoriented. Off his beat, out of his depth: he was hating this. And he thought there was humiliation coming, and he was barefoot and defenceless, and he'd hate that worse, he thought.

I thought he was probably right.

"Yeah. We don't want the exit. I told you, we're just changing trains."

Down to the end of the platform, and here was a passage with no signs and no advertisements, just one bare flickering fluorescent light bouncing off the grimy tiling. Puddles on the cracked concrete floor, that looked and smelled suspiciously just like exactly what they were.

"Oh, great. Now I have to wade through a toilet?"

"Hush, and come on..." And *yes, you do*. Poor Jacey. He was learning fast, but he really wasn't used to this. At least he wasn't trying to pull back, though; he grumbled, but he didn't resist. Most likely he still thought he was protecting me, and he hadn't changed his mind – yet – about whether I was worth it.

The low arched roof of the passage closed over our heads, that juddering light embraced us. We plotted a course that kept his feet more or less dry, though it meant skipping and weaving from one side to the other; then the passage turned a corner, and here was a very solid gate of iron bars, very firmly locked against us.

"Well, then." He was very ready to give up, even though it meant another skip around the puddles. "I don't know where you thought you were taking us, Desi, but you can't get there from here."

I just looked at him. "Got your card?"

These two I carry are not the regular kind that you can pick up at a station or order down the phone. These you can only find online, at an address that Google doesn't know. Registration is complex and can prove expensive, sometimes in other ways than money. But sometimes – well, sometimes you just have to see a friend to safety. Or take yourself there, suddenly and without warning.

The lock on the gate was in a big old-fashioned cast iron case, with a keyhole hiding behind a brass escutcheon. It looked deliberately unfriendly, disinclined to open under any circumstances, key or no key.

No key needed. I said, "One at a time now. Do what I do."

What I did was swipe my card down between the lock and the jamb, as if it were a credit-card reader.

There was a brief pause, then a heavy *clunk,* and the gate swung marginally open. I heaved it wider and slithered through; it closed firmly in poor Jacey's face.

"Now you. Swipe and go."

He blinked at me through the bars, then obediently swiped. The gate unlocked; I pulled it open and beckoned him through. It slammed shut at his back, more violently than any spring could close it, or any human hand.

Jacey blinked again. I wanted to muss his hair and kiss him and call him a good boy just to make his eyes snap with temper, just to call him back into himself; it was disturbing, seeing him so uncertain and out of place. Good for him, perhaps, but not so good for me just now.

He said, "Why couldn't we both come through together?"

"Two people on one card? Can't be done." It couldn't be done upstairs, at the regular barriers with the regular cards; it certainly couldn't be done down here. "You don't imagine the lock is the only safeguard on that gate, do you?"

He shrugged. "I hadn't thought about it. I don't know what the gate is protecting."

"No. I'm sorry, Jacey. I'm not keeping you deliberately in the dark." Though of course I was – or at least in the flicker of an unreliable light, giving him only flashes of insight. "You're used to the mundane world and the Overworld, and this is something else. This is the underworld, where people tread more carefully." And pronounce it without a capital, to save confusion. "We have to." *I'm one of these,* I was saying, before he even met them, *and you're not.*

*You made me this way,* I could've said, or *your family did.* I thought I'd leave it, let him figure that out for himself.

At least the floor was dry, this side of the gate. Here was another sharp turn, and now the light was better; here were steps leading down, and now he had smooth tiling underfoot and everything was clean.

And now the passage debouched onto a platform just like the one above, only older. No ads, no vending machines, no electronic destination boards. No electronics of any sort, and no announcements. Just the platform, and benches made of wood and cast iron, and us. No other passengers.

Jacey looked up and down and said, "What happens now?"

"We wait. Not too long."

"And if trouble comes in the meantime? Say if the Corbies followed us regardless, underground or not? A flock of birds could get through that gate, even if a man didn't have a clever card."

I wasn't so sure; I thought a flock of birds might find itself unexpectedly swallowed. He needed something else, though, so I said, "Well, then I guess we find out if you're right, when you think you can take a Corbie. Or two. One at a time, I'd recommend. If they both come, I'll keep one busy as best I can, until you're ready."

He looked at me narrowly. "Are you laughing at me?"

"Only a little," and only because I didn't want to do the other thing. I sat down then and patted the bench beside me. He was still being good; he stopped pacing, and sat beside me.

"The Tube is full of old abandoned stations," I said. When in doubt, lecture. "Thirty, forty? I don't know how many. Some were never finished, some were superseded, some were abandoned because they never had the traffic."

"Mornington Crescent," he said, nodding. Playing along.

"Exactly – though they reopened that one. People pressure. Anyway. One or two found themselves stranded at the end of a line that didn't go anywhere, and keeping up a shuttle service back and forth is too expensive, just not worth the trouble."

"Except...?"

"Except," I said, nodding firmly. "For some of us, it's worth the trouble. Welcome to the Ghost Train." Immaculately timed, just as its lights appeared around the bend of the tunnel, with a blast of warm air to herald its arrival.

"Whoo," he said, determinedly cheerfully ironic. "Should I be scared?"

*Actually, Jacey? Yes, I think you should.* But I didn't say so. We stood up and moved to the platform edge as the train drew to a halt. It was a short one, just two carriages; it looked out of scale with the platform, stranded almost, like a toy on the wrong gauge of track. But nobody was playing here, and looks weren't important. It was big enough to take the traffic; that was all that mattered.

Jacey said, "Christ alive. Did you see the driver?"

"It's better not to look. And don't ask questions. I said that, remember? And keep your voice down"

– as the doors slid apart and we stepped aboard – "these are real people. Hurt and frightened people, mostly. They're entitled to a bit of respect."

That would be a new and a strange notion to the people Jacey went around with ordinarily, his clubbing crowd, the gilded youth of the Overworld. He was trying, or at least, prepared to try; he took it on board in silence, as the train took us.

There were maybe half a dozen people in the carriage, scattered in ones and twos with plenty of distance between them. I didn't imagine they'd been talking much in any case, but they watched us on and didn't say a word.

I could feel Jacey's distracted puzzlement, the way he knew that something more was odd here and didn't understand what it was, one extra thing where everything was strange. I said, "This is old-style rolling stock. I don't know how long it's been running this line. Not quite from the days of steam, I guess, but..."

But there would still have been steam trains overhead, at any rate, when this stock first ran, even though the carriage doors down here slid closed with a hiss of air and the train pulled away in an electric silence. The upholstery was red and green, plush velvet and leather worn to a warm softness; shaded lamps glowed against the dark of the tunnel that swallowed us.

The carriage swayed and rattled. We found seats as far away as possible from everybody else, as everybody else had in their turn; it was probably a mathematical problem, reducible to a formula. Like tossing monopole magnets into a dish and watching them repel each other.

Jacey said, "Come on, then. Straight answers now.

Where have you brought me, and where is this train going?"

"It's not about the place, it's about the people. It's just a short run to a station that never opened, because the line dead-ends. They wanted to call it Savoy, because it was meant to serve the hotel, and one of the exits would take you straight into the lobby, with a flunkey standing by to take your luggage; but of course anybody heading for the Savoy with luggage takes a taxi, so it was all wasted effort. We call it Stranded, because it is and we are and it's under the Strand, ho ho."

"We?"

I shrugged. "The runaways, the broken. People who've met the Overworld, and need a place to hide up for a while. Us."

He flinched. "Desi." He was still trying that name out, learning the shape of it in his mouth, wondering if it would ever mean the shape of me. "Do we really do that much harm?"

"What, you think you're a boon and a blessing to men?"

"No, but – well, no worse than the merely mortal. Kings and millionaires, industrialists, profiteers. There always have been bad people at the top, and not everyone at the top has to be bad."

"Oh, boy," I said, "do you have a lot to learn." But he was maybe ready to learn it, him with no shoes on and nothing in his pockets, nothing to fall back on: reduced to the pure essence of himself, Jacey alone. I thought he was rather nice, actually. But then, I always had. He was a little miracle, given where he came from.

Didn't stop him being arrogant, heedless, extravagant, self-indulgent, half a dozen other character flaws I could mention. Spoiled rotten, basically. But that really wasn't his fault; and compared with the people whose fault it was, they really were minor sins. I might have blamed him more if he'd contrived to spoil me too, the way he'd have liked to, early on. He let me think the Overworld was all champagne and roses, all the way for everyone, the way it was for him. But his parents disabused me fairly swiftly; and then I was on a mission, I wanted to save him.

And then I had to run and hide, and it was as much as I could do to save myself. I saw the underside of the Overworld, up close and extremely personal; and Fay turned into Desi, who was at least not so simple-minded; and now I wouldn't try to change him if I could. Oh, there were lessons to be learned, and I'd teach them willingly, but I'd let him build them into what he had already, the man he was making of himself. By himself, I thought he was doing okay. Today, in the circumstances, I actually thought he was doing spectacularly well.

Right now, he was getting to his feet first as the train pulled in at Savoy, even though he was the stranger here. Holding out a hand to hoick me up the way he used to, frail girlie that I was.

I used to love that gesture. And cling to it, cling to him, because as often as not he was taking me into curious and frightening places, to meet curious people who were only not frightening because I was with him.

Now – well, he wasn't frightened, but perhaps he ought to be. At any rate he was utterly out of place here, and if he wanted to pretend he was taking the lead, that was fine by me. It meant I could keep hold of his hand and see him through the tough stuff, nudge him when necessary. Push my own worries to the back of my mind, stop looking over my shoulder, focus on keeping Jacey straight. Yes.

Off the train, then, unhurriedly, letting everyone else go first because we could. Some days everybody wanted to do that, when it was a trainful of first-timers; the driver never hurried away. The doors stayed open until the last person finally found the courage to step down, or else irrevocably changed their mind and went back into the world.

Not us, not today. It wasn't about courage, just keeping away from the world for a while. Having a place to be.

Here was the platform, like a recreation for a 'twenties movie, *SAVOY* spelled out in tiling on the wall. Original posters that were probably worth a mint, only nobody here would touch them.

One exitway, where everyone was headed. Old hands, perhaps; they didn't dawdle, there was no reluctance in their shuffling, only the weight that the left-behind world had left on them.

Here was the stairway. Here was a boy not busking, just blowing a sad horn because that was what he did and what he could do, a boy with his face peeled off. Some Overworldly creature had taken it for a trophy, most likely, and left him with red-raw flesh exposed like dry meat at the butcher's, with cartilage and bone and tendons showing through. He had no lips; he gripped the mouthpiece of his saxophone between his revealed teeth, which must make dentistry easier but music probably harder. I figured he had to be making some kind of seal with his tongue and the roof of his mouth – but what did I know? Maybe he wasn't human and never had been; maybe he'd grown that way and not been hurt at all. Maybe he kept his lips behind his teeth. This was the underworld, these were the Stranded.

Beyond the boy, another brief tiled tunnel-passage led to another platform, the way the other passengers were heading. "That's the dormitory," I told Jacey. "Everybody builds their own nest, and we all bunk down together." *Us too, if we stay.* I could read the unasked question on his face; I guess he could read the unspoken answer on my own. "We don't go that way yet," I went on, as though the whole silent conversation had been explicit, dealt with, shared. "Up first, to see Reno."

*Who's Reno?* – it was another of those inevitable questions that he managed not to ask. I wanted to applaud, only then I'd have to let go of his hand and I didn't want to do that.

So his effort went unrewarded, if not unappreciated, as we started up the long straight flight of stairs. There were escalators on either side, the original old wooden kind, but they didn't actually run; I wasn't sure they ever had, and climbing a dead escalator is no fun at all. Even with your Aspect on. I'd let that slip since the train came, just keeping it at a low maintenance level, present but not obtrusive. Not in charge.

Hell, it was never in charge. It was a tool, that was all. And not addictive, either. No way. No.

"I don't know what it is about escalators," I said, to distract myself as much as him. "When they're not running, I mean. The pitch is just wrong or something. It feels unnatural, not shaped for the human body. And they're *tiring*."

"Says the girl who's just run fifty miles without getting out of breath."

"Oh, hush, that's different. Maybe I mean mentally tiring. Maybe it's because they're supposed to carry you, it just feels so much more effort when they don't. Like having to push a bike when you should be riding it, or –"

"Or having to push a conversation one way, to stop it taking you another way that you don't want to go, maybe? Desi, when you talk about this place you always say *we*. We do this, we do that. When did you become one of these people?"

"When I had to run away from you, of course."

# CHAPTER FIVE

"IT HAPPENS ALL the time," I said – *it's not just you, not just you and me* – "that people find themselves in trouble with the Overworld. Someone's after them, or someone's broken their heart or taken their place, stolen their life or their reputation or their lover, and they just need space, they need to step away and hole up for a while.

"The kind of places that people go, the hostels and the hideaways, the all-night cafes and the all-night buses" – the places I'd tracked Jordan through – "there's always someone there who knows about this place and how to get here. Where to pick up an Oyster-knife." That's what we call the special cards, because they slip through the cracks and open this place up to you, and maybe if you're lucky you'll find a pearl. "You wouldn't ever have heard about it, because you've never been needy that way." And he still wasn't, of course, and probably I shouldn't have brought him here, but I couldn't have left him to the Corbies. Power or not. He might be right, that he could take them – but he might not. Asher was still dead.

If I was going to be in trouble for bringing him along, I'd find out soon enough. Here we were at the top of the stairs. No barriers here, to touch our cards against for rights of passage: straight out into the old ticketing hall, all gloss green walls and immaculate 'twenties styling, lovely ironwork everywhere: from the lamps to the balustrades to the illuminated signs to the doorhandles.

"Right," he said. "It's a refuge. Got it. How long can people stay?"

"As long as they like." That boy with the sax might never leave. Where else could he go, who would take him in? What would he do? Here he had a life of sorts, a horn to blow, a place to stand. A place to sleep, among his own people, the brutalised and the terrified and the torn-apart, all the most needy refugees from the worlds above. "But it's more than just a shelter for the homeless, it's a sort of employment agency too. Reno likes to find places for us back in the world, where we can be safe and make a life again. Nothing's compulsory, but – yeah. Come on. Let's check in."

I was fairly sure that Reno would know already that I was back, and who I'd brought in tow. Not sure how, but sure, oh, yes. Even so: new arrivals always did do this.

Down to the end of the hall, past the shuttered windows, each of them framed like a painting in tiles of darker green, each with its sign hung above on an iron curlicue bracket, proclaiming *Tickets*; down to where a full door was similarly framed, where the sign said *Stationmaster's Office*.

A quick formal rap of the knuckles on one panel of the door, though again I was quite sure that Reno knew we were here. There's no CCTV, but even so. Reno knows everything that happens at Savoy, and a lot that doesn't. Pretty much everything the Stranded get up to, here and elsewhere. If it's known anywhere, if it's knowledge, it belongs to Reno, pretty much. As we do, pretty much.

As I still do, pretty much, though it's been years.

As I always will, a little bit, most likely. You can take the girl out of the Savoy, but.

ANYWAY.

*Rap-rap* and in we go.

The decor outside may be all bright and open and Charles Rennie Mackintosh, but the office feels pure Victorian, wood-lined and sombre. I guess that's the way they thought offices should be back then, even when they were ready to be freethinkers with their public spaces.

Reno was behind the desk, as ever.

I still had hold of Jacey with my non-knocking hand. I wasn't looking at him, but I didn't need to; I could feel his sudden hesitation, I knew exactly the abrupt blink of surprise, the moment of unpreparedness, the swift recovery. Knock him back on his heels and he rocks right up again, that's how it goes.

Probably I should have warned him, probably I should be feeling guilty. But we never do, and I never would. Not about this.

Reno said, "Not expecting a woman, huh?"

It's her standard joke. It's a test, I think, to see if people laugh. Learn how they laugh, meanly or forcedly or hysterically or what.

Jacey was being good. He said, "Well, it does say *Stationmaster* outside your door." He played it as po-faced as she did, as if he was enjoying himself just as much.

Reno's an angel, and she likes to make a pun of it. In the way of a West End theatrical angel, she invests in us and hopes for a return, even while she's hoping never to see us again. Never to need to.

But that really is just for the pun of it. Reno really is an angel.

Or rather, she's a woman with wings. That's as good as it gets down under, as much as you can hope for.

Or rather, she isn't. A woman with wings.

She used to be, but that was long ago. Somebody's been unkind to her, cruel and unkind. She's the other thing now, a woman without wings. But still nothing like the rest of us.

I'm guessing that they plucked her first, quill and barb: every pinfeather and every flight ripped individually out. There must have been a number of them – she's a big woman, even sitting down she's taller than me, and she wouldn't have sat still for this – and they will have needed tools, pliers of some kind. But they did have tools. I know that, because plucking wasn't enough. They cut away her wings, what they'd left of them, the naked bleeding ruins that they were;

broke them, crushed the bones and hacked off what was left. What she has now are splintered stumps, just too unkindly long to hide beneath a shirt. They jut from holes she rips in anything she wears, and twitch with remembered life when she's forgetful.

I think they must hurt her appallingly, all the time. She doesn't show it, but even the healed skin shows brutal scars where she was torn deep inside. The visible bone, all the serrated living shards that push out through fresh scabs, fresh runs of blood like dribbles of congealed ruby – well. It doesn't bear thinking about, so I don't. Much.

She said, "Jacey Cathar. I never thought to see you here. I don't imagine you're looking for work."

"No," he said. "Nor shelter, actually. I only came because... because Desi brought me." He was still tripping over the name, but still being good, making the effort. I squeezed his hand.

"Well, never mind. You're welcome anyway." And then she turned to me and said, "I didn't expect to see you back. I thought we'd got you settled."

"You did. But, you know. Stuff happens."

"Stuff. Yes. It must do. Someone was asking after you just recently. Asking *for* you, actually. Did I know where you'd gone, how to find you. I said no."

"Uh, thanks, Reno..."

She shrugged. And didn't wince, but I thought that was practised. I thought a shrug was like red-hot irons in her shoulders, biting deep. "What I do. Client confidentiality. But I did think you were settled. Well, no matter. You're here now. Make yourselves a space, settle in. Find your boy some

boots if he's staying, don't let him make trouble if
he's not. Are you looking for another position?"

"No. Thanks, but no. I'm really not. Who was
asking for me?"

"Client confidentiality," she said again. "I can't
tell you that. Only – well. Perhaps I shouldn't be
surprised to see you back. Go on, now." And her
long, long arm was already reaching for a sheaf of
papers in a cubby-hole, her head and her attention
were already turned away.

Too busy to linger, too well-informed to gossip,
too well-connected to be impressed: that was Reno,
through and through. As instructed, I took my boy
away to find him boots.

Poor Jacey. His day had become a succession
of bewilderments, and what he was possibly –
probably – thinking now were bad decisions.
Especially the big ones: to come with me when I
ran, and to let me choose where we ran to. Here
he was off balance and unexpectedly out of his
depth, feeling disrespected, disregarded, almost
dismissed. He wasn't used to playing second fiddle,
to having the girl he was with seem inherently more
interesting than he was. He certainly wasn't used to
being called somebody else's boy.

And I was no help, leading him around by the
hand with my thoughts all too obviously elsewhere,
wondering who'd been enquiring for me here, who
I needed to be afraid of now. Not the Cathars, or
not directly. One of their mercenaries was still a
likely choice, but that was also the lazy choice, the
one that didn't trouble to think things through.
Occam's Razor can do that to you. You make quick

assumptions and act as if they're true, and more often than not you're right, and the times that you're not – well. Those are the times that you can end up dead.

Dead or worse, naturally. There's always something worse.

So I was thinking mostly about that and hardly at all about Jacey, just tugging him along like a grown-up with a little boy in tow. Until my thoughts stumbled over something I really didn't want to think about, and that brought my head up and my mind back to where I was and what I was doing, right here and right now. I was taking Jacey utterly for granted, treating him like a tiresome duty while I considered far more important matters in the privacy of my own skull – and he was *letting* me. Allowing that to happen. Playing along.

Being good.

I glanced up at him, and just that little physical gesture was deeply familiar and deeply wrong, both at once: like a sudden startling reminder of how much had changed this morning, between one boy and another. Jordan was shorter than me. And not with me any more, and maybe hunting me by now, and that was what I really didn't want to think about. So: right here, right now. Think about Jacey instead.

He was waiting exactly for that glance, that moment when I remembered that he was there, and that he mattered. He met it with a smile, as though I were the one suddenly being good. Living up to expectations, shaving with Occam's Razor.

I said, "Why aren't you spitting mad?"

He shrugged. "Too easy." His version of *that's the lazy choice*. "And, look." His hand swung mine back and forth. "You're here, and we're having an adventure. That's got to be worth something. I guess we'll find out later, just how much."

I didn't think it was worth all his lovely cars and his fancy bikes; I was damn sure it wasn't worth his life, which was the other thing he'd flung into the balance. Knowingly or not. But, yes. Something. It really hadn't occurred to me before that perhaps all this time, he'd been missing me as sharply as I missed him. All the time he chased me, all the time I ran. Both of us spinning dizzy around the same black hole.

I said, "We need to talk," I needed to tell him everything, I owed him that at least. Lay out the razor and the other blades, see what amounted to a shave. "Not up here, though. This isn't the place to start claiming private space or special privileges." Especially not with him. "Come on, boy. Boots."

HERE WAS ANOTHER door, one with no illuminated sign, nothing to draw the public's attention. Beside it, though, was another hatch like the ticket-windows, similarly boarded up. This one, its sign said *Lost Property*.

Jacey looked up at that, and balked before I could get him through the door. "You're kidding, aren't you?"

"Nope, not at all."

"Second-hand boots?"

"Second-foot, I think you mean – but probably not. This isn't charity gear. This is the stuff the charity shops don't see." I tugged at him tentatively, but he still wasn't moving. I may have rolled my eyes a little, but it wasn't really his fault. He'd probably never had to consider putting something on his precious body that had been used before. So I bit back *well, if you'd really rather go barefoot* – no point giving hostages to fortune; it would be all too easy for him to say *yes, I would* – and instead I said, "What you don't know, Jacey" – *among the vast scads of things that you don't know, a few of which I guess I get to teach you* – "is that everything that gets lost or dropped or left behind anywhere in the London transport system is all routed to the same place. Tube, buses, black cabs, it doesn't matter. Some of it goes through the police first, some of it sits in local offices for a week or so; then it heads for Baker Street. There's a normal-looking storefront at street level and vasty underground rooms beneath, all stuffed with stuff.

"They keep things for three months, and do what they can to reunite them with their owners; but you'd be amazed what doesn't get claimed. Eventually, that all goes for auction or else to charity.

"Except that Reno has her own people in the system, people who passed through here themselves until she found a place for them outside. Savoyards, we're everywhere. And the Baker Street Irregulars divert what they can, what they think she can use. It's another kind of charity, I guess, but – no. Not second-hand boots. You'll see."

He was still looking unconvinced. I just opened the door and beckoned him through.

\* \* \*

ONE THING ABOUT building underground, there's plenty of space. That unassuming door led into a long windowless store-room, lined and mazed with shelving. Shelves and shelves.

There were boxes and boxes all along the shelves, and every box was labelled. Shirts and jeans and skirts and underwear, all scrupulously clean. We knew; we did the work, picking and sorting and laundering, pressing and folding and boxing away. With labels. Often the laundering wasn't strictly necessary; much of this was new. Fresh from the shop, in its original wrapping, mislaid or forgotten and somehow never asked for. Of course people lose brollies and bras, but they lose ballgowns too. And wedding-rings and keys and brooches, yes – and telescopes and dartboards and voodoo masks and wheelchairs and you wouldn't believe what else.

We all knew our way around in here. We all did our stints, helping newcomers to find what they needed, hunting things down for ourselves. Making free, dressing to impress or dressing up to play, whatever. It wasn't always solemn and it surely wasn't uniform.

On the lower shelves, boxes and boxes of shoes and boots. Most of them new, unworn; many of them costly. Men's and women's and children's too, divided that way just for convenience. Some who came this way were indeterminate or uncertain or very certain indeed about how they meant to dress. Not all the skirts and stilettos went to girls.

Poor Jacey, he was still very uncertain. Charity boots. I didn't suppose for a moment that he'd ever tried to walk a step in someone else's shoes, and now he thought he had to. But we found his size and he picked through a few boxes reluctantly, and then with growing enthusiasm as he began to understand, as brand names peeped through tissue-paper. Soon enough we found one pair that he allowed that he could bear to wear; and he sat on the floor in new socks and gamely tried them on, laced them up, held his hand out to me for a teasing tug up. I just gripped him palm to palm and let him do the work, pulling against my solidity.

He blinked a little, as he rose. His body still remembered how mine used to be; he hadn't bargained for my Aspect, even that shred of it I was holding on to. I was a lot more solid, apparently, than he had budgeted for.

Still. He stamped his feet, paced back and forth, tried not to grin as soft leather folded itself around his feet. "Well," he said, "I suppose that'll throw the dogs off my scent." And then, "Are there any dogs down there?"

"Bound to be." I was just playing along, but chances were there'd be some werewolves among the Stranded. Or other shapeshifters, but those were the most common. I guess dog-kinds still seek out humankind for company or comfort. Cats walk by themselves, and birds can always fly away from trouble.

"Come on, then. Let's go and measure their confusion."

"Hang on. We'll find you a jacket first, just in case."

"In case of what? It's not going to rain today."

*No, but you may not be going home today. Or tomorrow, or the next day after. You may not have a home to go to any more.* Granted that he could always go to his parents, or any number of other houses, and know that he'd be taken in and looked after – but I couldn't. My best guess said that I was being hunted twice, by Jordan and the Cathars' mercenaries. That made two good reasons not to go to any of Jacey's regular hang-outs. I'd just be too easy to find, and I really didn't want to bring any more trouble down on him or his.

"In case you need the pockets," I said lightly. "Start lifting those boxes down, will you, tall boy? There's a hierarchy of clothing, and jackets are the peak of the pyramid, top shelf material. Don't ask me in what world it makes sense to put the heaviest things highest up. That's just what we do. Really I guess we ought to get a rack and hang them, but I don't know where we'd put it..."

Linen jackets, leather jackets. Nothing suited, until I found what looked like a genuine World War Two sheepskin flying jacket, worn and warm and romantic. Definitely second-hand, but. He protested, and I made him try it on anyway. As soon as the weight of it embraced him, he stopped fussing. Even before he saw the mirror on the back of the door, and checked out what he looked like.

The last of the few, that was what he looked like. Tousled and diffident and indomitable, like a mighty schoolboy.

Disturbingly much like the boy he'd been when we'd first entangled each other's lives.

That was something else not to be thinking about. I opened one more box on a shelf by the door, and started filling his useful pockets with useful things.

"Hey, what...?"

"What? Just because we're Stranded here, doesn't mean we have to beg like monks. Whatever we find, whatever comes in, Reno lets us use – and most of us don't go out much, so there's not much use for cash, so..." So there was money in the box here, money for the taking. I wasn't touching it, but he needed cash to feel comfortable. He could pay it back later, if it hung on his conscience. I'd show him how.

Folding money, then, a wad of notes taken uncounted from a fatter wad, all the cash that accumulates from jackets and jeans, pockets and purses and other stranger places; and a wallet to keep it in, people are always losing wallets; and a Swiss Army knife because he's a boy and besides you never can tell when a tool may be actually handy. And a pay-as-you-go phone all loaded up with credit, in case I lost him and he had to call for help or for a friend or for a taxi. A bubble-strip of painkillers in case of need – someone else's need, most likely; his kind aren't much bothered by headaches – and a notebook and pen in case he felt old-fashioned.

And then I was about done, but apparently he wasn't. He reached an arm above the mirror, and hooked down one of a dozen caps that hung up there.

Tried it on, checked the mirror, jauntified the angle and turned to me.

"What do you think?"

"Oh, absolutely. I think you need that." I did think it, too. He needed something that he'd picked out for himself. I didn't think a cap would cut it for long, but as a stopgap it was a fine idea.

And besides, it made him just that little bit more anonymous, less easy to spot; and besides, he did look really rather wonderful in it. Actually, I thought we looked really rather wonderful together, in the mirror there – but then, I always had thought so.

And besides, Jordan did hair of many colours, dyed or shaven, but he never wore a hat. That was good too, one more way to underscore the difference between one boy and another.

I didn't need it – it was the last thing I needed, the last thing that would ever happen, that I should confuse one Jay with another – but even so. Visual signals. Good to have.

Oh, yes.

Not thinking about that or the need for that, oh, no.

"Come on, then. Down we go."

This time, going down, we did use the dead escalator rather than the stairs. Because I was in the lead, and because the pitch of those steps was still wrong and would give each of us something else to think about, keep us rooted just a little in our bodies. Even if the effect was only marginal for both of us, given my Aspect and his – well. I don't like to say *natural superiority*, but. There it was. His body came easily to him. He danced down that escalator behind me, and grinned when I turned around, and said, "Why do they call it an escalator, anyway? The last thing it does is speed anybody up."

"I dunno. I guess when they're working, they escalate people's progress through the building, as an average, traffic management; some people are slow on stairs, going up or coming down. Never mind. Come and see the dorm."

The boy with no face was still blowing his melancholy riff. He was new since my day, but it felt like he had properly belonged there for ever, like nothing ever changed for him or for us or for anyone. I was here, wasn't I? Even with Jacey physically at my side instead of just oppressively in my head and frighteningly behind me, it wasn't that different. Hunted on the outside, hiding in here. Wondering just how to get away.

Last time, I'd found an answer – but it hadn't lasted long. I was here, wasn't I? And not on false pretences, not faking it. If the Cathars called it off, there was still Jordan; if Jordan decided that he really didn't care, there were still the Corbies, and whoever else had been set on my trail and unleashed.

Maybe Jacey could talk to the Corbies; they might listen to him – but they'd broken into his home and chased him out. They'd made him run away. Or I had, but it came to the same thing in the end. I didn't think he was in a talking mood, as far as the Corbies were concerned.

Besides, he thought he could take them. He might be right – but I didn't want to give him the chance to find out he was wrong. The way that Asher did, that sudden brutal revelation that even the immortals aren't actually that. Not even the young ones who ought to be immortal anyway, who often think they are.

It was odd, finding myself protective of Jacey, trying to keep him safe against his own worse judgement. I used to think that he'd keep me, safe and protected for ever. Then I fled him in terror: down the nights and down the days, down the arches of the years. I thought he was Death incarnate, or the promise of it. His father's representative. I thought he carried Hell in his back pocket, and would take me there.

I get things wrong, too. Turned out that was Asher, and he did that and he died for it.

Now it was Jordan, and I could die for it. If he could be bothered.

Turns out Hell is a heritable condition. Who knew?

WE TURNED RIGHT by Little Boy Blue, and let his horn-music wash us down the short connecting passageway into the dormitory at Savoy.

Onto the other platform, if you want to put it that way. It hadn't ever been used for trains, but it did still look the part.

Actually, mostly what it looked like was Henry Moore's wartime sketches, back when people used Tube stations routinely for bomb shelters and slept down there every night. Huddled, shrouded figures, somehow private and communal both at once: each little personal space like a single tesseract in a mosaic, helping to make a bigger picture.

There were no rails for a train to run along, down on the track below the platform edge. Even so, we had never colonised the railbed, either here in the lights of the open station or in the tunnel beyond. Stairs at each end of the platform offered an easy way down, and even so. People made their beds along the platform, and kept to it. Kids would race up and down the track, play cricket and their own more imaginative games, shriek and holler from one end to the other and dare each other into the tunnel's dark – but never for too long, and they'd come back, come up when they were called. I think there's something inadvertent in the human psyche, something ingrained. Tunnels are caves, and tigers lurk within; canyons are river-beds, only waiting for the flood.

Sometimes the kids seemed only too happy to be called away.

"What do you do for toilets, showers, laundry? Lunch, come to that?"

I grinned at him. "What, you think we're a dirty people? Or a hungry one?"

"No, I just think you'll have a solution, you must have. Only I can't see it here."

"Come with me. A tour of the facilities, courtesy of your willing guide."

I wanted to take him out of earshot anyway. Nobody here would spy for anyone outside – or at least I thought not, and so did Reno, or she wouldn't take them in. But I'd been wrong before. I'd missed a spy, so had other people, and trouble happened. For other people, mostly, then and later. Responsible was how I felt.

Learn from your own mistakes, and other people's trouble. I was a lot more cautious now.

Other people, in their troubles. Coincidences happen, that's why we have the word; it's not all fate or physics, it doesn't have to be inevitable. Sometimes it's just chance.

Like when you're walking along thinking about one person in particular, and suddenly there they are.

I'd been thinking about caves, and modern substitutes, and what you still might find inside them. And about spies, and the spied-upon, and what trouble that had led to. Dead people, in the end.

And here was a bench with someone sprawled along it, even their face covered with a blanket, which of course only made me think about the dead again though I'm sure they were only sleeping; and just beyond, huddled up against the foot of the bench was a figure shrouded in a blanket of his own, only he lifted his head as we passed and gazed up at me in a kind of bleak disintegration.

And I looked down at him and knew him, even in pieces as he was, just a shard of what he used to be; and what he used to be was resplendent and terrible beyond measure, cruel and generous and true. I had run away from him before, when he was the Sybil in her cave; but then she had been the one to run away, driven by foreknowledge, that day her cave was broken open and we were all dragged down to Hell. That day that Asher died, and Salomon too, and –

Gods, was it only yesterday? Really? Was that even possible?

Possible or not, we'd come a long way since then. Not in time, perhaps, and not in distance travelled, but a long way none the less.

Mostly down, I thought, for most of us.

For her, most certainly. For him, I mean. I thought I ought to mean. There wasn't a trace of drag about him here; he was only a man in middle age, in torment. In a suit and tie beneath his blanket, because I guess that was what he did, how he dressed without thinking when he wasn't being Sybil. Not being a voice in the wilderness, not singing out.

His suit and tie were doing him no good. Classic Englishman's armour, but nothing can defend against destruction from within. His eyes were hollow horrors. If Sybil the *grande dame* still lurked anywhere inside him, that was where she showed, crouched in the cavern of his skull. Still seeing the world as it was and as it would be, her twin curse; still unable to change a thing.

I didn't know, I couldn't guess what song she would sing for herself, but I thought it was probably going around and around in her head now, the most vicious of earworms, chewing and chewing as it went.

There may be a thousand songs all called 'Cassandra.' Perhaps it was a medley.

There was nothing I could say, to ease her. Nothing true. She knew the truth. That was her trouble in a nutshell, and it always would be.

I'd barely even hesitated, when our eyes met; just long enough to know her – *him!* – and to know how lost he was.

Just enough for Jacey to feel it through the hand he still held, and to check in his turn and glance around; which was just time enough for me to recover, and nod, and move on.

A little tug had stopped him; another brought him back to my side again as we negotiated our way along the platform, around one nest and another. Some people had hung screens around their beds or built walls of cardboard boxes, some mock of privacy that everyone respected. I didn't need to tell Jacey; he stepped as lightly as I did myself, with that same trick of seeming not to see.

At the far end of the platform were the stairs going down to the track, which we ignored. Also, there was a service door propped open.

"I don't know if this was always the plan," I said, "or if it cropped up in the digging. Maybe it was just accidental, someone hadn't done the survey right and they broke through without warning and everybody blushed; but –"

But beyond the service door was a plain brick corridor that must run parallel to the tunnel proper, and must presumably give access to it through the various businesslike iron-framed doors we could see spaced out as far as the light reached ahead, until a curve cut it off.

Closer at hand, though, and on the other side of the corridor was another door. It didn't promise much, maybe – it was plain wood and unadorned – but neither did it have the unappealing utility of the tunnel doors. And it was oddly warm to the touch when I laid my palm against it, and there was an inviting lamp on a bracket overhead. All in all, there was enough to say that something a little unexpected lay this way, without opening up at all what that might be. Like finding Narnia at the back of the wardrobe, and all those fur coats not having a thing to say about it.

I pushed the door open, and a billow of steam came out.

Jacey grunted. "What is this, the boiler-room? I'm not scrubbing down with a bucket drawn from the copper, girl…"

He didn't need to scrub down at all, he was freshly showered; and in any case his nose was better than that, he could smell that it was no industrial furnace pumping out that fragrant steam.

I didn't think either one of us would know Bay Rum if we smelled it, but I was fairly sure that was what we were smelling.

I said, "Not quite the boiler-room, no" – and ushered him through into what was, quite clearly, a boiler-room. Just, not for any Tube station or anything like it, except that this too was tiled floor to ceiling. Here the tiles were all white, and the boilers sat in the middle of the floor like gauche strangers in a private club, not knowing quite what to do with themselves; and there were benches and niches around the walls that all spoke about a different purpose before these great boilers came to squat and their fat black pipes broke through all the walls, and...

"It looks like a Turkish bath," Jacey said slowly. "Or it used to, before."

"Smart boy." In olden days, I would have kissed him for reward. Not now. Not nowhere near now. Though I still kept hold of his hand. "It is a Turkish bath. This used to be the sweat-room, until the diggers broke through. With or without notice, I don't know. But they must have wanted to keep the connection; maybe they figured that gentlemen heading up to the Savoy might like an hour to wash and brush up first. Only you couldn't just step from the platform into the sweat-room, not in your nice heavy City suit, not where other customers were naked; so they changed things around and made this be the boiler-room instead. Which is a bit déclassé, maybe, making gentlemen walk through the coal-dust and the stokers – so actually maybe they did this for the workers, the navvies who dug out the tunnels, let them scrub off the day's filth before they went home to the East End. Except it's all a bit grand for navvies, so – oh, I don't know. It's a mystery. Ask Reno.

"Anyway," I went on determinedly, tugging him past the boilers – all oil-fired and automatic now, no stoking required – and towards the further door, "this whole building was a Turkish bath below and a gentlemen's club above, and it closed down back in the '70s because there just weren't any gentlemen left, and it's never been open since. Mostly that's because Reno holds the lease. Maybe she bribes the council, I wouldn't know; maybe they're on the board and it's all legit. Anyway. At street level it's all boarded-up and dark, we don't use the upper storeys; but down here we get the best toilets, the best showers, the best baths in Westminster. And kitchens, too, of course; and there's a back way out into an old graveyard that nobody goes near because of all the dodgy kids who hang out there. Actually that's us, and that's how we come and go if we don't want to use the train. If we just want lunch somewhere that isn't here, or a coffee with a friend, or a breath of air that hasn't been breathed half a dozen times already. Are you hungry?"

He shook his head.

"Good, then. We've only just got here, and maybe I'm just being paranoid, but I'd really rather not show my face outside again this soon. I feel like half of London is looking for me. And I'm sure half the Overworld knows all about Savoy, but at least they can't get there. Not without Reno's consent, and she never gives that. Never ever."

"Um. She, um, doesn't look that formidable, Desi. Or at least, she most surely met someone more formidable than she is."

"She did. Or a pack of someones, I always reckon – but even so. She made me feel safe, when almost nothing could." *When you were trying so hard to find me, and your parents were trying harder.* "It's not just Reno, after all, who guards Savoy. You saw the train driver."

He shivered suddenly and violently, and I didn't think he was shamming that at all. "I did. What – no, never mind. You're right, I don't want to know. If he's on my side, I'm grateful, that's all. I think I'm grateful."

There were a lot of people in Savoy who would never accept that Jacey's side was the same as ours, not under any circumstances. But I didn't need to get into that right now. I tucked my arm through his as we came out into the central hall of the baths, and gave him a quick guided tour: lavatories, laundry-room, steam-room, plunge pool. "If you want a massage, there's usually someone around. If they're willing, they're probably pretty good. Some people spend pretty much all their time in here." Why wouldn't they? It was hot, it was clean, it was safe. Massage was a skill, and people were glad to have it, glad to use it, glad to feel the benefit. For some Savoyards, that was enough right now. For some, perhaps it always would be.

By definition, that made this not such a good place to be talking privately. It was our hang-out spot, because where can you be comfortable in a Tube station? We soaked and sweated, we dozed and splashed and shivered, we groaned beneath hard fingers that found out all our sore spots – and, yes, we talked. Inevitably, we talked. And listened, that too. It seemed not to matter so much back when I truly belonged here, when I saw the same faces every day and could just assume that everyone knew my secrets already. Now, though, I was an interloper, however hard I tried to pretend otherwise; and I'd brought Jacey here, and Jacey was worse. Jacey was from the Overworld, and nobody's victim at all, at least as far as anybody here was aware. Which made him totally fair game, and I wouldn't let them loom around him like shadows in the steam, tapping into the losses of his day. His home might be gone and his motors too, I think we were both assuming that; his self-respect was severely dented, standing in borrowed boots. No stranger was going to pry into his privacy too, as long as I had anything to do with it.

I had a plan; of course I did. I showed him all around the subterranean baths, and the busy kitchens beyond, another hang-out spot no use to us right now; and then I took him up.

Up a winding spiral marble staircase, into the hallway of the old club.

"I thought you said you didn't come up here?"

"I said it was all boarded up, and we didn't use it. Which is true. Sort of. But."

But for a building long abandoned, the floor was oddly well-swept, and the air was fresh. Perhaps there were broken windows and missing boards – but then one would look for birds' nests on the high ledges and droppings clustered underneath, and there was none of that. A person might think, perhaps, that people might come up here quite often. And might want to hide that fact, might sweep out the whole hallway to disguise the tracks their feet made through dust and grit, up from below and going higher yet, up the grand sweeping staircase to the upper floors.

Up, and up again: to where a glass dome stood above the stairwell, circled by an iron gallery. Here was the only daylight in the building, the bright sun making the most of its chance; here we could know we were alone. Here I could perch on the railing with the long fall at my back; I could wind my legs around his as though I were afraid of falling, the way I used to when we were kids, when we were lovers; I could smile at him a little twistedly, a little ruefully, and say, "We're safe to talk up here."

"You sure?" He looked down into the well, a little doubtfully. "If you whisper up in the dome in St Paul's, they can hear you all over."

"Not down in the basement, they can't. There's no one between here and there." This was the other place we came to hang out, as witness all the cigarette-stubs on the ironwork beneath our feet. It was astonishing the whole place hadn't burned down yet, though I thought Reno probably had something to do with that. Fire doesn't work too well around angels, perhaps.

"If there's an Ear around, they'd hear us."

"Yes – but that's true anywhere." An Ear is just what the name suggests, anyone with hypersensitive or directional hearing. They don't even have to be magical. Most of them are, of course, given the company, the nature of the Overworld – but half the young of the Overworld are geeks, one way or another. A kid with an electronics kit can be an Ear too. "All I'm saying is, this is as safe as anywhere I know. Even Reno doesn't hear us up here. As far as we know." If she did, she'd never acted on what she overheard.

As far as we knew, she hadn't.

It's hard to tell, with angels. Everything's conditional.

"Go on, then," he said. "Talk to me."

So I did. Mostly I told him about my morning, Jordan's parents, what I'd done. How Jordan had reacted.

He whistled softly through his teeth – then looked briefly pleased at the echo-effect as it rolled around the gallery, and did it again. Then shook his head and looked back at me all solemn and said, "You betrayed him? *You* did?"

"Yes. I suppose. I just – no. It's not betrayal. Someone had to stop him, that's all. Sometime. He couldn't go on for ever, tearing his parents apart and never being whole himself. Always on the run from who he really is. Someone had to stop him, and – well, it fell to me. It felt like mine to do, I was right there, you know? And Ash was dead, and…"

And I seemed to have stopped; that was the limit of my justification, a rock wall that I ran into every time.

He shook his head again and said, "I guess… Well, I guess I don't know, Desi. Fay wouldn't have done that. I thought you and he…"

Never mind what he thought, and never mind the truth of it. My turn to shake my head, just to shut him up. His hands were locked around the railing, on either side of me: not actually touching, but ready to grab in case I toppled. Just in case I toppled, I thought he was making that quite clear. I wasn't going to topple. My own hands had found their way around his waist, which I hadn't meant to happen; I was undoubtedly only holding on, arms and legs together, because of that lethal drop behind me. Just in case I toppled.

"So it's Jordan chasing you?" he said. "That makes sense." *Why you would come to me,* he meant. I thought he meant.

"One of," I said. "He didn't send the Corbies." He didn't have time; they were surely hunting me before ever he had cause to. And he wouldn't do that anyway. If he came for me, he'd come himself. If he could still be bothered.

"No," Jacey agreed. "No, I'm sure not." Even though that still left his parents as favourites for our current predicament, willy-nilly.

Except that the Corbies must have known whose flat they were breaking into, who I had run to. If their commission came from his father – well, they weren't stupid. They might stop to check. To check back, *do you still want us to...?*

They might even talk to Jacey. *That girl: do you know your parents want us to...?*

They hadn't done that, though. They'd just blasted in like he was nothing, one more mundane to be brushed aside. Which made no sense in that scenario.

I said slowly, "Reno said she shouldn't be surprised, to see me back. Given who had been asking for me, she meant."

He said, "What does that mean?"

"I don't know, but – well, when I left here, it was Reno found me the gig." She was the only one who knew, the only one I'd ever trusted to know where I'd gone after Savoy. Who I'd gone to serve.

"Wait. You mean, when you went to be a daemon? This is where the change happened?"

"That's right. Fay in, Desi out." Poor frightened desperate Fay had run to Reno, or been led that way.

She'd stayed a while, but she never meant to linger. A conversation, an interview, a contract: Fay disappeared, and Desi took her place. No less frightened, maybe no less desperate – you'd have to be desperate to sign that contract, but of course it was Fay's name at the bottom; yes, signed in Fay's own blood just for the drama of it, for the gesture, because she was a silly young girl and sure to be impressed – but cooler, that at least. Stronger already, and focused. Employed.

Not quite protected any more, but even so: beginning to think she could maybe look after herself. So long as no one found her for a while.

So she left Fay behind, and Desi went out into the world, and you could argue a long time over whether she was trying to find herself or lose herself entirely. Both at once, I think, and not a little bit of each but altogether.

"So who, then? Who took you into service?"

Did I hesitate? I'm not sure. Maybe I was only waiting while the conviction grew, feeling it happen, knowing that I did need to tell him now. Discovering that I trusted him, still or again.

Maybe that. Or maybe I did just hesitate, maybe it was as big a step that faced me as that fall that lurked behind. At any rate, I was silent long enough for his face to change, for him to think that I wasn't going to tell him.

His hands shifted, from the rail to my hips. Maybe that was meant to be persuasive, the familiar touch to help me over that last difficult hurdle; maybe he meant to shake the truth out of me. Or to lift me down off the railing, make me disentangle myself from him and stand on my own two feet, face him directly, only so that he could push me away as I seemed to be pushing him. Maybe. I don't know; I didn't ask.

I didn't get the chance to ask.

His face changed again, to a sudden sharp focus as he stared up over my shoulder.

Hullo Aspect, my old friend.

It was something in Jacey's expression, I suppose, hurling me into alert mode before I knew that there was any reason for it. My Aspect snapped around me, settled into the very bone of me, unsummoned but absolutely there as I flung myself backward across the railing.

No time to turn around, to peer, to have him point. I just locked my legs around his waist and hung upside down over that long fall to the hallway far below, feeling his hands' grip tighten, feeling utterly secure. Trusting him entirely after all, immediately and no question.

As a teenager I danced, I did gymnastics, even before I ever heard of Aspects. I've always been good at knowing just how I stood in the world. Or hung, or spun, or dangled. Proprioception, they call it. Upside down was no problem, it was only the quickest way to get a sight of the glass dome overhead; and I only needed to find what it was that had alerted Jacey.

Even knowing where to look, though, it still took me a moment. That was infuriating. He was a Power, sure, where I was just a daemon – but, hell, I'd been *designed* for work like this. Designed and trained and aimed like an arrow. What he had, he was only born with, and it wasn't like he worked it much. Or at all. Or –

There. Barely more than a speck, a fleck against the sun's bright glare. It could almost have been a flaw in the glass, a bubble in the curve of the pane; it could almost have been dirt on the outside, a smut of soot or a crow's feather, anything. It could almost have been a sunspot, massive and deadly and endlessly distant, nothing to worry about. But it wasn't.

It was dark and living, growing. Coming.

*Beware the Hun in the Sun.* They must have been reading Biggles.

Out of that fierce light it came, and of course it was a bird, a black bird, a crow, diving like a gull, like a missile, wings folded. All beak and thrust, and utterly unnatural.

It struck a single small pane dead centre – aimed like an arrow, yes – and there was a shatter of glass and blood and feathers, a falling and a drifting and presumably a death.

I was barely paying attention, except in so far as the Aspect logs everything. What concerned me more was what was coming after.

This time there was no looming shadow, no acrobatics in the air, no show for us to watch and wonder at. Just that narrow cast in the sun's eye like a squint, like a promise not yet realised. One bird wasn't it.

One bird and another, and another, and another: like links in a chain drawn taut, all diving on the same line, firing like bullets rat-a-tat through that same broken window, supreme marksmanship.

One by one they burst into that lofty space, and flung their wings out to lift themselves abruptly, bone-breakingly out of their plummet; and one by one they survived that brutal deceleration, and circled high in the dome there as more and more of them threaded through the window, tugged like knots through the eye of a needle on a thread invisibly fine. They massed together until it was hard to make out individual birds among those clots of black.

Then all those separate clots eddied into one, and came to settle on the gallery and were a man, just one man, one Corbie coming striding over the ironwork towards us.

It hadn't taken long, but time enough to think, that much at least. I don't know about Jacey, but for me it was time enough to make a choice.

I didn't give Jacey any choice at all.

He thought he could take them both, but there was no way I was letting him face even a single Corbie, if there was any chance at all that he was wrong.

I reckoned up the risks, made a decision and went further.

Further over.

All the way.

People often say that when I have my Aspect on, it makes me feel more solid, heavier, as if I acquired gravity with a flick of thought. Maybe they're right; it can feel that way to me, too. When you can punch your fingers into brick, you need another way to think about the world, and physics, and physicality.

But I think it's mental more than aspectual. Aspective. Aspectant. Whatever. Or maybe it's instinctual. Instinctive. Cats can do it. Tybs can be so light on his feet in your lap that you think he's all fluff and no body; then he curls himself up for a sleep and suddenly you're cuddling a cannonball in a fur coat.

Anyway. I had been hanging back over the edge there, trusting Jacey to counterbalance me, both of us caught in equipoise, almost no work at all for either one.

I trusted him; I guess he trusted me.

Now I made myself abruptly heavy. You wouldn't have moved me, if I'd been standing on the ground. Suspended in mid-air, nobody could have held me then: not even a Power.

Jacey would have let me go, except I didn't let him.

With my legs locked tight around his waist and my hands reaching up now to grab his arms, there was no way he was slithering free to be left behind for the Corbie.

I toppled backwards, and he came too: over the railing and down, down and down into that long waiting fall.

# CHAPTER SIX

HOW FAR WAS it?

Thirty feet or so, I guess. I wasn't really counting.

Mostly, as we fell, I was unhooking myself from Jacey, fending him off. Either one of us would make a softer landing for the other, but – well, sometimes it's not about sacrifice. Not when one of you is feeling particularly... concentrated, and the other is an unknown quantity. On an earthly scale, Jacey outweighed me by a distance; add that he's the son of two Powers, possibly the sum of two Powers, and I wasn't sure that he couldn't push his fingers into solid marble if he felt like it.

Into solid marble, or into solid me.

I just didn't know. I'd pulled him off the balcony in case we were wrong one way; I pushed him away from me as we fell in case we were wrong the other way. I didn't want to break his ribs, landing on him; I really didn't want him to shatter mine.

Two young fit people who know what they're doing shouldn't be too shaken by a thirty-foot drop. We'd both done parachute jumps, individually and together; we'd both done martial arts. We knew how to fall, in a simply human way – as witness, here we were, falling – but we knew how to land, too.

Besides which, he was Jacey Cathar and I was Desdaemona. I really wasn't worried about the fall, or the coming to ground after.

So long as I wasn't wrong about Jacey the other way. So long as we didn't find out the hard way – the extremely hard way – that actually he had human-normal bones in there. Thirty feet onto parquet is really quite a long way to fall, if you're not ready for it. Perhaps I should be pulling him close, falling beneath him, giving him that softer landing after all...

Thirty feet is plenty of time to second-guess yourself. If you remember your high-school physics, maybe it doesn't seem so much – thirty-two feet per second per second, it only takes a second to fall that far – but trust me. Second thoughts don't take as long as that. Your mind fills fast when it's flooding with fret and regret.

Still. I'd done what I could, or at least what I'd done; it was done now. Nothing to do but fall, until we hit.

Then nothing to do but "Oof!" – daemon or Power or not. Oof is an active verb, all about impact. Flesh and bone, decelerating hard. From 32 fps squared to nothing, in nothing flat. Hope not to be *too* flat.

Then nothing to do but ride that impact, roll with it, spend a little of that vicious energy in movement.

More of it had gone straight into the floor. I'd never broken parquet before; I hadn't known that thick wooden blocks could splinter.

Having an Aspect doesn't give me a soft landing, it doesn't give me anything soft. I hit just as hard as anyone; just then, as hard as Jacey. It's not that I don't feel it, it's just that I don't break.

Not as easily, at any rate. Little bits of me still break under sufficient provocation, blood vessels and such. I was going to be bruised, come morning.

It would have been totally mean of me to hope that the same was true of Jacey.

Totally mean.

So of course I didn't do that.

Of course not.

No.

I rolled to my feet and never mind the ouchie in my back, I wasn't going to show him that. Really I should have checked for the enemy first – it's a bad combat move to worry about your wounded before you know for sure you won't be joining them – but I did just glance aside, just to make sure Jacey wasn't lying broken on the floor there, all our guesses wrong.

Not he. He was coming easy to his feet, much as I was. Looking round, much as I was, rather than looking up. Just to be sure of me.

I frowned at him for being frivolous, and lifted my head ostentatiously.

Crows are bright birds, they learn fast. I'd hoped to see a figure of shadow and bulk flowing down the long turns of the stairs, quicker than any real man reasonably might. Instead, here came a shadow of birds, enough to darken that whole high hallway: hurtling down at us, seeming faster even than we had been. Is it possible to fly faster than you can fall? I don't know, my physics doesn't stretch so far.

But here they came, diving like cormorants, right for us. Crows love eyeballs, and I'd never wished my Aspect to be more like a coat that I could wrap around my head for cover, and it had never felt less like that. Nothing was going to save my eyes unless I did it my own self, swift and aggressive and hyper-aware.

Which is actually what the Aspect is really all about. What it's for, pretty much. It didn't really settle in on my shoulders with a happy sigh, *now you're talking*, but it did sort of feel that way as the first crow-missile reached me and my hand batted it aside.

I could write a list – actually, I think I am writing a list – of all the things an Aspect doesn't feel like or act like. Sometimes I used to think that what I really needed was another list for the thing itself to read, telling it all the things it really wasn't despite whatever it thought or wanted to be.

Except that of course it couldn't read, because it really wasn't aware. Certainly not self-aware.

Certainly not *enjoying* itself as we played crazy-cricket in the hall there, birds coming at us from any angle, both my hands independently deadly as I dashed them to the floor or swatted them into walls and pillars and newel-posts. If one of those birds had got through, I could have been in trouble; two could have finished me, one eye each. But I could, just about, handle this. Moment by moment, bird by bird.

By definition, if they wanted my eyes, they had to come where I could see them. That helped. The ones that attacked me from behind, that battered my head with their wings or tangled in my hair to peck and scratch at my scalp, I pretty much ignored. There wasn't too much damage they could do back there. It did hurt but only distantly, folded away, to be considered later. I worried more that they might think to coalesce into a man again behind my back, where I wouldn't see until he was manifest and deadly.

Which gave me the excuse I needed – no, the good military tactical reason – to check on Jacey and how he was doing. Peripherally, I was aware that he was on his feet and hurling crows around, much as I was; we weren't exactly tag-teaming, but every now and then one of his came my way, and vice versa. I didn't really need to concern myself with his, post-Jacey; they weren't up to much. And vice, I hoped, versa.

Still, I stole a better look in the first instant I could afford to – and nearly lost an eye but not quite, just snared the vicious thing in the air a moment before its kamikaze plunge could drive its beak deep into my skull – and saw him carving birds out of the air with a banister-post that he must have kicked out from under the graceful curving rail. With that in his hands he really did look like a cricketer, elegant in motion, lethal in contact.

"Wish I'd thought of that!" I yelled, between blows. And then, "Back to back?"

"Right."

The fighting had drawn us apart, more or less unheeding; now, deliberately, we drew back together, slaughtering as we went. The floor was deep in feathers and corpses now; bird-bones crunched underboot for both of us.

"How the hell many more?" Jacey demanded, flailing away. It was mean of me to wish that he might sound at least a little breathless. So I didn't, obviously.

"As many as they can recruit, I think." I wasn't gasping at all. Of course not. "All the crows in London, if they need 'em. I think they're conscripts, not constituents."

"How – no, never mind." He was right; this really wasn't the time to wonder how actual living birds could become part of some supernatural gestalt were-crow, in and out of form, an independent bird or a fragment of a human-seeming man, depending. "I don't suppose we can really go on doing this for ever."

"No." Sooner or later, when we did inevitably get tired or careless or lose the light, one or another of those birds would get lucky. A beak would find an eye.

"We should move, then."

"Yes." So long as we stayed here, the Corbies could carry on funnelling a constant stream of crows through the broken pane overhead. "The stairs would be easier." Birds could still come at us there, but only from one direction; we could spell each other, maybe even fetch some kind of help. I was slightly surprised that no one else had come up yet from the kitchens or the baths below. We were surely making noise enough to spur someone's curiosity.

"Do you think this is all of them? Both of them?"

"I'm hoping so." We'd only seen one human figure above – but I figured that if they could build themselves from birds, the Twa Corbies could build their twin selves into a single awesome man. Which was a neat trick, and maybe what they'd been doing before on the jib outside Jacey's window, to make a body massive enough to walk in through his window.

Step by step, like some four-limbed crablike creature, we shuffled sideways towards the tight spiral staircase that would lead us back below. Birds molested us all the way, but Jacey's batsmanship and my flying hands kept us safe until we reached the shelter of the stairhead.

More or less safe, and the approximate shelter. Jacey was bleeding from several gashes to his fingers, where they peeped from the sleeves of that heavy flying jacket. My hands were okay, but I could feel trickles of blood meandering across my scalp, ready to clot horribly among the roots. I still had one bloody bird knotted up in my hair; Jacey found the time to reach out a hand and yank it out.

That yanked enough hair with it to make me yelp. Which made us both grin, in the circumstances. He crushed it to rags of flesh and feather, dropped it on the stone steps, and for a little while we stood shoulder to shoulder just in the turn of the stair there, just far enough down that the birds couldn't come at us from above, they had to funnel through the narrow doorway.

Where they met Jacey's banister-post, which he handled like a quarterstaff now as there really wasn't room to swing. I didn't know he'd studied staff. I did know that there wouldn't be room for two of us without my getting in his way, so I dropped down a couple of steps to give him space. Took a couple of seconds to watch, to be sure he knew what he was doing – which he did: either he was a natural or else he really had studied quarterstaff – and then I left him to it.

That was actually harder than pulling him over the gallery rail. Trust just doesn't come easy, not to me.

Still watchful up the staircase just in case – what is it they say, *trust, but verify?* – I walked pretty much backwards down the steps into the loitering steam of the baths below.

AND LEARNED VERY quickly why that's always a bad idea, and why nobody had been coming up to see what all the noise was about.

Actually I knew already, that it was a bad idea. I've seen enough horror movies. When a character's going one way but looking another, you just know they're heading into trouble. Turns out that people do it anyway, despite all those movies. Despite their Aspect positively screaming at them, at least in so far as a mute insensate artefact can scream: which is not quite far enough, apparently.

I was warned, as I should have been. Distracted and anxious, I was just that little too slow to react, which I never should have been.

Though to be fair, he was bloody fast. And bloody quiet, that too.

There was blood in the steam. I could smell it now, too late. Now that his arm had closed around my throat, so that I couldn't even yell a warning up the stairs to Jacey.

Damn, I was supposed to be better than this. Jacey could look after himself; I certainly couldn't look after him without first doing the same thing, getting myself sorted. Breaking free of this chokehold. Basic stuff, except when the choke comes from something frail under your fingers and yet intolerably strong, like bones of slender steel wrapped in some cool matter that might look like flesh from a distance, at a glance, but really wasn't to the touch. More like iron filings, when they cling to a magnet: individual shifting barbs making a stubborn whole, like uncounted birds joining into a man.

There was another smell to cloak the blood, more immediate, right there beneath my nose: a mustiness and a wildness together, the smell of a thousand nests of old dead twigs and moss and shed hair, fallen feathers, detritus.

How many Corbies make a man? Just the one, apparently, that we'd seen above. The other must have come in through the tunnels, he would never have survived the train; and he'd been waiting down here for exactly this, for exactly me.

As above, so below. One came as birds, one came as a man, both the same thing. Manageable to themselves. Jacey could manage the one, I thought, at least for now; this one was for me. There was no one here now who could manage him. Blood in the steam. Bodies that I didn't want to look for. *Damn it, Reno! This place is meant to be safe, it's why we come...*

Too late to protest now. Everything's unfair, and nothing is secure.

My fingers can punch through brick. This was bird-bone: impossibly dense, compounded of impossible numbers of birds, and even so.

It was like a steel bar across my throat, pressing hard enough to cut off air and blood together, and even so.

I still need air, but not that much, not right that moment; my blood still pumps around, but it's... special. It works hard.

Just as well.

I set my legs, grounding myself as solidly as I could when I didn't stand on solid ground, when my senses were catching echo or vibration or something to say that there was hollow tunnel underneath me. One of the other Tube lines, that must be; London's clay is woven through with them, it's like an ant-hill, like a hive, a three-dimensional city.

Then I bent and twisted, to hurl this bird-man over my shoulder and away.

Tried to.

He wasn't shifting, as it turned out.

I thought I grew heavy, when my Aspect was upon me. I was nothing, a lightweight next to this guy. Next to this guy now. He'd been a featherweight before, when I'd hurled him off the towpath; how many birds had he filled up with, since then? He must have swallowed whole aviaries, whole species. Maybe he was the one I flung into the river; maybe he'd taken half the Thames on board for ballast, though it hadn't washed away the smell of him. A thousand thousand nests, it might have been.

Whatever. I couldn't budge him. Me with all my Aspect turned up to eleven.

He *laughed* at me, he did. In a bird-voice, a bird's

laugh, harsh and hollow. And then leaned close to my ear and made words with his troubled mouth, clashing his jaw on them as though he had a beak yet:

"Oz wants to talk to you."

Six words, and they were an answer to all my questions of the day. Mine and Jacey's too.

Actually, one word would have been enough. Just the name, one shrunken syllable, Oz: that's plenty.

It stopped me fighting. Trying to fight. Stopped me dead, in my useless straining. Instead I stood very, very still. The Corbie laughed again, like a made man, like a gangster satisfied; and then I stamped.

Aspect up to eleven, I stamped. And stamped again, brought my foot crashing down in its good boot, again and again on that tiled floor.

Maybe understanding gave me a whole new notch on the dial, turned me all the way up to twelve.

I did not want to go and see Oz. No.

I stamped out the urgency of that, the fury and the fear all together; and the outrage too, that these damn birds should make themselves so free of our lives, our time, our choices. Jacey's *home*, where I'd gone to be safe; here where I'd brought him, where we should both of us be safer...

I stamped.

When it was a gentlemen's club with a bathing-house below, it was likely kept up spruce, in good repair. Since it was abandoned, not so much. Not at all, to be honest. We kept it as clean as we liked it and the boilers working, but the building wasn't our responsibility. Reno's, perhaps – I didn't know the terms of her lease, if she had one – but she had other things on her mind. So long as we weren't complaining, she wasn't interested what went on over here. This wasn't even technically Savoy; I'd never seen her out here. Come to that, I'd never seen her outside her office, night or day. It might be difficult for her, coming and going, the size she had to be standing up; if she had no other damage than the wings, I was still sure it would be painful, walking about. No blame to her if she chose not to do that, if she could contrive to avoid it.

What's the internal economy of an angel? I didn't know. Perhaps she lived on sunbeams. Bottled sunbeams, fetched down underground and kept in one of her filing-drawers like a subterfuge whisky.

Whatever. If she didn't check the state of the building, no one did. And this floor wasn't laid on solid rock, or even rubble. I knew it, I could feel it: flagstones beneath the tiling, maybe, but those flags lay on wooden joists. And what with all the water dribbling down through cracks, through decades, with oozing clay beneath to keep everything good and damp...

I stamped, and stamped again.

The tiles were long since shattered. The flag we stood on tilted and fell back. I stamped again.

The stone cracked, but the joists beneath just splintered. The whole floor came apart, and through we fell.

There was clay, I said, beneath the joists – but no great depth of it. Under that was a tunnel. And we fell and were heavy, too heavy for Victorian engineering not built with the Overworld in mind. We fell through, in a slimy mess of sticky clay and crumbling brick.

And I thought we'd come down in a railway tunnel, probably with a Tube train bearing down on us.

As we fell – as we fell apart, which I guess was a blessing, and had always been part of the plan, in so far as there was one – I remembered about the live rail. And wondered if we'd both fall directly onto it or only one of us, and if so, which one, and whether my Aspect could absorb six hundred and fifty volts of current, and whether the Corbie could fly apart into all his separate birds before he hit, and –

AND THEN WE struck.

Struck *water*.

Struck and sank, heavy and unexpectant.

It took me a moment of cold startled shock before I could recover enough to remember that I'd probably need to swim, I wasn't going to get far just thinking myself buoyant. I might not need as much oxygen as often as a regular unenhanced girl, but that didn't mean I could just wade underwater until this culvert spewed out into the air...

No, it was more than a culvert. It was over my head; I kicked out and broke the surface and found myself in a positive river. It was almost black dark, but my eyes are as good as anything I have, and that hole we'd made in the tunnel roof let fall enough light to see by. There was a current, but the water was foul and sluggish with city corruption; I swam to the side, and here was a walkway and a ladder leading up to it. Old and rotten with rust, but even so. I thought myself as light as possible, and hung from a rung of the ladder while I scanned the water for any sign of my enemy.

This was the second time today I'd dunked a Corbie. I was guessing that they wouldn't like it much.

Frankly, neither did I. I wasn't sure if that mephitic atmosphere was explosive – but I wasn't sure that it wasn't, either. I tried not to breathe too deeply, and just hoped nobody came down here with a candle.

Nobody seemed to be coming down at all, despite the hole in the floor above. Nor was there any sign of the Corbie coming up. If he was still down there, he must be in trouble.

Well, good.

I hauled myself out, and right by the ladder was a door in the ancient brickwork. It was locked, but I didn't even need to set my shoulder to it; there's strength enough in Aspected fingers to break most locks with a twist of the handle.

The other side of the door was a short brick passageway that smelled of damp, then stairs rising up to another door.

Beyond that was the janitor's room. We didn't have a janitor, and I guess we'd never had a key or enough curiosity to find out what lay down below. Mostly we just used this as a laundry room.

Squelching, I walked out into the broken hallway.

People were gathering: not from the baths as they should have been, I think everyone who'd been in the baths or the kitchen was dead now, but they came from Savoy, through the boiler-room, puzzled and afraid.

One came down from the club above, and oh, was I glad to see him.

Jacey wasn't the only one staring at the state of me, but he was the only one I cared about. I skirted the hole and everyone else and went to him and said, "Don't ask. What's the state of things upstairs?"

"Don't ask," he said. "Knee-deep in feathers and corpses, since you did. But they went away eventually. Not the feathers, not the corpses. Don't get clever. All that muck's still up there, a nice job for someone, bags not me. I mean the endless bloody birds. After we heard the ruckus down here, they just wheeled up and flew away."

I supposed that was a blessing. Temporary one, maybe. "They'll be back," I said, as ominous as I could make it, just to stop him getting cocky. "Or someone will. One way or another. I know what they want now, and they won't stop."

"Okay. What do they want?"

"Me."

"Well, yes. I think we knew that. What do they want you for?"

"Confession. Punishment. Revenge... Something like that. Look, I'll tell you, okay?" I really didn't want to – it was going to sound like an accusation, *this is what you drove me to* – but there wasn't any help for it, as far as I could see. "Just, not like this. Not sodden, and not stinking. You go up to Reno, tell her what's been happening, if she doesn't know already. Then raid Lost Property for me, will you? Clothes, boots, everything. Bring it down here. I'm going to take all the hot water that there is, and scrub myself from the inside out."

Poor Jacey. I might be the only person on the planet who felt sorry for the guy – or who would dare to – and I seemed to be making a habit of it today. He knew my size intimately, and he had a good eye – he used to love buying me clothes when we were new together, when I was all unused to designer labels and fittings with the actual designers – but he was all unused to being ordered about, by me or anyone. He'd just been a heroic warrior upstairs, and he probably wanted praise for it; I was sure he wanted a bath himself, preferably with a drink attached. And instead here I was sending him off on errands. No wonder he looked bemused.

Still, he agreed placidly enough, once he'd reassured himself by word and eye that I really wasn't hurt. And once he'd done what he could to wedge that door shut, that I'd come through. Nothing he could do would have stopped me, and I didn't think for a moment that it would stop a Corbie, but it made him feel better. He peeled off his new jacket first, then started ripping great baulks of timber from the broken floor and slamming them into place with his bare hands. I left him to it, shedding my own clothes unheedingly as I headed towards a long and scalding soak. If the Corbies came back – well, they needed a bath too, but they'd just have to wait their turn.

# CHAPTER SEVEN

JACEY ALWAYS WAS fastidious. It was no surprise when he did come to find me in the steam room that he came towelled and scrubbed, with his thick hair dripping wet. Everyone else was long gone, the shocked and the helpful and the dead. Whatever came next – and something surely would – I figured it would be different; birds just weren't cutting it today. Hopefully, arranging something else would take time. I was determined to take time anyway, no more fighting till I really felt clean all the way through. Fastidious might have been one more thing I picked up from Jacey.

That meant I couldn't dodge it, though, as he settled down beside me and said, "Come on, then. Give. What's this all about? That's not Jordan sending the Corbies after you, or his family either; and I'm damn sure it's not mine. Whatever you think, or want to think. So who? Who else has a reason to be after you?"

"A better reason than anyone. Or he thinks so." I smiled a little thinly, and wanted just to nestle up against his shoulder, so that at least I wouldn't have to look at him while I confessed. And then thought, *sod it*, and did just that.

Damp hair on bare skin: he didn't seem to mind. I inhaled the old familiar smell of him, as his arm settled around my sweaty shoulders. Neither one of us was going to worry about the sweat, or the fact that I didn't even have a towel on. We'd come too far, too strangely to be body-shy with each other now.

Even so, it wasn't only the situation that had me keeping a tight hold on my Aspect. Let that slip, and – well. So would his towel, if being hurled aside counts as slippage.

"Don't go to sleep, girl. Talk to me."

"I'm not. I was just... organising my thoughts," and never mind what thoughts, or in what order.

"Come on, then. Trot 'em out. Tell me who's been sending bad people to ruin my life."

I could feel his lips moving in my hair. We used to talk like this all the time, but that was long ago, back when I never wanted to peel apart from him, when I'd have melted into his skin if it was only possible.

Now I only wanted to apologise, for being the one who was ruining his life. He'd deny it, of course, but I couldn't. I wasn't quite sure that I was bad, exactly, but dangerous to know, oh, yes. Trouble didn't follow me, so much as the other way around. I stalked it down dark and obviously untrustworthy alleyways, picked its pockets for the hell of it, tapped it on the shoulder and ran away like a kid playing games, led it inexorably into other people's paths and let them face its fury.

"When I –" I said, and stopped. And tried again: "When you and I..." And stopped again, because that was just dishonest; and so, back again, "When I left you, when I... had to hole up for a while, I did that thing that kids do, sinking down into the streets, getting lower and lower." Finding trouble, more and more. "I was lucky; I ended up here." Lucky, or well-connected. I didn't dare use any of my connections, because they'd all lead back to Jacey and the Cathars, but – well, call it well-informed. I knew all about the Overworld, so I knew what to avoid and what to be afraid of; and when I'd sunk far enough, when I'd found my way down to the underworld and the Savoy, I wasn't fazed by an angel with shattered wings. I wouldn't have trusted her either, except that so many of those she'd gathered here – *under my wing*, she liked to say, deliberately ironic, cruel only to herself – were in the same state, distrustful and holing up. And not betrayed. And moving on, some of them, one by one as Reno found them safe passage; and coming back every now and then, an act of kindness, just to reassure us that they really were safe and not sold down the river, and –

"One day Reno called me upstairs, because she had something for me. Better than hiding, she said. She says there's always something better, always a way to live if you can find it. Or if she can. That's the best thing about Savoy, that it's like the hotel overhead; you can stay as long as you like, as long as you need to, but it's only ever meant to be a stopover. People come and go and you can see that happening, it's like a constant reminder that the same thing can happen to you, your life can change, there's always somewere else to be if you can get there. If she can get you there.

"What it was, she had a client looking for a girl. That's... not unusual. Sometimes it means just what you think it means. Reno isn't judgemental; if a girl is willing – or a boy – then that's fine, so long as they know what they're getting into. And how to get out of it again, that too.

"This time it wasn't about sex, though. Not just about sex. He was offering a full makeover, a daemonic Aspect with all the bells and whistles, enough to help me feel safe in the world." As much as anybody could feel safe, with the Cathars hunting them. I leaned harder into my own Cathar, and didn't feel safe at all, and went on talking.

"What he wanted... Well. Put plain, he wanted an assassin.

"An assassination, rather, it was a one-time deal. Seduce someone, get inside their guard – and kill them."

"Fay wouldn't do that." His objection was immediate and absolute, as if it had been jerked out of him on a string, or just utterly physically rejected by his body: projectile vomiting of a thought.

I said, "No, of course she wouldn't. But I wouldn't be Fay, would I? I'd be Desdaemona: cool and strong and not bothered. In my head, Desdaemona was like hatching from a caterpillar to a butterfly, she wouldn't be like me at all. Not recognisable. I thought I could write her like a song, make her amoral and magnificent...

"And besides, that isn't what he said. He didn't put it plain like that, he didn't say 'assassin.' I don't know what Reno would have done, if he had. Maybe she'd just shrug and say okay, she'd find him someone. I think maybe my dream of Desdaemona was quite a lot like Reno. I wanted to be... not human, I think. As far from Fay as it was possible to get. If he had said 'assassin,' I might have stepped up anyway, just to prove to myself that I could do that.

"But all he said was 'thief,' he said get into this man's bed, get into his house and steal something from him – and that was easy. It should've been easy. It was easy enough to agree to, anyway. If you're going to sleep with somebody for gain, why wouldn't you steal from him too? If you're a cool romantic outlaw type who keeps her desperation simmering just below the surface, where everyone could see it anyway? Of course I agreed. What did I have to lose, when I'd lost it all already? Gods forgive me, but I was almost grateful."

I'd told the story before, here and there, or parts of it: just often enough that the old ways of telling it, the old words came easily to my tongue. A little too easily. They were out before I understood how much they must be hurting him. I wanted to bite them back, too late; I wanted to apologise, but for what? For telling the truth about the girl I was, the girl he made of me? Nothing would get any better, if I went that way. If I took us down that road.

Besides, I'd made something different of myself, and that was all on me. Nothing to do with him, no choice of his. My burden to bear, my guilt to confess. All in a rush I said, "So that's what I did. I signed

up, I got my Aspect on, I tracked down my target
and seduced him, all as per instructions. Yeah. Only
then I figured out that what the client wanted me
to steal was his oxygen, and... Well. Apparently I
wasn't so cool after all, or I still had too much of Fay
left in me, or whatever. Because I didn't want to do
that. So I didn't." Which would obviously be why
my erstwhile employer was in pursuit of me now.
There. All wrapped up, in one neat burst of speech.

Jacey took his time, thinking it through. Then he
said, "Sweetheart."

I said, "Don't call me that. That was Fay, not me.
And a long time ago."

"Not that long," but he was immortal, what did
he know about time? "And – well, here you are,"
tucked into his shoulder, under his arm, just the way
I used to be. Skin on skin, in the sweat and the heat
and the solitude, whispering secrets. Just the way we
used to be. "And there are some holes in your story,"
he went on sternly, kind of the way I'd just been
hoping he wouldn't be. "Like names, and details,
and like that. Tell me what actually happened?"

"You don't need to know the poor guy's name. It
wouldn't mean anything to you anyway. He was...
just a pawn." *Like me.* "It's what you Powers do,
you use us to fight your battles for you. Yeah, yeah,
I know: you wouldn't use me. But others would.
Others did. Him, and me too."

"So who...?"

"Oz Trumby," I said; and Jacey was quiet then,
very still, and apparently there were names that
could make even a Cathar hold his breath, and
who knew?

Then, "Wait, what? You were *working* for *Oz Trumby?*"

"Yeah." *I had to do something.* "And I guess he just found out that I didn't do what he asked. What he paid me for." What he had most generously paid for, with money in the bank and a house and a boat, none of which mattered all that much, all of which I could walk away from at need – as witness, here I was – and with my Aspect, which mattered a great deal, at least to me.

None of that meant anything to Oz, of course. The money, the power: they were just small change to him, the kind of life-changing benefit he handed out like tips for good service. He didn't even look for gratitude. But good service, yes. He expected people to deliver what he'd paid for.

Nobody ever cheated him, nobody would dare – but I had. And now he'd found out.

And he knew where I was, or his agents did; and of course he knew all about Savoy; and talking it through with Jacey was the same as working it out on my fingers, and –

"We need to get out of here."

"Yes." No argument, no hesitation. Jacey's mind was tracking my own thoughts, which was one of his best tricks way back when. I used to think it was magic, but not really. Mostly I expect I was just pretty obvious. Fay's life had been so simple; I didn't often want to go back – what, and give up my Aspect? No way! – but right now, oh, I might have given a lot to be stripped back to basics. One girl, one boy, one place to be and no one chasing me...

Dream on. We didn't even stop for the traditional

cold plunge; we just tipped a bucket of water over each other to rinse the sweat away and reached for towels, grabbed clothes when we were only half dry, skirted the hole in the hallway floor and headed back into the tunnel with our hair still dripping.

Hand in hand like a statement, the one thing we really wanted to say to each other, the one thing we really didn't need to: *hurry, hurry...*

Two hurries, because there were two things we needed to do. The second was the one we'd said aloud: to get moving, be somewhere else, oh, yes. Savoy was a sanctuary, sure – but not against Oz Trumby.

The first was to warn Reno. She was suddenly not safe, in her own refuge. Nobody was safe. Which wasn't fair, but life isn't; which was my own fault all down the line, and there was nothing new in that either.

Trouble. I bring it. You should probably not take me in.

Jacey surely shouldn't. Perhaps he was having second thoughts, constructing a wall of regrets; as we went, he said, "Maybe you should go back to Jordan's people."

"Oh, what?"

"No, I'm serious. The Lord of Hell and his lady? Even Oz Trumby couldn't move against those two. And they'll be feeling very grateful to you just now."

"They'll be with their precious son just now. And Jordan wants to kill me."

"Perhaps. Perhaps not, now. He might be grateful too, by now; you've given him back a lot of what he'd lost. And you're right, he did have to grow up sometime. He knows that too; I think he's always known it. Anyway, even if he's still, what, lingeringly murderous, his parents will nip that in the bud. You shouldn't be running from everybody at once, it's too complicated."

Which was my thought again, echoed back at me as we hustled along the walkway to the dormitory platform. But everything about Jordan was complicated, and not everything could be cancelled out by his father's word. I didn't know how I felt, even, only that I didn't want to be facing him again today. Especially with Jacey so firmly attached to my right hand, and so welcome there.

I said, "I'd rather go to your folks than his," just to make the point; he knew exactly how I felt about his family.

"Okay, deal," he said immediately. "We'll go there."

Had I just been snookered, or stymied, or sold a dummy? Or some other sporty metaphor to prove that he was playing me for a sucker? I wasn't sure, and we were in too much rush to jerk him to a halt right now and interrogate the slippery drip, but – yeah. I was fairly sure, actually.

Still. Rush. One thing at a time. Warn Reno; get the hell out of here; then take Jacey apart, make him sorry he'd ever tried to put one over on me.

Heh. If I only could. Dream on – though I might enjoy trying.

Safe in the knowledge that he'd enjoy it too, and then take me apart entirely, and...

No. Let's not go there. Not now, not today. Not the day I ran from Jordan.

The day I did to him what Trumby had paid me to do to someone else: seduced him and took advantage of his trust, took something from him that he couldn't live without, that left him with his throat open to the knife. Funny, the parallels hadn't struck me before.

Right now, it was like being hit by a train.

Sometimes, a parallel is just painfully apt. There we were picking our way along the platform, between huddles of stressed and frightened Savoyards not sure where their greater safety lay. I guess metaphorical trains can jump metaphorical tracks; I felt the impact, the thought of it so hard, I almost stopped moving. I did hesitate, just long enough for the crouched figure against the wall there to lift his head and find me.

One more time, the Sibyl saw me; one more time, the Sibyl sang.

> *Ride a cock horse to Banbury Cross*
> *To see a fine lady upon a white horse...*

It was a child's nursery rhyme, and I didn't understand it. I didn't want to hear it: that thin reedy voice, haunting me like a monument of loss as we hurried away.

"Should we be telling them?" Jacey's voice was just a murmur, but his eyes were a giveaway. "Give them time to get packed up, start moving. They can't stay."

"Of course they can't – but let Reno tell them. If we start a panic now, there'll be a stampede. There'll be deaths." *More* deaths. "She'll know how to handle it; she'll get the train organised, evacuate them properly..."

*If she has the time.* It was the thought we both shared, and neither one of us uttered.

\* \* \*

AS IT HAPPENED, she didn't have the time. None of us did. It was still the right choice we made, but people could have suffered for it regardless. That's one of the hard lessons of being grown-up, that sometimes the right thing can go very, very wrong.

We were through the crowds and off the platform, past the boy still blowing his lonesome horn, halfway up the dead escalator – taking the escalator without discussion, without need for words, because it was fewer steps and we were both ramped up, leaping easily – when we started to hear screams.

Behind us, below.

I stopped dead, we both did, and gazed at each other with a dreadful surmise. Neither one of us wanted to make that full turn around, to go back down and see just what had followed us onto the platform.

Only, there didn't seem to be enough screaming for the horrors we imagined; and when someone came running, he came from the other platform, where the train still shuttled back and forth into the network proper.

Young man, nothing to pick him out from the crowd, nothing in the least strange about him bar his evident terror. People like him washed up at Savoy all the time, and seldom stayed for long. Likely it was their first encounter with the non-human world, and for most of them it would be their last. If they had their way, at least, it would.

This boy, I thought he would jump under a train sooner than meet anyone – anything – else from the Overworld. Whatever it was that followed him, I thought he'd lead it straight through onto the dormitory platform, where so many people were gathered. I thought it'd be a slaughter.

I'd already taken the first step back down, that way you do, only missing the slam of my Aspect all around me because actually it was all there already. Jacey checked me, though. Just his hand in mine, enough to hold me against my firm intent: it was like a casual reminder that this was a Power at my side. No mortal boy could have stopped me so easily. Or at all.

He said, "Wait. You think it's after him?"

"No, but he'll –"

"No, he won't. See?"

So I looked, and no: he wasn't running through to the other platform. I should have known that without looking, just from the sudden silence down below. Apparently just having an Aspect wasn't enough; I needed to pay attention.

The boy with no face had let his horn drop on a thong around his neck, and grabbed the screaming boy as he tried to pass; and now they stood there head-to-head. The faceless one was saying something, anything, it didn't matter what. I did briefly wish that he might have gone on playing instead; there might be some kind of protective magic in music, and I knew for sure there was none in any words. Friends talk to each other all the time, and bad things happen anyway.

And here came the thing that he'd been running from, and no blame to him for that. I thought he should still be running, and his friend too.

Jacey thought we should still be running, on up the steep wooden steps. His insistent tug said so, and his voice too, "Christ, come *on*...!"

"Wait, shouldn't we...?"

"Shouldn't we *what*? You think you can fight that?"

Well, no, but he wasn't giving me the chance to prove it. With his hand locked around my wrist, he marched upward and I went with him, willy-nilly.

Speaking truth to power all the way, cursing him blindly in a sullen monotone. Not really trying to fight him, though: not pulling back against his relentless tug, not in the grip of a toddler tantrum, not having a meltdown, no.

I hated it, but he was right. We couldn't fight that. Even working together, a daemon and a Power. No chance.

Even so, I watched over my shoulder as we climbed. I wanted to cry *Fly, you fools!* but there was no point. It was – well, just too big. People think they know what to do when an earthquake hits, but the first time they're actually in one, mostly they just stand abstracted while the world shakes underneath them and everything falls down all around.

Okay, maybe they fall down too. Even if nothing falls on top of them. It's hard to keep your feet when the ground's turned to jelly, but it's harder still to take positive action, get moving, get out of there. Something gets cut between the mind and the muscles: the paralysis of shock, it's very real.

Those boys were really only standing there, waiting for the wyrm to eat them.

\* \* \*

SEE, YOU SAY "dragon" and everybody knows what you mean: bright colours, flame and flight and glory. Virgins and sacrifice, terror and greed and death like a promise, everybody looking around for a hero on horseback.

That's just the story we tell ourselves; it's really not very English. Hell, we even had to steal St George from Palestine. The dragons of legend come from much further afield.

Our home-grown, English dragons? It'd save time and trouble if we'd just learn to call them wyrms.

And where else would you look for a wyrm, than under the earth...?


FLIGHTLESS AND FURIOUS about it, this wyrm came barrelling out into the stairway, and you did just have to hope that it hadn't met any trains coming or going. It was pretty much the size of a train itself, and a hell of a lot nastier. If I'd been standing waiting for a ride, and seen that coming up the tunnel towards me – yeah, I think I'd have screamed too. Run too.

I still thought the boy should shut up now.

So did his faceless friend, I guess. His hand clamped over the other boy's mouth, he could manage that much, though between them they still didn't have the strength or the wit to get out of there.

Nor did I, of course. Jacey was running for both of us, dragging me along in his wake.

The wyrm was sludge-grey and slimy, absolutely right for a life under London, with a mouth that could doubtless chew its own holes through London clay if we hadn't kindly dug them for it, sewer and Tube. Actually its front end was pretty much all mouth. It could only see where it was going if it puckered up; open wide, and its own jaws would block its mean little eyes altogether.

Maybe that's what saved the boys. Maybe it knew from experience that a mouthful that small wasn't worth gaping for, it was too hard to catch, snapping blind.

Or maybe it was just more directed than that. More driven. A wyrm on a mission, not to be distracted by casual passing snacks.

If so, its mission was us. But we knew that already; it was no surprise to see the thing head straight for the stairs, the dull half-buried eyes turned absolutely and intentionally onto us.

Okay, not the stairs: the escalator. Never mind that that wasn't working, it would work well enough to snake up by. Besides, the creature was following us. Maybe its primitive mind couldn't handle the notion of parallel courses.

It would have fitted better on the stairs, but – okay, maybe I exaggerated before. Not the size of a train, it only seemed that way. Maybe not even the length of a train, though its pulsing body still trailed back onto the platform while its head came oozing up the escalator. I was still surprised that it could fit into the narrow gap between the rubber handrails, barely two people wide. Maybe a wyrm's body is rubbery itself. For sure it's flexible; it has to flex to move. No legs to carry it, just its own undulating self.

I was surprised too how fast it had covered the ground between the platform entrance and the foot of the escalator. It seemed slower now, squeezing up behind us. Maybe it really was struggling to fit, like toothpaste trying to crush itself into the tube. Like dough, massively overflowing the bread-tin. Muffin-top.

Anyway: we were at the top suddenly, bursting out into the ticketing hall – and now at last Jacey let go of my arm. And didn't sprint for Reno's office, didn't yell. Instead he turned back to the escalator, bent down, gripped the wooden slats of those unmoving stairs and *heaved*.

A Power, in his strength. Yeah. He ripped those slats away.

I could have done the same thing if I'd wanted to, if I'd seen the point. A daemon, in her strength. Yeah.

Only then Jacey plunged his arms deep into the mechanism beneath, found something more resistant to grip, and heaved again.

"Uh, Jacey...?"

"You could help," he gasped. "If you wanted to. This thing's bloody heavy."

I wasn't sure if he meant the escalator or the wyrm. Either way, really.

I was willing enough, but there wasn't room for the two of us at the head of the escalator. They are two people wide, just barely, but not if one person is straddling that whole width to get good purchase.

Besides, he might be puffing and blowing a bit, but he didn't really need me. One more heave, and he tore the whole linked chain of steps loose from its tracks. And then began to pace backward as he hauled, drawing the wyrm ever higher as he went, as it squirmed. Higher, closer...

"Uh, *Jacey...?*" I was starting to sound like a sampled loop, except that my voice too was getting ever higher, while I was no closer to understanding.

"What?" He grinned at me mirthlessly, mercilessly. "You want me to shake the thing loose, is that it?"

"Well, yeah..." I didn't see the point, else.

"And what, send it down among the little people, let it eat them instead?"

It was what his father would do, coldly and deliberately, no question. Apparently it's what I would have done without meaning to, without thinking. Not what Jacey would do, even in crisis, even when he'd already said we couldn't fight the thing.

There are reasons why I like that boy. Why I always did. I have good instincts, maybe. Or he does.

Okay, self-immolation it was, then, for the sake of those below who really couldn't help themselves. Neither could we, of course, but at least we'd make some noise about it. At least some people would want to know what had happened.

I pictured the Cathars coming to ask questions, and maybe that wasn't such a good idea after all – but it was too late for second thoughts, even if Jacey was willing to stop long enough to allow them. Here came the wyrm, dragged up from below like a worm in a bird's beak; here was its head, rising up above the handrails while Jacey trudged back and back, doing his conveyor-belt trick.

Leaving me, eye to eye with the beast, and suddenly, oh, yes. Size of a train again.

Size of a train that was looking at me, turning its head to keep me fixed in its sights, utterly focused now. I thought likely it had the brain of a dinosaur, tiny and tailwards, but that was no disadvantage now. This was Oz's second-tier message, an escalator in its own right. First he sent the Corbies to fetch me, now he sent a wyrm to eat me.

There wasn't much point wondering what the third tier might prove to be, or when he'd actually come himself, like Jabba the Hutt in a director's cut. I really wasn't likely to survive this one.

Still. Even if I'd been willing to stand still and let myself be swallowed, apparently my Aspect wasn't. It must just be instinct or training, the readiness is all – I really didn't think it was my Aspect taking over, for all that it felt that way – but I'd already launched myself, feet-first, go down fighting.

I've done martial arts training since I turned daemon, but mostly for the opposite reason, to learn control, how not to hurt people. Even with the Aspect on. Especially with the Aspect on, I guess. Sometimes I needed it, sometimes I just wanted it, sometimes it was hard to let it go. Poor Jordan – I'd used it shamelessly, with him. Misused it, probably. I didn't think I'd ever hurt him, but even so...

Right now it was using me, or that's how it felt: how it often felt, at the height of action. Hurling me feet-first across that space, to land like a missile between the wyrm's deep-sunken eyes. One thudding impact, good boots with immeasurable energy behind them. I didn't jump, nothing so crude or simple, so human and inadequate. I really did feel gripped, lifted, hurled.

I struck and fell away, like a missile spent; and rolled neatly and came up ready for anything, and really there wasn't any point.

It might have a brain the size of a pea, or else the size of a planet; it might keep the thing anywhere, in its skull or in its tail or offworld or ex-dimensional. It really made no difference. It didn't bother to shake its head, it didn't shrug me off; its head did turn to follow me, but it seemed not to have felt the blow at all.

Damn. That was the best I had, guaranteed to carry me through concrete bunker walls. That was my break-into-bank-vaults hurtle. Not that I ever had, but now I guessed I never would.

There was a noise like all the noise that engineering has ever made, all wrapped up into a single shattering effect. That must be Jacey, tossing aside the innards of the escalator. I didn't flinch at the ruinous catastrophic sound of it, I didn't glance around. My Aspect has me far too well-trained for that. I kept my gaze on the enemy, my feet grounded and my balance poised. Alert, prepared, pointless.

Something flew by my shoulder and struck the wyrm more or less where my boots had marked the spot. Something the colour of cold steel, with glittery edges: ripped cold steel, then, something torn from the mechanism and thrown with all the power of a Power behind it.

Just for that little moment, it was good not to be fighting alone. Not to be the best we had.

That hunk of metal should have split the creature's hide, shattered its skull, buried itself deep in flesh and bone and maybe-brain beyond.

Shouldn't have just bounced off, the way I had a moment earlier.

Hey-ho.

Jacey was at my shoulder now. Following up like a warrior, checking that surge like a warrior frustrated, seeing his first best attack fail utterly.

Standing with me like a boy, helpless and protective.

We glanced at each other, that way you do: half a smile, half a shrug, *I'm sorry it came to this but I'm glad you're here with me, I'm glad it's you.* We probably both learned it from the same damn movies.

The wyrm was fixing us with its coldly savage eye, starting to open its mouth.

Then there was another of those ultimate noises, this one like the sound of all doors everywhere being slammed open all at once.

This time, of course I looked. We both did. Why not, how not...?

I think the wyrm looked too.

That was the door to Reno's office that was flung wide, and there stood Reno.

No: *here* stood Reno, this side of the doorway. Way too big for the doorway, she stood maybe eight foot tall, eight or nine.

I didn't suppose she had stooped. I didn't think she'd bothered with the door at all, I thought it had done that all by itself as a courtesy, an announcement, like a flunkey calling out arrivals at the head of the stairs, *Reno has arrived.*

She looked... bitterly shiny, like an angel flung down through no fault of her own. I could hardly bear to look at her. For a moment there, I almost pitied the wyrm.

She gazed at the wyrm but spoke to us, which I think surprised Jacey as much as it did me.

She said, "Do you know who has sent this... worm... into my place, against my people?"

That made us her people; I felt Jacey's hesitation at that, but she was right, of course. We'd come here, and she'd taken us in. And we'd been attacked already, but next door didn't count as her place, not quite Savoy. We were on our own out there.

Not here. Again, I felt that surge of warm relief. *Not alone*. Not even the two of us.

I said, "Yes. It was Oz, Oz Trumby."

"Well." She noted that, accepted it. Filed it away. I didn't know if there was anything she could do about it, even if she got the chance. Oz was... well, he was the kind of man who could send wyrms to do his work.

The kind of man who could send them and they'd actually, y'know. Go.

She said, "You two should leave now."

I don't think either of us wanted to. For that little moment we'd been a different thing, *not alone*, and we didn't want to change that. If you were feeling generous you might say we didn't want to leave her alone, but actually it was more complicated than that, and probably less heroic.

Jacey maybe made a move to argue: lifted his hand, took a breath.

She cut him off brutally. "Go. There is nothing you can do here. This is my place. Go."

No chance to be a hero and die gloriously, not this time. I'd have dragged him away by main force, quickly down the stairs to shepherd unhappy Savoyards onto the train when it came, away to somewhere that had to be safer than this – but they could shepherd themselves, they'd come this far on their own and if there was one thing they knew, it was when to abandon a sinking ship. They could trust the driver to see them through the tunnels and back into the light. They didn't need us, we'd be no help to them – at best no help, and likely worse than that, likely we'd draw the wyrm down after us – and we couldn't get to them anyway. Deliberately or otherwise, the wyrm had spread its long grey oozing body between us and the stair-head. No clambering over that.

I said, "Uh, Reno, I don't know how...?"

There must be an exit from up here, surely – but at street level the building was all boarded up, doors and windows both. We could bust through any boards, of course we could, but Reno might not appreciate that. I was seeing an angel in her wrath, in her absolute power; I wanted to keep her neutral at least, if not appreciative.

I don't know how the wyrm felt, but she scared me skewy.

"There." One arm flung out, one finger pointing. Her eyes never shifted from the wyrm's. Excellent technique. "Go."

One thing about Jacey and me, we don't need telling four times. We went.

I was quite proud of us for not actually running. From either of them. We backed off slowly, following the course of her finger.

At some point, I realised, we'd started holding hands again.

Good. I clung on, quite fiercely.

That pointing finger sent us to a far corner of the ticketing hall. I didn't think I'd ever explored this way; this was Reno's territory up here, and we just didn't.

Another of those ubiquitous tiled passageways, only with more colour in the tiles, green and brown and gold – and suddenly it ended in an old-fashioned lift shaft, with those iron trellis gates drawn back.

Jacey laughed, brief and sharp and painful.

I said, "Shouldn't we...?" with a glance back over my shoulder: not because I thought we should, only because one of us had to raise it.

"No," he said, bless him. Being the reliable one, so that I didn't have to. "No, we really shouldn't. She'll be fine." *Or nobody will*, one or the other, not needing to be said.

So we stepped into the open lift, and drew the gates closed behind us, and looked at the control panel.

"I guess we're going up," Jacey said, and pressed the solitary button.

# CHAPTER EIGHT

REALLY, I GUESS we should have known. Not expected it, perhaps, in the circumstances, but we should have worked it out.

I think there's something about modern transport, though, whether it's a bus or an airplane or just a lift: the less contact you have with the world outside, the less curiosity it engenders. In a bus I'll watch through the windows all the time, keep myself oriented, track the route, even argue with the driver if I think he's missed a turn. On a plane, you hand yourself over to the unseen aircrew and find ways to pass the time with nothing on your mind except landing and what comes after. The windows are hopeless: too small and at the wrong height and there's no useful data to be gained anyway. Nothing you can do about it, you can't stop the plane and get off. Me, I just stretch my legs out into the aisle and never bother to look outside.

A lift? Doesn't usually even have a window, doesn't have a human hand in the operation anywhere. I think lifts stultify the mind. Deliberately, or we'd never get into them. Step in; don't think about it; step out. Everything fixed beforehand, no hope of control or persuasion or influence. It does what it does, and so do you.

WE STEPPED IN, we went up. We stepped out.

Into – of course! – the lobby of the Savoy Hotel.

Into an obscure corner of the lobby, at least, where we could stand still for a moment and get our bearings, get caught up with where she'd sent us.

Vivid marble flooring, black-and-white chequer-board designs stretching away from one strong pillar to the next. Sofas and table-lamps, ormolu, wood and brass everywhere. And people too, people everywhere: staff in dark and sober suits with discreet badges, customers in vivid frocks and traditional robes and Savile Row tailoring.

And us. Me in black denim – of course! Jacey's a quick learner, he'd found me the kind of clothes that Desi wore, not tried to remake Fay – and him dressed as I had dressed him, hunkered into his flying jacket, looking lean and mean and the kind of guy who'd only hang out in the Savoy if he were a film star meeting his agent and the press. Except that even the most louche of film stars would take time to dry his hair before he ventured into the public eye.

Or the private eye, come to that. Reno's lift might debouch into a shadowy corner, and might be used seldom, but a watchful staff kept an eye on it none the less. That, or they had an alarm fitted to the gate. Neither of us needed long to orient ourselves, but someone was already on their way before we'd taken three steps across the marble, from black to white to black again.

A brisk blonde woman, in fashionably sensible shoes and a trouser suit of severe cut, her hair trained to the millimetre; it was almost a surprise to see that she could smile in that get-up, and a serious surprise to see that the smile was entirely genuine.

No surprise at all, that the smile was not directed at me.

"Mr Cathar," she said, while everything in her body language said, *Jacey!* "Welcome back to the Savoy. It's been a while." *Too long,* her hands said, both of them reaching to take one of his in a gesture that was – just about – on this side of a handshake. By this time I might, just possibly, have been glowering.

"Julie. Good to see you. This is, um, Desdaemona..."

At least he'd remembered that much, my nom-de-guerre. I still had my Aspect on; this was still wartime, even if we'd fled the enemy. Her eyes assessed me, she freed his hand to take mine politely, I swear I saw her hesitate between "miss" or "ma'am," a chilling put-down either way. In the end she simply nodded, professionally pleasant, with never a twitch of either eyebrow at the damp dishevelled state of me.

"What can I do for you today, Mr Cathar?" Anything that lay within her power, apparently. Presumably she'd done it all before. Though she hadn't seen him here before, coming out of this lift; now that eyebrow did twitch in its direction, putting the question as politely as she could manage, a way that he might entirely ignore if he chose to.

Not he, not now. This day had rubbed away all his boundaries and all his protections; now he was raw and open, hoarse and direct. "We could use the suite, if it's free. Or – well, just a room, I guess. Anything. And, uh, Reno could use some help down there, maybe. If you've got...?"

"Of course." Of course they knew up here about Reno: how not? They kept that lift working and accessible. And of course they had people prepared to go down there, even in times of trouble. You always keep a watch on the back door. They might even have known that there was trouble brewing. The Overworld responds to unusual occasions; sometimes the aether just twangs with tension, you can smell it. Even I can smell it, me with my all too mortal nose.

At any rate, here came a man and a woman. I looked at them once and thought *bodyguards*; looked again, and thought, *Oh!*

Since when has a hotel been keeping daemons on its staff?

Since it's been hosting a broken angel, probably, beneath its cellars.

I thought perhaps I ought to warn them about the wyrm, just as a professional courtesy. But I didn't like their strict haircuts and their formal suits, and I really didn't like the way they looked at me and saw me, knew me for what I was and still dismissed me.

*Good luck with it, then,* I thought sourly, watching them go down. Didn't quite hope that they'd find the wyrm still in fine fig, I couldn't wish that on Reno, but even so. If it slimed up their sobersided costumes, the way it had ours – "damp and dishevelled" really didn't cut it as a description, now that I could see myself in mirrors – I wouldn't care a bit.

Meanwhile, Jacey's friend Julie was leaving them to it, asking no more questions, leading us away. Towards a bank of other lifts, more regular but not too much so, not the common lifts for common people. A swipe of her ID card commandeered one; she punched buttons herself and rode up with us, walked us along a corridor, swiped the card again to let us through a double door.

And then didn't come in, left us there on the threshold with a smile and, "If there's anything else, Mr Cathar, you know my number."

I was sure he did. But she was gone and he wasn't watching her clip away, silent on the carpeting like a muted pair of scissors. All his attention was on me, and I thought we'd been here before.

Not literally, not in this suite together, though it was obviously familiar to him. But his attitude was intimately familiar to me, and after a moment I pinned it down. He was like this when he took me to the family home, the house that he'd grown up in: sort of proprietorial but tense, not sure how I would like it, not knowing where I'd find my comfort in all this ostentatious wealth and luxury.

Like the young prince bringing a revolutionary into the palace and hoping that she wouldn't make a scene.

I wasn't going to make a scene. I was just curious. "A suite, Jacey? In the Savoy?" And on retainer, clearly, always accessible. I couldn't begin to imagine what that cost.

"Not mine," he said hastily, though I'd worked that out already. "Dad keeps it, for business. You need somewhere to meet people..."

I was sure of it. When you had fingers in as many pies – and as many upper crusts – as the Cathar clan, no doubt you needed somewhere impressive and imperturbable. The Savoy would meet both those criteria handsomely: so, no, the people here would be no strangers to the Overworld. Of course they'd keep a couple of daemons on the staff.

I eyed my own particular scion of the Cathar clan, closed the door determinedly at our backs – and let my daemonic Aspect slip.

For a moment there, I thought it didn't want to go. Didn't want to let go.

Then it slithered off my shoulders like an old coat shrugged away. I almost looked down to see if it lay puddled on the carpet at my feet.

Almost. Not quite. I still wasn't taking my eyes off Jacey.

My own particular Cathar. Still that, apparently. To me, at least, and maybe to him too, however many Julies there might have been in the meantime.

I'd woken up this morning with Jordan, my other Jay, but morning was a long time ago and a long way away. And now –

Well. Now I stood there with him, alone, door closed against the world and all my defences stripped away, and –

Well. I had all these unfamiliar clothes on, and God, I'd never felt so naked.

Never so wanted to be naked.

Oh. Yes. *Every time you let your Aspect go,*

*remember?* It was hard enough, hot enough last time, when he was the one with no clothes on. Since then I'd kept it close all this time, hours, and – oh, yes. Hot wasn't even a measure any more.

When I looked down, there really were clothes puddling on the floor around my feet. Apparently I was doing that. He wasn't moving, so it must have been me. He was – well, just standing there. Looking at me. Not staring, exactly, just really focused. Intent. Like me.

Breathing quite hard now, like me.

Shivering a little under my hands, when I abandoned my own clothes and moved on to his.

Either my body shoves out enough pheromones post-Aspect that whatever male I focus on gets caught up in the backdraught, or else Powers have the same side-effect when the action's over, or else everybody does and it's nothing special after all, or–

Well. He was still my Cathar, my own particular boy. Maybe it was just us, suddenly flung together after way too long apart, suddenly alone and maybe safe with a door closed against the world and a whole empty suite of luxury to explore and –

WELL. WE DIDN'T get to do much exploring, just then.

We didn't actually get out of the hallway.

There was a nice soft rug right there on the polished wood of the floor, and that was good enough.

Actually, up against the wall would've been good enough for me. I guess the rug was his idea, while the urgency was mine. We wouldn't have made it as far as any bedroom; if we'd moved at all, if he'd tried to move me, things would've got frantic. Things would've got broken. Better a rug in the hallway than bending him backwards over an antique table and hearing the joints all splinter.

Later – not actually that much later, but later enough – I lay there with the pile of that rug under my cheek and the colours of it all out of focus in my eye, almost literally in my eye, and I thought, *Mmm. Feels like silk. Oh – it probably is silk, isn't it? It's probably Bokhara, or some such. Or Persian. Valuable, anyway. Expensive. Antique...*

What did I know from rugs? Absolutely nothing, except a few iconic phrases; but I knew where I was. Whose suite this was. Of course it would be valuable, if this was where Jacey's dad did business. Of course it would be expensive.

Well. Okay, then.

It was just a rug. He could always have it cleaned – expensively – if necessary.

He'd probably never notice. I doubted if he ever looked down, once he'd tied his shoelaces of a morning. That would be beneath him. If you owned a fancy rug, to the Cathar way of thinking, what mattered was that other people should see you walk on it.

I may possibly have giggled, at that point. It's undaemonic and undignified, but – yeah. Might've done.

"Hey. What's funny?"

Oops. If there's anything more wounded than a boy who thinks he's being laughed at, just at the very wrong time, I hope I never have to hear it.

He was mostly faking for effect – of course he

was! this being not exactly our first time, after all –
but even so. I did need to turn my head.

Which should've been a pleasure. Would've been.
Was, in many ways – *oh, look: there's Jacey, back
where he belongs, his head cushioned on my shoulder
and that long body stretching away, too far, beyond
my toes' best reach* – but oh, it was an effort.

And *oh, look, that's just where Jordan's head was,
just a day ago* – that was a fact I couldn't deny, a
thought I couldn't squeeze out of my head.

Nothing to be done about it now. I was too tired
anyway, and – no. Nothing to be done. Just a fact.
Live with it.

I said, "Nothing, just..."

I shrugged against his side, mostly for the pleasure
of watching how his head shifted when I did it. He
waited, while I remembered that he never used to
let me get away with that, he'd just ask again, *well,
what?* until I told him.

Boys don't change, apparently. So I surrendered
to the inevitable, and blinded him with literature.
"You know that Orwell thing, his vision of
the future as a boot stamping on a human face,
forever?"

Jacey was used to the way my mind worked. Used
to be used to it. He said, "Uh-huh," in a very non-
committal kind of way.

"Well, I just thought of a more subtle version,
that's all." *Your dad, walking on a costly carpet* –
but I wouldn't need to spell that out. I was used to
him, too – used to be used to him – and I knew where
his mind would go. He wasn't that much interested
in books.

He said, "That's what you're thinking about, is it? Here we are" – together after years of the other thing, lying on a rug in a suite in London's grandest hotel with his finger tracing patterns idly on my breast – "and you're thinking about rewriting old books. Have I ever said before, how downright bloody odd you are?"

"Once or twice, maybe." It was his constant chorus, even back when I was Fay, when I was just this girl that he delighted in. That was a thing to be, a fine thing, but it was a lot less complicated than what I was now, Desdaemona with a whole other history he hardly knew. "Never mind, Jacey love. You'll get used to me. Eventually."

"I doubt that. Seriously." He propped himself up on one elbow, looked down at me and said, "So on a scale of one to ten, how comfy are you feeling right now, and how much d'you fancy taking this somewhere else, like to the bedroom, maybe?"

I can take a hint, but sometimes I can't carry it. I said, "Eleven and one."

"Huh?"

"Bed sounds better than this." *Better even than this.* "I just don't think I can move, is all." There's always a crash, at the back end of extreme effort. Carrying an Aspect is, well, a new definition of extreme. Letting my Aspect carry me, for the better part of a day – or the worse part, more like – had left me exhausted past counting, almost past caring. I was drained, absolutely; my bones felt hollow and leaden, both at once.

I was, emphatically, blaming the day and the Aspect and nothing more. Nothing to do with a frantic fuck on a fancy rug, no. Nothing to do with Jacey, nor with Jordan neither. Just the day.

"Huh." Jacey surveyed me thoughtfully. "Well, you're not exactly a frail flower, but hey. You never were. I reckon I'm still up to your weight. Hold still."

And he scooped me up and carried me, all through the suite; and I didn't see any part of it, I was all too utterly tired to be curious. Just my head on his shoulder now, and it was like lying on the rug except for being smooth living skin beneath my cheek and not so colourful, even more expensive, just as out of focus.

And then he laid me on a bed, a blessed bed; and he lay down again beside me, on the proper side, his side – and I barely had time to register that Jordan had always been on the other side, because that was where I'd put him, where I'd wanted him, and I didn't know if that was significant or not but actually I was already pretty much asleep, so let it go.


"WHAT TIME IS it?"

"Night-time. Darktime. Go back to sleep."

"What are you doing?"

"Turning the lights off, so they don't disturb you. Go to *sleep*."

"Oh. Okay, then."


HE'D TURNED THE lights off all through the suite, and drawn the curtains too – and all of that could only help so much, not enough, against the bright coming of the day.

I did eventually, reluctantly, have to wake up. And all but crawl in that half-light from the bed to the bathroom, where on another day, another time, in another world I would have loved to linger and play, but not now. I contemplated a hard cold shower, just to underscore that whole waking-up idea. It might be my turn. I did, briefly, contemplate it.

And then oozed back to bed, slithered under the covers, nestled up against the slumped and slumbrous warmth of my Cathar, mine – *mine!* – and was asleep again, as I deserved to be.

AND WOKE AGAIN the best way, roused by a curious, enquiring, suggestive hand, an impertinent hand; and bit its owner, complementarily hard; and one thing led to another, as it does.

SO THEN HE was asleep again, as boys do, and for a wonder I was not. I felt... slept, quite exhaustively slept. Not enough, of course, never enough when sleep is such an all-consuming pleasure, but maybe enough for now.

I poked a toe out into the world, a whole foot, and then another. Sat up cautiously on the edge of the bed, and Jacey never stirred; so okay, I tried standing up. Found I could manage that, more or less, at least for the short stagger to the bathroom. Not that short, not in the Savoy – it wasn't so much en-suite as distantly related – but still, I made it. And the door between the two was solid enough that the sound of rushing water shouldn't disturb a sleeping male, so I closed it on him firmly and ran a bath, deep and hot, while I soaped and rinsed and shampooed in the shower.

Then I just soaked in the bath till I was wrinkly, and just a little longer. And finally, reluctantly, hauled myself out and dried off with the world's fluffiest towels and spoiled myself entirely among the lotions and the unguents supplied; and then slipped out and checked on Jacey – yup, still sleeping: how do they do that, men, like sex was an anaesthetic? – and went to explore the suite.

SOME SUITE. SOME neck, my even being here, even under Jacey's aegis, under his arm, under his shadow.

There were three bedrooms as big as ours, each with its luxury bathroom in attendance if you could find it, if you could walk that far. They all three inhabited their own passageway, to give a sense of privacy, detachment from the business end of the suite.

At the end of that passage was the main sitting-room, a lounge area bigger than a lot of hotel foyers I had known. Opening directly off it I found a conference-room with a long table, a dozen chairs and as many screens hung like portraits around the walls to allow for off-site attendees, and an office with computers and faxes and phones, several desks for secretaries and PAs.

Not opening off it was another door, which I didn't even think of leaning into with even a hint of Aspect-strength. In honesty, I'd be just as happy not to touch my Aspect for a day or two, or a week or two, or more. Besides, it would be rude to go breaking

Savoy doors when they'd been so quick to welcome us in. And besides again, I thought I knew what lay the other side of this particular door. I thought it was probably the boss's private office, and he probably had reasons to keep it locked. Even against family. Maybe especially against family. *Jacey, love, I just had a look through your dad's files, and –*

And no. Just, no. I wasn't going there; that wasn't anywhere I wanted to find myself, no matter what else I might find.

Besides, I'd already found something else. Not the spectacular view of the Thames from Canary Wharf to the Houses of Parliament, that long march of bridges that came visible when I drew back the sitting-room curtains. Also coming visible in the fall of light was a small dark pile on a side-table, which was all our clothes, Jacey's and mine, picked up from where we must've left them strewn in the hallway over there.

Picked up and laundered, pressed and folded and delivered back to us. Jacey didn't do all that when he was pulling curtains and switching off the lights.

Jacey didn't do *any* of that. He'd been way too privileged all his life, he'd never think of it.

I thought about it, briefly. This was the Savoy, a private suite in the Savoy. Nobody here was going to be disturbed by a swift rap on the door and a voice that called "Housekeeping!"

Even so. Likely the suite came with its own housekeeper.

Even so…

After a bit, I picked up the phone and didn't even have to dial. A voice that managed to be both warm and deferential at the same time – which is a neat trick if you can do it – said, "Good morning. How may I help you?"

"Um," I said. "This is –"

"Yes, Miss Desdaemona. How can I help?"

Okay, that's a neat trick too, but it's just technology tipping them off. I don't know how it works, but I do know what it does. Even when it takes me by surprise. Even when I can hear that extra 'a' being pronounced very carefully in the middle there. I said, "When we... arrived yesterday" – you couldn't exactly say we'd checked in, but I didn't suppose anyone in this suite ever would – "we were greeted by a, a" – a miss? a ma'am? a clerk, a manager, a what? – "by someone called Julie," I said, ducking all the questions frantically. "I wondered if she might –"

"One moment, please."

Of course she might. Even if she was off duty, at home, in the bath or in bed or in mid-fuck on the rug: this was the Savoy. Very, very quickly, I heard her voice on the line. Not out of breath, not caught on the hop, not disturbed in the least. Of course not; this was the Savoy.

"Good morning. How may I help?"

The same formula, but short of warmth: all crisp efficiency. As she was in person, immaculate and prompt and professional. I was suddenly very aware of standing naked by the window, in full view of any passing helicopter, any paparazzo with a zoom lens, any creature with enhanced sight...

No matter. Sometimes nakedness is strength. *I can do this, I can wander around this time of the morning with no clothes on. You can't. Guess who's*

*doing better? Even before you take one sleeping
Cathar into account?*

Stop it. We weren't in competition: not for Jacey,
not for anything. I said, "I suspect that you're the
one I need to thank for having our clothes cleaned."

"It's all part of the service," she said, which was
likely true, but... I thought about strangers letting
themselves into the suite while we slept, and would
have felt deeply unhappy about it except that this
was the Savoy, and we were guests, and they'd go
to any measure to keep us safe. Or she would. I was
fairly sure that she was the one who'd picked our
things up, personally. Not a stranger, then.

I suddenly wanted to talk to her about Jacey, but
I was damned if my own life was going to fail the
Bechdel test. Instead I said, "Julie," in hopes that she
would reply in kind, "tell me what happened down
in the station. Is Reno all right?"

"She's fine. It takes more than a wyrm to get by
an angel in her wrath. Our people didn't have to
do much; stood and watched, mostly, by their own
report, while she took it apart. I sent them to haul
the pieces up a side tunnel and butcher them more
thoroughly, just in case. They think it's a penance."

"Isn't it?"

"Good Lord, no. I wouldn't send a pair of daemons
down against a wyrm. Not and expect to see them
come up again. I wanted intel, not action; I'd have been
livid if they hadn't hung back, in the circumstances."

Despite myself, I found that I was warming to
her. Human or Overworld, mostly people look on
daemons as cannon-fodder, more or less. I said,
"So why...?"

"Why the butchery? Because I've heard too many stories about wyrms regenerating from any random fragment, and I don't want to find a nest of the nasty things breeding directly beneath us. Tolk and Carter will strip it flesh from bone, in so far as it has either, and treat the pieces so that I can be quite sure there's no hint of life left in them. Then we can safely leave it to the dark; there are scavengers down there that even a wyrm is right to be afraid of."

"Daemons too," I said pointedly.

"Oh, yes. They'll be careful, and they'll be quick. They'd be quick anyway, it's a foul job, but someone's got to do it. And they won't be fit for human company afterwards. They can clean up in Reno's bath-house if that's still operable, but even so. When they come back I'm sending them on a week's leave, effective immediately. With tickets to the Maldives. I think that should be far enough."

"There's water enough to soak the slime off," I agreed. And then, because I couldn't keep up that neutral tone that seemed so natural in her, "Some daemons get all the luck. Why didn't I ever – ? No, never mind. I wouldn't have liked it anyway. Well, the corporate side of it. I could've handled the Maldives." And the butchery, if necessary. But, "Are you sure you can spare them both? Someone's got his eye on this place now, bound to have."

"I'm sure," she confirmed. "They're not the only two on the payroll, and the Savoy is... not short of protection in other ways."

Well, no. Not with Cathars in a top-floor suite and Reno watching the underway. Even so, I was anxious now. And reluctant to confess it, or to press my case.

"What else can I do for you?" she asked. "Are you ready for breakfast?"

"Jacey will be, when he wakes up." He'd be starving. It's another male attribute, seemingly. First they sleep, then they eat. "He'll want the works, full English with American pancakes on the side. And cereal, toast, all the coffee that there is. You know."

"I do know," she said. Drily, I thought. "And for yourself?"

"Um, no. I really need to be going." Now, quickly, while he slept; while I still could. While I was steeled to it, and before he started to argue. "I've brought enough trouble on my friends, this last twenty-four hours. Do you have a back way out that you could show me? Something more private than Reno's, if possible. They know about that."

"Of course." Diplomats and presidents passed through this place; so did mobsters. So did the Overworld. Privacy must be inherent. "I'll meet you at the lift."

"Thanks, Julie. I'll be two minutes. I just have to dress."


IF I WAS any longer than that, it was only because I couldn't find my jacket. Until I figured out that of course the mirror in the hallway was a sliding door, and of course there was a wardrobe behind it, and of course that was where she'd hung our brand new jackets, after she'd had them cleaned. His was so much bigger and friendlier, it looked like it was reaching out to hug mine, or at least dip its sleeves into my pockets. I had to bite my lip, and steel myself all over again.

Steely, then, I took the lift down, half anticipating an argument at the bottom: the kind of argument I was slipping away, leaving him snoring, to avoid.

I underestimated her. A bloke, I think, any bloke would have argued. *It's dangerous to go alone. At least wait till he wakes up, talk to him, make plans. Let him know where you'll be, who you'll be with. Who'll be looking out for you, who's got your back. He'll want it to be him. You can't just go off into the blue this way, not when he's just found you again.* Like that. Lots of common sense, lots of heartstring-tugging, none of it any use to me at all.

The blessed Julie was made of sterner stuff, girl-stuff. The lift doors opened and she was there as promised, with her arms full of gifts.

"Breakfast," she said, handing me a heavyweight paper sack that oozed warmth into my fingers. "Fresh from the bakery, easy to eat on the move. And the biggest, strongest coffee we can do. You look like a coffee girl to me, and Jacey can't have it all. And I cleaned your phone up and charged it for you. What else, now – do you need money?"

"No," I said. "I'm good for cash, thanks." Realising as I said it that chances were she knew exactly how much cash I was carrying, she'd obviously been through all my pockets, and she was offering anyway. I could have asked for anything, I think she would have found it. And maybe charged it to the room, but I wouldn't have cared about that; Jacey's dad could afford me.

Jacey's dad was getting me cheap, if he was getting me at all. I stood firm, and she nodded.

"All right, then. Laptop? MP3 player? Anything? We get a lot of kit left behind, one way or another."

I was sure they did. And it struck a resonant blow as she said it, and, "As above, so below, eh?"

"Yes." Her quick controlled smile flickered into place. "We are... something of a mirror image," though she still wouldn't let Reno disgrace her hallowed halls if she could help it. More than her job was worth, perhaps, to have a mutilated angel blunder into public view – except that I was starting to wonder about that job. Her name badge only said her name, which meant that she was either very junior, which I didn't believe for a moment, or else she was very specialised and everyone who needed her would know just what she did, she wouldn't need a label to explain it.

Might as well just ask, then. "Are you, um, are the Cathars your particular responsibility?"

"That's right." That smile again: snapped on, snapped off. "I suppose technically I come with the suite; but the suite is exclusive to the Cathars and their guests, so... So am I."

If she was a man, they'd probably call her a butler. As she was a woman – well, I thought she'd refuse *housekeeper*. I thought she probably had.

"Uh-huh. And, what, that includes Jacey, does it? Coming with the suite, and being exclusive?"

Oh. Oops. Apparently that was my out-loud voice. Yesterday must've taken more out of me than I'd realised. Including my tact, my good judgement, my good manners. Either that or I was counting on my Aspect to intervene, but sadly I'd left that on the floor upstairs.

Weirdly, it didn't seem to matter. Her first response was a stiff silence, the pure professional, remembering her badge and her position; but that didn't last. It was followed by a smile that didn't flicker so much as flare, that was pure wickedness and not at all Savoy for the brief moment that I saw it.

She said, "Actually, no. It was the other way around: first Jacey, then the job. I... was somewhere else, before. He put me in here."

He might have found her the place, but she got to keep it – I could see – by being very, very good at what she did. No doubt she'd have a manager, someone she reported to, who'd be in charge of all Savoy/Overworld interactions; she was young yet, but in five years, I was willing to bet, she'd have that job. Maybe not so many, maybe she wouldn't wait so long.

I did briefly consider being nasty again, out loud again, something about how Jacey making a servant of her was somehow a promotion – but my heart wasn't in it, and the words died with the impulse. I liked her too much already, to want to sting that sharply.

She really was very, very good at what she did. Making random women like her, enough to be polite? Yes, that would be a part of what she did.

It could simply be true, anyway, that thought I might have stung her with. Some of the places he might have found her, the things she might have been doing – yes, this could be a promotion. Better than that. This could be a rescue. Even it it meant picking up Jacey's filthy clothes and doing his laundry for him.

His and hers, whichever random woman he'd brought with him...

"This way, now," she said. "It may not look like it, but this is the VIP exit."

She led me through a staff door, hidden behind another mirror. I was expecting to feel like Alice stepping through the glass, finding a completely other world the other side; but not so much, actually. It didn't seem that different. Broad corridor, soft lights, soft carpet underfoot. The doors had people's names on them instead of numbers, Mr This and Mrs That, but even so. Everything still said high-end hotel. You could still positively smell the money.

Again, that feral smile from Julie. She knew just what I was thinking. "It should be seedier than this, right? What the public don't see: cramped quarters, bare brickwork, sordid conditions. But the public do see this, that's the point. At least our public do, our guests. Our favoured guests. We used to take them through the kitchens, but... Well. That's no way to treat the super-rich. So the last renovation, this happened. The managers got an upgrade, and nobody has to tread in anything nasty. Not that we have anything nasty, you understand: not in the Savoy. Not any more. Everything got an upgrade."

It didn't really matter whether I believed her or not, whether she was telling the truth or not. Maybe she was just being properly corporate, but I didn't imagine I'd get the chance to catch her out. I didn't imagine I'd be coming back.

*Goodbye, Jacey.* Again.

She was still reading my mind, apparently. "Did you leave him a note?"

"Uh, no." I was a bit ashamed of that, and a bit defensive. I wasn't sure which was worse, to sneak away without a word or leave a Dear-John letter on the mantelpiece. After a moment, I said that, all of that in my out-loud voice; and then, "I was kind of hoping you'd say goodbye for me." *Help him understand. If he needs the help. I'm sure you'd do that, it's probably part of your job.* "And to Reno too, tell her I'm sorry I can't stay to help with the clean-up, but..."

"But you're a part of the problem, not a part of the solution. Quite. If you stay, something else will come, and it can only be an escalation."

It occurred to me, a little belatedly, that I was being hustled out of here. Certainly this was a part of her job. As long as I stayed with Jacey, I was a guest, and she and everyone here would do everything they could to protect me. As soon as I started to leave – well. For the hotel's sake, for Jacey's and everyone's, the sooner I was gone the better. She'd do everything she could to speed that happy moment.

That was fine by me. Two minds with but a single thought. Even when she went on, "You do realise, though, that Jacey's going to be coming after you? As soon as he wakes up?"

"Not before breakfast." But yes, of course I did. That was fine too. Of course it was. "If there's one thing I've grown good at over the years, it's keeping ahead of Jacey."

She eyed me askance, and said, "That was when you didn't want him to catch up with you."

Ouch. Not just askance, astute with it. Even so...

"Even so," I said determinedly. "Try to misdirect him if you can, distract him, anything." Not that I have much of a martyr complex, but – well. Maybe a bit. There was this total turn-around in my head.

I used to be all about protecting myself from him, I thought I had to do that; now I just wanted to protect him from me, my influence, what was coming after me. What I'd done. One long day, one too-short night wasted mostly in sleeping: twenty-four hours was enough to turn me around, but the end result put me exactly back where I'd started. Needing distance still, between him and me.

Making a gift of him, apparently, as if he really were still mine to give away.

This time it was the professional smile she gave me, and I wasn't sure what that meant. "I'll do my best," she said, which wasn't enlightening either. I didn't know whether to feel encouraged, or dissolve in a burning, blistering, boiling lava of jealousy and hatred. One or the other, and it was quite hard to choose.

"Here we are," she said, opening a door and leading me out into a private underground garage. The car that waited there looked like a perfectly standard black cab. "We find they attract less attention than a limousine," she went on smoothly. "The driver will take you anywhere you want to go. Shetland, if you want to go that far. And we'll charge it to Mr Cathar." In context, that meant Jacey's dad. Which did at least give me a flicker of pleasure, even if it wasn't enough to lift the gloom that gripped me; and she said it with not so much as the hint of a conspiratorial wink, and I wanted to applaud, if only that wouldn't spoil the effect.

"Thanks. Um, it had better be Heathrow, then, put an ocean between us." Jacey, and Jordan, and Oz: none of them would be expecting that.

Her eyebrow flickered. "Passport?" She knew I didn't have one on me; she'd been through all my pockets.

"Stashed at the airport," I said. "Just in case I ever had to cut and run."

She nodded. "Good luck, then. Here" – her card, pressed into my hand – "keep in touch. I can be a point of contact, if you need it."

"Good. Thanks..."

And the car door slammed, and we were away.

# CHAPTER NINE

THE LITTLE TWIST of road in front of the Savoy is famously the only street in England where you have to drive on the right. I kept quiet while he did that, let him concentrate until we pulled out into the Strand; then I leaned forward, tapped on the glass and said, "I'm sorry, I've changed my mind. Make it London City Airport, will you?"

Julie might work for the Savoy, she might have discretion tattooed on her soul; she still worked for the Cathars on a daily basis, and she still harboured a soft spot for Jacey. And no, I was not about to trust her. One scenario played out in my head, where we rolled up to Heathrow and I stepped out of the cab and there was Jacey to meet me, forewarned and sneakily come ahead on the Tube. And there was a crow overhead to spot us, what more likely than aerial surveillance at an airport?

And then something devastating fell upon us both, all because I'd trusted Julie...

No. Distraction, misdirection, all the tricks I knew. While I was still this close, all the lies I could tell.

"Got another passport stashed there, have you, love?"

"As it happens, yes." This might look like a regular London cab, but; he might look like a regular London cabbie, but. I've read enough spy fiction to know that you never take the first that offers. He might be working for the Savoy or for the Cathars, or both; he might be working for anyone.

He might be a truthsayer. I was going to be very careful, just in case. As it happens, I have passports stashed at various airports, in various names. Just in case.

Then I started in on breakfast, my best excuse not to talk at all. Warm flaky pastries and hot strong coffee: I chewed and slurruped with a kind of honest greed – not a word of a lie, even when I wasn't saying anything – while the streets of the city unwound around us, with Jacey – I hoped! – left further and further behind.

If he tugged at my heart like a fish on a line, well. Let it unreel. All the way.

He wasn't the only one, and I'd run from Jordan yesterday, and it had hurt just as much. Today was Jacey's turn, that was all.

Jacey's and mine. It was always my turn.

Gods, but I was sick of running.

\* \* \*

BRIEFLY, I DID think about Shetland. Or heading north, at least, and a long way north. One cab was hard to pick out from the air, hard to tell from another; I might be safe from crow-spies, and I could get a good long way and know that the driver wasn't ratting me out. Except that he'd need toilet breaks, and I could hardly frisk him for a phone before he vanished into the gents, out of sight and out of my control. And his cab might have an electronic tracer in any case, something beeping even now in Julie's private office to tell her just exactly where we were.

So no, the City Airport it was, and dump him too. Be on my own again, with everyone that I could trust.

He dropped me at the terminal, and I thanked him, and tried to tip him, but he wouldn't take my money. "That's all covered, love. Don't worry."

And then I stood and watched him drive away; and as soon as he was gone I walked boldly into the terminal in case he had some degree of farsight and was still watching. Suddenly I was utterly paranoid, trusting nobody even in their humanity, let alone their motives or their loyalties.

Paranoid might save my life, maybe. It might save more than mine.

First thing I did inside was turn my phone off, like a good airline passenger ought to.

The second thing I did was pull the battery and dump the phone in a waste bin. It was still new to me, untouched and empty – but it had been through Julie's hands, and I had no idea what she might have left inside it, an extra microchip or a hidden instruction, anything. All phones are bugs, when you don't know who might be listening.

Then I buried myself in a sudden surge of people, enough – I hoped – to confuse any watcher, whether or not they were physically present, whether or not they were a bird peering in through a window; and then I followed signs to the Docklands Light Railway, rather than the planes. No way I was flying anywhere today. *Sauve qui peut*, but I had someone else to save first.

Not a martyr complex, no – but a massive guilt complex, oh, yes. I'd brought down trouble enough on other people; just once I was going to get ahead of it, do somebody some good.

If I could manage that much, if I wasn't only fooling myself one more time, dragging trouble one more time in my wake.

I'd never know, if I didn't go.


I LOVE THE DLR. No driver equals one person fewer to distrust, one way less for something wicked to come at me. There's still a ticket inspector, and there's still all the other passengers, but even so. It's a step.

And I'm sure there are plenty of ways to make an automated system betray me, and I know it has CCTV so it was watching me anyway, and even so. I still rode away from there with a lighter feeling in my heart. Slightly lighter. I'd shed that sense of being crowded by spies; I'd done what I could to make people safer, by leaving them behind me; I was doing what I could for one person more, heading that way.

Convolutedly. I did still need to be sure I wasn't being distantly followed, or caught up with. Jacey would be prompt; Jordan could be devious; Oz was...

Oz. Which didn't mean ubiquitous, he only wanted people to think it did. Eyes everywhere, though, for true. Too many people too nervous to be anything other than sneaks and stool pigeons. Stool crows.

I really did need to be sure that I'd lost them. And then keep my head down, not let anybody pick me up again. Discretion, thy name must be Desi.

Maybe I should've brought Julie along. For the ride, for the lesson. Discreet has never been my middle name.

(Maria. Since you ask. Back when I was Fay, I was Fay Maria. Desi? Doesn't have a middle name, unless that's the *daemon* bit. Mostly she gets by on just the one, and you don't get to shorten it without consent. I guess Julie had picked up on that; she didn't know what to call me, so she didn't call me anything. If we met again, I ought to do something about that – but I wasn't planning ever to meet her again, so.)

So anyway. DLR, sweet little toy-train, carrying me away from anyone who might be watching.

I hoped.

I was planning to ride it all the way back to Bank and jump a bus from there – no more Tube trains, not for a while, not if there were wyrms in the system – only the thing about the DLR, it runs above ground, sometimes quite high above, so you can look down and see the people in the streets, and...

I JUMPED OUT unexpectedly at a station halfway, surprising even me; and ran down to street level and stopped a total stranger and thrust money in his face.

Discreet, yeah. Tell me about it.

But he was a young man in the kind of suit he shouldn't have been wearing yet, all pinstripes and formality. The jacket was slung over the strap of his messenger bag; the trousers had costly kneepads buckled over them, and the cuffs tucked into a serious pair of rollerblades. "Inline skates" we're supposed to call them, but nah – these were blades. Designed to cut through traffic, cut through anything.

Anything except me, slamming into his way, slamming him to a sudden halt just in time. I didn't even need to use my Aspect; I guess blading through London hones your reactions.

He was good; he didn't even wobble, let alone grab at me to keep himself upright.

He was also furious. That was probably part of his technique, to hate all pedestrians and all cyclists, all roadworks and all traffic-lights and all vehicles indiscriminately. And then he'd weave and slice around them and think himself even better than he was, leaving empires in his dust.

He worked in the City; his suit said so, and so did his trendy satchel, and so did his vicious attitude, his hurry, his contemptuous skill.

That's how I knew he'd stop, when he saw money.

He did stop. His lip twisted in a sneer; his eyes glittered scathingly; his belly – I was sure – boiled with indignation, that somebody should deliberately seek to stop him. And that they would know the way to do it.

I said, "Sell me your skates."

"What?"

"Your skates. Take them off your feet, give them to me." He'd be my height, more or less, if we were standing level. I was fairly sure they'd fit me, more or less. "I will give you money."

"Don't be absurd." He tried to slide around me, but it's hard without momentum; blades are awkward to get going, if you've got no room to move. I was deliberately standing too close, denying him that room.

"No, I'm serious." My hand on his arm said so, startling him back into stillness. I still didn't need my Aspect, this was just my regular physical self. I'm quite springy. He could feel that. Enough at least to let him know that he didn't want to wrestle me. Not on skates. "You've got regular shoes in your bag there" – I could see the shape of them beneath the fabric – "so I'm not going to leave you barefoot in the street. You're not far from your office, or you wouldn't be wearing your business suit; wouldn't want to spend the day at your desk all sweaty and smelly, your colleagues wouldn't like it. Your boss would get complaints. You couldn't live with that. So. Sell me your skates. Chop-chop."

I tried a smile, to make this easier on him: *you're right, this is absurd, but let's just do it anyway, shall we?*

He wasn't playing. "Have you any idea how much these skates cost?"

"Yes, actually. Which is why I'm offering you this much" – a ruffle of notes under his nose – "which is more than you will have paid. Come on. It's called profit. You're supposed to be keen on that."

He said, "What do you take me for?"

It's an old joke, but I cracked it anyway: "We've already established that. Now we're just dickering over the price."

I didn't say, *Would you rather I simply turned you upside down and stripped them off your feet for you? I could do that. I'm trying to be nice.*

I didn't say it, but perhaps I let him glimpse it, just a hint. I might have twitched oh-so-reluctantly at my Aspect, just a touch, enough to have it show itself in my face, to have him feel it in my fingers.

He buckled then. And bent over, unbuckled the boots; said, "Do you – do you want the kneepads too?"

"No, that's okay, thanks. I don't fall. I'll take your shades, though, if you can spare them."

GIVE HIM CREDIT – or maybe just give him cash – he even lingered while I tried them for size. I don't know what he would have done if they hadn't fitted: claimed them back again, perhaps? Offered me a refund? Maybe an apology? No worries, though: warm insoles embraced my feet, sturdy boots supported them, and I stood three inches taller than I had been.

Three inches and a hell of a lot faster, freer, happier.

Technically more exposed, sure, but hell: you take what you can get. I may love the DLR, but it's still a tin box on rails. Now I was on my own in a different way, fuelled and wheeled and fit for anything, my regular boots hung from their laces around my neck.

"Thanks," I said. "Have a nice day."

And then I was off, and whatever he offered in return – wishes, curses, gestures; pheromones, maybe, if I'd showed him a little more of my Aspect than I'd meant – was wasted in the wind of my departing.

\*   \*   \*

DID I MAYBE suggest that he was arrogant, did I, as he incised his perfect line around all obstacles in his path?

You should see me.

No, you should. Me on skates, I'm an object lesson in how to be objectionable. That same perfect line, shaved to a finer hair's-breadth: carving heedlessly by you, close enough that you feel my slipstream like a tug on your sleeve, your feet stutter and you shy at that sudden body in your eyeline and maybe you cry out but there's really no point, I'm long gone already. That same seething fury, aimed equally at you and everybody else, everything else, every lamp-post and letterbox, every bollard, every car. That's half the fun, is the bottled rage that drives me; and oh, yes, it is fun. I love it.

I love how good I am and how mean, how fast and how disturbing, how close to peril and how neat in recovery. Blades feed everything about me that's selfish and unkind and elitist. They almost fit me to join the Overworld, for what little time I'm wearing them.

That day, they were just what I needed.


FOR THE FIRST mile or so, I simply let myself play. Get up to speed, get in the groove; rediscover just how entitled you can feel when you're the fastest thing on the street, just how much of a dick you can be.

Spot the pensioner couple holding hands up ahead, see how they're blocking the entire width of the pavement. Hate them.

Hate them *but*. See how the woman's hitching up

her handbag, about to let go her husband's hand so she can rummage. Ride the moment, trust yourself. Glide up behind them, and, yes: now. Now a gap opens between them, barely wide enough. Turn side-on and seize it, slam between them like a malevolent breath, nudge each just a fraction as you go: not enough to topple them, just to teach them. To the victor, the spoils; the sidewalk is yours. They ought to know that. Now they do.

Young mothers, with their buggies on parade. They feel entitled too, but they're not. So they reproduced; so what? It's not big and it's not clever, it doesn't qualify them for special consideration. They're still in the way. Except they're not, of course, because you can slalom. Twist, crouch, turn: all grace and power, the opposite of what they are in their awkward indignation, their screeching protests as they react too slow and too late, pointlessly jerking their buggies this way and that when you're already on your way and gone. Never mind that they end up with a wheel in the gutter and a wailing baby; they deserve it, if only for not being as cool as you.

Dogs. Dogs on leads, let dash unpredictably from wall to kerb. Be ready to cut around them, this way or that; be ready as a last resort to leap stuntwise over that taut tripwire of a lead, or else fall in a tangle of legs and leather, chain and dog and moron.

*I don't fall.*

No, indeed.

Besides which, the leap is fun. Kicking off without warning, soaring high above the street, tucking your legs up one side or the other to pass over the dog rather than hit their human, however much the idiot deserves hitting. Timing is everything, timing and speed of attack, speed of reaction. Don't even think about your Aspect, not for this. Do it yourself, it feels so much better that way. Having an Aspect is nothing to be arrogant about, though a lot of people think it is. Having this, now, this seething lava-rage that drives you to excel: oh, yes. That's worth all the fuss and all the effort, all the sweat and the cleaving wind, the grind of wheels on paviors and the shrill of exaltation that you hold behind your teeth because really, let's be cool, okay?

THAT, ALL OF that; a mile of that, just to get warmed up and work through the thrill of it, make believe that I was only doing this because I could.

Then I got serious, because I had to.

The Twa Corbies had found me before, when I'd been out loose and running free. Granted, it had hardly been a tricky thing, just then. All the Overworld would have known it, the moment I cut Jordan free of his amulet. Call it the Jordian knot, if you like. I cut it, and his mother's cry of discovery must have shivered mountains to their roots. For a little while there, I must have been famous. Or put it another way, say I was exposed, in that same light as Jordan was; and one person at least turned out to be looking for me, and sent his henchbirds after me straight off. Rubbing his hands, no doubt, with satisfaction, if his hands had still been free to rub.

And we ducked the birds and the henchwyrm too, we found shelter for the night; and now here I was, out again in the open. This time at least I knew that he was looking, and I'd played three-card monte just a little, this way and that under cover of cabs and carriages. Even so: I might have been betrayed, deliberately or otherwise. I might be spied on even now, and chased, and caught, and...

More reluctantly than I ever had before, I reached for my Aspect.

Just a twitch, I only wanted a touch of it.

And felt it settle over my shoulders like a too-friendly hug from someone you can't rebuff, and *ahhh, at last,* I heard that too. Or felt it, rather, deep in my bones, because of course my Aspect had no actual voice of its own. Hell, it had no actual existence of its own: no life, no opinions, no feelings. This was just another sign that I'd overdone it yesterday, relied on the thing too much for too long. Maybe it was like alcohol or caffeine, any drug; maybe you could chart the course of it from hangover to need to addiction. Maybe I needed therapy. Oops.

Right now, I needed what it had to offer, more than I needed to worry about what that was doing to me long-term. I blanked out my wilder fancies, and let my awareness stretch above, either side, below me as I zoomed along.

It's a neat trick if you can do it: not quite like radar and not quite like that sense we all get when someone's watching us, but somewhere between the two. If someone's watching me then I can find them, so long as I think to look. To check, rather. I shouldn't call it looking, when it doesn't use my eyes. When it can reach down as well as up, into the earth as far as into the air.

No one was watching me, unless they were better at this than I was. Of course, someone would be. Inevitably, someone would know how to use their Aspect or their Power to hide themselves even while they kept tabs on me. There was nothing I could do about that. It was endlessly recursive, and I would lose on every turn. So: pretend it couldn't happen and carry on as though it didn't, as though nobody really was there.

And be stubborn with your Aspect, don't let it rule your life. I shrugged it off, more or less, though that took more of an effort than I liked. I held on only to that whisper I'd originally reached for, enough to keep my legs from tiring as I skated on and on; enough to keep a tendril's reach trailing into the sky, in anticipation of any passing bird. I could make like a jellyfish, sting the damn thing if I distrusted it.

Otherwise, I just buckled down. No more playing with pedestrians, no more stoking an artificial temper. I was in the road now, swooping along with steady strides, faster than any car could go in London traffic. Careful at junctions and heedless of lights, just going when I could: cutting it as fine as I cared to, speed and angle of attack, hurtling under the nose of a passing truck or tailgating around a corner when a tail presented itself, grabbing a tow from any useful bus and then zooming on by at the next stop.

It's one thing about an Aspect, about being adopted into the Overworld and gifted strengths you'd never even dreamed of. Of course it changes you, but mostly what bubbles up is what was there already, lying dormant. It's a chance to express yourself, the truth of you; a chance to open doors you never dared before.

Fay was quiet, girly, shy before she met Jacey. Privately, though, she always did think bike messengers and skateboarders were cool. Not the cocky, confident, look-at-me boys; she looked for girls, and seldom saw them. It was the life, the speed, the skill she envied. Body-consciousness, strength and judgement and control.

Then, well. Fay dated Jacey, and that in itself was a process of discovery, and yes, very much about the body. And then Fay became Desi, and oh, yes. Strength and judgement and control beyond measure, beyond anything human. Turned out that Desi liked machines – and that came from Fay too, a little secret buried part of her that had always wanted a motorbike of her own, however much she loved riding pillion behind her boy – but underneath the kick and roar of an engine was always this, the kick and surge of effort, of speed earned, deserved, achieved.

It's easy just to live in the moment, in your muscles, in the work. It's another kind of displacement activity, *I'm going for a walk* or *a ride* or *a drive*, movement without purpose – but not for me, not that day. I did have to go somewhere, after all; I couldn't just be not-with-Jacey. That was Jordan's thing, to run for the sake of running, just to get away.

And besides, I did have somewhere to go. It was only a question of how to get there, which way was best.

By train, I thought, was probably best. Quickest and safest both. *Get out from under the sky*, I thought, and *cover the ground*, that too. Expand my love of the DLR, learn to love the real thing. But all the big mainline stations were too close, too easy to watch, birds flapping in and out of those high Victorian arches. And I'd be there too soon: before my legs had had a real work-out, before my mind had sunk into the mindlessness of exercise. I wanted to be Zen, and I wasn't even in the zone. So far all I'd managed was exhibitionism. Which went well with my Aspect, but not so much with being discreet.

So. One of the suburban stations, then, somewhere on the margins of the city. A good long stretch, and I'd let my Aspect go before I got there, wear myself out thoroughly and then spend hours changing trains in unexpected places where nobody would think to look for me.

Undetectable, progressing. Getting there.

# CHAPTER TEN

BEING HERE, FOR now. Being in the moment, in the movement, in the stride and drive and flow of it: all smooth power and supple strength, stretch and balance, confidence and devil-may-care. The kind of girl that Fay had always yearned to be. There was a satisfaction in that.

Except that Fay was nicer, and didn't drag a broken heart in the dust behind her until the end there, when she really had no choice. Me, I seemed to make a practice of it. Three broken hearts, maybe; three damaged lives, at least. Sometimes I thought I'd sooner be Fay again. She was so... uncomplicated. Desi tried to be brisk and brutal with the world, to skate over it hard and fast, but everything always tangled up around me. Too many dogs on leads, I guess, and you can't jump them all.

Never mind. I was out of the city's heart now, the worst of the traffic was behind me, I couldn't find anything spying; birds were just birds, as far as I could tell. I could put my head down and bull along. Reel in my Aspect, that too, do the work myself. Work up an honest sweat, like a real mortal girl...

SOMETIMES, A DOORWAY takes you by surprise.

People have done studies, how you can walk into a room and abruptly forget why you came there. It's all in the doorway, in the process of passing through, it's like you reboot your mind. Like there are magnets in the frame, to wipe your short-term memory.

Or a doorway makes itself a metaphor, however solid and substantial and really in the world it is. You step through, and your life will never be the same.

Or never mind the metaphors and never mind the brainshift, it's just a physical actual doorway and you go from here to there, one place to another, and things are different.

Whichever: you can be ready for any of that, if you only see the doorway coming. If you know it's there. If you *choose*. If it lets you make the choice, in or out, this side or that.

Sometimes you're just bulling along, head down, working up a sweat, and someone sticks a doorway right in front of you, and everything changes.

HEAT IS WORK and work is heat. Not a metaphor, that's a rule.

Basically, Fay always wanted to be hot. Okay, that's a metaphor.

Desi? Likes it both ways. Metaphorical and otherwise. It's hot to be cool, but regular heat is also good. Sunshine or sauna, fresh air or pheromones, dance-time or double-time, it's always good to be getting sweaty.

The sun beat down on the back of my neck and even the air tasted hot in my mouth, even the road beneath my wheels had stored up enough heat to be radiating back at me.

It felt gritty too, that road, like I was rolling over hot, hard, gravelly sand rather than laid tarmac. I hadn't really looked for a while, I'd been zoning out, automating; but I looked now, and –

Oh.

Hot hard gravelly sand, oh, yes.

*I don't think we're in Kansas any more.*


ACTUALLY, KANSAS MIGHT be more like this than London ever was. I lifted my head and saw open plain, with a promise of distant mountains. The sky was... not the right colour. Not the right sky. There was dust in the air, lifted by that hot wind even before my wheels stirred it up from the red, red road.

There were green things growing by the roadside, but I didn't want to call them crops. I didn't think they'd been *planted*.

Self-sowing suddenly acquired a whole new meaning.

Never mind.

There was something else that mattered a whole lot more, that I was already trying to avoid.

Some*one* else.

I didn't stop skating, not immediately. That made no difference. He kept pace without effort, and without skates. I wasn't certain sure that he was even walking. He was just... there. This was his kingdom; of course he was there. I was his guest, and of course he'd come to make me welcome.

To open the door for me.

Soon enough, I slewed to an elegant halt and turned to face him directly.

We stood about on a level, me on my skates and him just standing in the road there. He might have been barefoot; I didn't look down to see. He might have been wearing a suit like yesterday, or something anciently appropriate, or nothing at all; I wasn't really paying attention to his dress, any more than he was to mine.

I said, "Hell of a place to waylay a girl." Just to get the groundrules clear: *I know where I am* and *I'm not afraid of you*. At least one of those was a lie.

He just smiled. He knew.

I said, "How did you find me?"

"Please," he said, with a little shrug. "This is my home. I know where everyone is, here."

*In Hell, sure – but in London? How did you find me there?* There was probably no point pursuing it, if he wasn't interested in telling me. It was just a thing he could do, that was all. He couldn't find his son without my help, but he could sure as hell find me.

I said, "Does Jordan?" I wasn't going to be suddenly looking around for him – was *not* – but it would be useful information. Might be. If he was still looking around for me.

He said, "My son is... a law unto himself. He's with his mother now." *Relax*, he was saying, *you're safe. For now. Here, with me.*

That was a little odd, perhaps, but I believed him. I thought he was still grateful, in so far as he understood that he ought to be.

I said, "Well, then...?" *Why did you bring me here, what do you want?*

One does not simply interrogate the Lord of Hell. But one can come perilously close to it. When one is in a hurry, say, with a message to deliver, a warning for an old friend; and has been hijacked, hoicked out of time and place at some immortal's whim.

I assumed he was being whimsical. What else? What manner of use could a mortal be to him?

He said, "My wife and I wanted to offer you an apology, over the way yesterday's events ended for you. Our son's reaction was not unexpected, perhaps, or should not have been; but it was unfortunate, and you deserved better of us all."

*My wife... our son... his mother.* He seemed to avoid names, when he could. To him it was all about relationships. I felt a mad urge to do the other thing, to resist him, to call him by his name – but which one? Dis, Pluto...?

Or none of the above. I still didn't understand what he was doing here, or what I was. What he wanted. Lord of the Underworld, he was a Power of the Overworld by definition: why in any world or all of them should he feel the need to apologise to me? I'd been no more than a messenger. A servant. What he'd expect, from the mortal world.

Unless...

Oh, wait.

Oh, hell.

The way he'd taken me aside, in his own way, somewhere we could be private together; the way he was talking to me, a little formal, a little conspiratorial; *for him it's all about relationships*, and two nights ago I'd been sharing a bed with his son. Suddenly he reminded me of nothing so much as an awkward father-in-law, trying to act as go-between in a family row.

*No. Just... no.*

If he could find me this easily – could he have found me last night? In bed with another of the golden boys, in defiance of whatever he was hoping for?

Probably, yes.

Had he found me then, like that? And held off, waited until I was alone, when he could maybe obscurely urge the interests of his own boy?

Maybe. No way to tell. If he had, at least he hadn't blasted us both in fury at our betrayal. That was something. I supposed.

If not, could he read my mind right now? Or my blushing, giveaway body?

Again, no way to tell. He was polite, mildly embarrassed, ungiveaway to the nth degree. I had no idea whether he knew about me and Jacey; or, if he did know, whether he cared. All I knew was that he did care about his son, and so about Jordan and me. He wanted peace between us; he expected peace to mean togetherness, because after all, who wouldn't want to be with his wonderful boy, now that the vagrant child had come at last into his inheritance? He suspected, perhaps, that Jordan's vicious reaction masked a deeper attachment. Likely he'd heard that such things happened among the young. Perhaps he and his wife had laughed about it, the way the laddie protested far too much. For sure – I was sure – this was a conspiracy. She was talking to the boy; he'd come after the girl. Strangeness and charm, a glimpse of power and a promise of life eternal in the Overworld: who wouldn't buy into that?

Well, I wouldn't. I for one. Not this way, not at his father's hand. It lay not in the old man's gift, my future.

Besides, there was Jacey. Now, again. Perhaps there always had been.

Besides, I had an errand to run. Urgent mercy. And I couldn't even ask for help, given how utterly I was about to refuse everything he offered.

I shook my head, and had to hope that he'd understand the breadth and depth of that, because I was talking almost randomly: "You don't owe me anything. Sir."

He looked a little taken aback, just for a moment, before ageless good manners cut in again. I replayed the last thing he'd said: the word was *offer*, not *owe*. Of course he didn't owe me anything, it would never have crossed his mind that he might. Noblesse oblige: it was his generosity that had brought us here, not any sense of a debt unpaid.

Oh, well. My mouth was dry, and that was nothing to do with the heat or the dust of the road. I licked my lips, which didn't help at all, and took a breath of that hot air which didn't help much either, and was all ready to try again, to say something, anything so long as it was *no*, but he forestalled me.

"How can we help you, Desdaemona? Anything that lies within our gift, you only need to name it." And then, in response perhaps to my astonished face, "You brought our son back to us." *The only one surviving.* "For that, we owe you the world."

Which indeed they held in their gift, more or less. I thought he was a little astonished himself, to find himself thinking that actually he'd been wrong and I was wrong and there was indeed a debt, however much we both tried to deny it.

I still thought he should ask Jordan about that, measure whatever was due by his son's gratitude rather than his own. That would keep things easy.

Here he was, though, and the offer was made; I only had to accept it. And decide what to ask for.

He gave me time, or took a little time for himself, perhaps, to recover from the enormity of laying himself so open to a mortal. He strolled to the side of the road, where something thistlish reached up almost to his head-height, and he was a tall man. Seemed to be, at least. I had no idea what he might be in truth. Heightwise or humanwise. He was one of the Great Powers, immortal and unchanging; did that mean he couldn't be human too? His son was human enough. And short, as it happens. Shorter than me, at least, which is the measure that I go by.

He reached a hand out and plucked a leaf from

the thistle-head, and my whole perspective changed.
Now it looked like a giant artichoke, salad grown
wild. A useful plant, contributory. I'd never heard of
an artichoke so tender that you could pluck and eat
it raw, but he nibbled his leaf with a thoughtful kind
of pleasure, as far as I could judge. But he was an
immortal, and... yeah. It's hard to judge them. And
hard to avoid it, when they're trying to look human-
normal and act that way.

And making crazy offers, holding out the world.

I didn't want the world. Not even a little bit of it. I
wasn't sure I wanted anything, from him.

What did I want? I wanted to feel safe, I wanted
to stop running. I wanted my friends safe too. If that
meant putting an end to Oz Trumby, then that was
what I wanted. I supposed.

If there was one... person... who could put an end to
Oz Trumby, I was probably looking at him right now.

He picked another leaf, wandered back, held it
out in offering. It was symbolic, of course, *whatever
I can do*. But it was real too, and I was terribly
tempted; only – well. I'm not immortal, and I can't
take everything they offer. I *can't*.

I shook my head firmly, hands behind my back
like a little stubborn girl.

"No? Well. Perhaps you're wise. I have no idea..."

No idea of what, the extent of my wisdom? Or
what a hellplant might do to a mortal human body?
It wasn't clear, and he didn't elaborate. He stopped
there, and ate the leaf himself – like an artichoke, yes,
stripping the flesh from it with a tug between bright
white teeth, and discarding the residue – and then
said, "So. What can I do for you, Desdaemona?"

*Tell your son to stop chasing me,* that was the first thing; except for *take care of your son,* actually that should come first. But of course they'd do that anyway now they had him back, they didn't need a girlfriend telling them to do it, and I wasn't his girlfriend anyway. Emphatically, not that.

*Tell Jacey not to come after me?* No, not that either. He didn't need to know about Jacey, if he didn't know already – and really there was something almost comforting in the idea of having Jacey at my heels. If he was. Not that I wanted him there, no, I'd run from him for a reason, to keep him as safe as I could manage; but – well. Let it lie. Don't mention Jacey.

Well, then. *Tell Oz Trumby to leave me alone. And my friends too, all my friends.* Then I wouldn't need to run any more, from anyone. I could even let Jacey catch up with me, if I wanted to. If I chose. And –

And for the rest of my life I'd know that my safety and everyone's around me hung on the word of an immortal Power, that none of us could actually look after ourselves. Which was true, of course, every way from Sunday, but even so...

I shook my head. Quite firmly, still. I was quite pleased with myself for that.

"Nothing, thank you. I'm good."

"You're sure?" One immaculate eyebrow lifted; I'd surprised him again. There was a satisfaction in that.

And no, of course I wasn't sure; but even so – *little stubborn girl,* and I'd never felt so small, or so young, or so helpless – I said, "Yes, I'm sure. Thank you."

"As you wish, then."

He nodded a polite farewell, and turned away. I hesitated – *um, how do I get home? Please?* – but figured he must have that in hand. This was his realm, and I didn't belong here; he'd spit me out like an orange-pip. One way or another.

So I turned round on the road there and began to skate back the way I'd come, slowly and distractedly. Wondering how much distance I was undoing here, how much would all need to be done again. Watching the scenery, that too: waiting to see it change, waiting to find myself back in London streets, going the wrong way and probably quite lost, unfocused, maybe a little afraid.

Maybe a lot afraid, if there were any sign of Oz's minions about. For all I knew this kind of Powerly interference in a girl's progress would act like a magnet, like a pillar of smoke, like a flame in the night, drawing all manner of immortal attention from the Overworld. Maybe I'd find myself skating back into the heart of a reception committee. Corbies and wyrms and Jacey and Jordan too, all wanting some contradictory part of me.

I skated and skated, and the sky grew dark. I hadn't known that Hell had nights and days, but –

Oh.

*I don't think we're in Kansas any more. Again.*

Only, not in London either. Not any more.

# CHAPTER ELEVEN

I COULD'VE DONE with a small dog to talk to, actually. It would have been a comfort.

I don't usually need that kind of comfort. Desi doesn't. But here I was suddenly in the dark, and – well, suddenly in the dark. Not knowing where the hell I was, except that it wasn't London and not Hell either. Nor was it daylight, as it ought to be. I couldn't even be sure this was the same day, or the same season. The same planet, I was fairly sure of that; and somewhere in England still, most likely – but these supercool rollerblades weren't quite so cool when they were embedded up to the ankles in mud, and frankly neither was I.

It's probably *lèse majesté* to become insanely irritated with one of the great Powers, but I did that anyway as I plodded down this squelchy rutted track he'd left me in. I'm a city girl, me. I don't do rural, except *in extremis*. Even my boat I kept moored near the bright lights; even my little cottage was in the heart of the Thames Valley, which is only country by courtesy, really just a dormitory playground for the better parts of London.

Still. You don't ever need to know where you are, so long as you know where you're going. You're just in transition, that's all. Speed and direction are what matters; location is incidental. Ask a particle, any particle.

I didn't need my Aspect to show me the lights down the valley there, simple human night-sight was good enough for that. I didn't need it to lift my heavy legs for me, despite all the day's exercise and the great mud weight of the boots, the claggy suck of the ground beneath. Above all, I didn't need it for reassurance, *I'm Desdaemona, the meanest bitch in the valley, and noli me tangere if you know what's good for you.*

I really was quite firm about that. I felt suddenly soured by the whole Overworld and all that therein is. Powers had been dicking me about all day – if this still was the same day, even – and I'd had enough of it. Didn't want to play any more.

Did still need to take a message to an old friend, that word of warning, *Oz is after you.*

*Me too, he's after me* – but that was the kind of news better kept to myself, frankly. Too many people would turn me in as soon as they heard it, for money or from fear or just because that's what you do, you do what Oz Trumby wants. It wouldn't make a difference, who they heard it from. I could give myself away as readily as I could be betrayed.

That's the Overworld in a nutshell. Fear and greed and tradition, all bound up together, inextricable. Is it any wonder I was sick of it?

So I left my Aspect alone, let it drag behind me in the mud as I hauled my weary self down towards those alluring lights.

First gateway I came to, I perched on the gate and worked the skates off my feet, put my regular boots back on again.

Left the skates there for the first passing farmhand who wanted them, because honestly, why not? Their time had come and gone, for me. They'd carried me to Hell and back; that was enough. Out here they were as silly as skis. Of course there was tarmac ahead of me, not every country road is mud and cowpats, but nevertheless.

Maybe I was being sensible, not wanting to draw attention to myself; zooming around on blades in country lanes is the opposite of concealment, perhaps. Or maybe I just didn't trust them any more. They'd carried me to Hell and back, when that was the last journey I'd have chosen to make.

Sometimes I can baffle myself, things get so complicated in my head. Trying to juggle three worlds, two boys, one hurry? Too much. I left the skates where they dropped, left my Aspect off however much it was nudging at the corners of my mind, went on as simply as I could. Just this girl, y'know...?

LIGHTS AT A junction in the country, by a bridge; of course there was an old inn there.

By luck or happenstance or someone else's good planning, the inn was still an inn. Pubs everywhere were closing down, being turned into family homes or offices or private clubs. The White Horse declared itself, though, proudly in the night: illuminated signs in the car park, in the hedgerows coming and going, and above the door.

The bridge took me over a gushing stream; my boots took me stompingly through the door and into the warm burr of local voices, the warm smells of beer and potatoes. Food, they did food! Of course they did, every surviving country pub these days is half a restaurant, but oh, I could have wept. I hadn't realised until that moment just how hungry I could be.

If they really were an inn still and not just a gastropub, if they had rooms upstairs, if they had room, a room for me, there could be a shower soon. Right now, though, a long glass of something cool, a plate of something hot: that was the height of my ambition.

I went to the bar and ordered almost without looking, almost without thinking. A pint of best and a plate of shepherd's pie. And chips. And crisps while I was waiting, ready-salted. Nuts? Yes, please. Nuts too. Anything salty, crunchy, immediate. Pork scratchings. Yes.

Order enough and you have to wait, even for what you want while you're waiting. He went this way and that, packets and pump and till; I let my eyes wander, so as not to stare at him like a scary ravenous ravening thing. Country pub, old low ceilings, beams and whitewash and mismatched furniture. Typical pub decor, horse brasses and repro prints, local views and old photographs, horse-drawn wagons and ploughs and...

Oh.

Wait.

The White *Horse*.

The *White* Horse.

*The White Horse.*


I'D BEEN HERE before.

If I'd come from the main road, I'd have known it. Plodging down a farm track, coming from the other side – well, no. Do you know how many inns in England are called The White Horse?

Me neither, but a lot.

Only one of them, though, was here. This place, *this*. I really should've known.

The road from Hell is rudely paved, and entirely at the mercy of its master. He thought I might be family, maybe; he was never going to dump me at random, however far the planet had turned while I was in his kingdom. There would be a reason, sure, for setting me here. And this, surely, would have to be it.

The Overworld and the mortal world are perilously intermingled, but there are places, confluences, where they lie more open to each other. Ley lines are like bastes, tacking-stitches, holding each to each but loosely. Stonehenge is a rivet.

Here, too. A rivet.

I still didn't know why he'd sent me here, only that he would have had a purpose. Even if it was nebulous, like his offer of help. I'd spurned that, but I thought perhaps he'd tried to help me anyway.

It would be silly to feel patronised. He was Lord of Hell, and I was a mortal girl; I should be grateful for his patronage, for anything. If he seriously wanted to take me into his family, I thought he'd be disappointed – it was Jordan's call, after all, or else it was mine, and either way I thought it wouldn't happen – but even so. For now, I should be feeling overwhelmed. And frantically taking advantage, if I was wise. I guess I never was that wise. At best, I found it slightly difficult to be grateful, not knowing what he'd had in mind to drop me here. Still, I'd been a Girl Guide; I did my best. I was here, at least, there was no changing that. And there was beer, and food, and more food soon enough. And no doubt there would be more beer afterwards, and I'd ask the nice landlord if he still had rooms, and if not he'd know a farmer or a pensioner who'd be glad of a paying guest, and no one knew where I was, and...

And the White Horse is a rivet.

For maybe twenty minutes there, the time it might've taken me to make my way down the valley, nobody knew where I was. Except Jordan's dad, of course, and anyone he chose to share it with. I did hope he hadn't told Jordan, but I probably shouldn't bet on that.

For maybe twenty seconds after I walked into the pub, still nobody knew where I was.

There was... a dog, call it a dog, sprawled vast and grey and shaggy on the flagstone hearth. No fire at this time of year, but even so: some places are warm by association, I guess. Hearthstones, Hell. Like that. All in the mind.

By the time I saw it, it had most emphatically seen me. It had lifted its head, and was looking.

I looked back. No collar on the beast, no sign of an owner; people were gathered in twos and threes, men mostly, and none of them was paying any attention to the dog.

Even when it got unhurriedly to its feet and padded out of the room. Watching me all the way.

This was an old place, still laid out like a coaching-inn with public bar and lounge and private parlours. It might have been going anywhere, in search of anything.

The more I looked at it, the less it looked like a dog. If I'd asked anyone, I guess they'd have called it a wolfhound.

That's almost a joke. I was almost laughing.

Never mind. I thought it was a fairly safe bet now that someone knew just where I was. A quick shift out of wolf-shape, a quick phone-call, *Hey, this girl just walked in and she doesn't smell right. Smells like a daemon to me, with the dust of Hell all over her. Guess who she's been talking to...? Yeah, I thought so too. And we know what daemon girl's been hanging out with that family, don't we...? Yeah. You want to tell him, or shall I...?*

Something like that, I thought was going on right now. Oz has, oh, let's call it an affinity with shapeshifters.

Okay, I guess I wasn't staying after all. Never mind. I'd wait for dinner anyway. Werewolves weren't a problem, being spied on was just an irritant, and even Oz Trumby would need a bit of notice to stir up something worse. By then I'd be gone. There were bikes as well as cars parked up outside. I'd stick to just the single beer, and once I'd eaten I'd steal something discreetly and be off. I didn't even need my Aspect for that, except maybe to break a security lock; you pick up skills, in the assassin trade.

I wasn't actually much of an assassin, never actually killed anyone for money, but hey. I had the skills.

Oh, and I did take the money, of course. Two out of three ain't bad.


THIS WAS AN old pub, but that didn't mean they'd done no work on it. There must have been a water-mill hereabouts, a little way upstream; now there was only the mill-race left, running right by the inn on its way to rejoin the river, and some architect had had the bright idea of building an annexe out above it. With a glass floor, so that diners and drinkers could sit and watch the water scoot beneath their feet. Illuminated, of course, to show the tangled weeds and the lurking fish and the dark stones of the bed.

So what do you do, when you're alone and tired and upset and a little scared, or more than a little perhaps?

You sit there with nothing to read while you wait for your dinner, with a pint of bitter when everyone knows that alcohol's a depressant, and you stare down between your feet at all that rushing water and you start to feel gloomy. Of course you do. You think of what you've left behind, what you've run away from, one boy and then another. You think how confusing that is, the way you want to knock both their heads together and then kiss them better, kiss them both.

More than kiss, perhaps.

You think about that, and you just grow more depressed.

And then you think about the future, all this running that lies ahead of you, and...

At least you have somewhere to run, short-term. Errand of urgent mercy. It's good to have goals.

After that... Well. Survival is a goal, I guess. But it's a bloody depressing one.


HERE CAME DINNER. Fork and fingers, and sod it: yes, I'd like another pint of bitter, please. Alcohol in my bloodstream wasn't going to be a problem, not with my Aspect on standby to burn it off; being breathalysed really wasn't a problem, as I wasn't planning to stop for any cop. Or any reason else. As soon as I was done here, I was off.

Meantime, apparently, I was still staring down through the floor. Spotting fishes.

Spotting a school, a flock, a flood of little fishes.

No, wait.

Those weren't fish.

Eels. Baby eels. Elvers.

Swarming elvers. They were meant to be delicious. And increasingly rare, and incredibly expensive. Someone should be out there netting them in the dark and flying them to Japan like living treasure.

Someone should tip off the landlord, if he didn't know already. But – nah, not me. He kept a werewolf in the house. It might be his son, or his son's friend; he might be giving it houseroom for all manner of decent reasons; and even so. There may be decent werewolves, but I've never met one. The clue's in the name, they do tend to be wolfish. Doglike, in a bad way: loyal to the strongest, not to the right. It wasn't the landlord this one had gone padding off to, but he gave it houseroom. I was giving him nothing for nothing.

Maybe I didn't need to; he might be getting something for nothing already. Those elvers were milling around beneath my feet, not moving on in a mad rush to the sea. These were country folk, they all had egg-sucking grandmothers; of course they'd know about the elvers. Of course they'd have a net across the stream, to pen the creatures here until they could be scooped out and bucketed up and sold on. They were a resource, and people are nothing if not resourceful.

Um. Elvers too, apparently. Finding themselves trapped, they were putting their time to good use, building up reserves for the journey ahead...

Put simply, they were eating the fish that lurked among the weeds there – but 'eating' was far too simple a word. Far too decorous. They were ripping those fish apart. I hadn't even known they were carnivorous, but that milling mass of elvers tore into their victims like sharks in a frenzy, scattering gobbets of flesh that tried to rise in the melee and tried to sink in the water and never got the chance either way, were snatched and fought over and swallowed by one ravening tooth-filled maw or another.

They were quite scary, those glimpses I had of one maw or another, rising out of the turmoil then spinning back into it again. Of course the elvers were only tiny, the length of a pencil, but even so. It was like watching piranhas in the schoolkid myth of a swarm, ripping horses to the bone in moments flat. I was a big strong human being even without my Aspect, and out in the air where they could never come, and even so I was weirdly glad to have that plate of glass between us. Thick glass, glass you could walk on, glass you could trust.

Even so, I couldn't take my eyes off what was happening down there.

Maybe slaughter's always been attractive, or maybe I'd just become a ghoul. Maybe years of using my Aspect had hardened me. I'd killed a lot of vampires, a lot of other creatures; maybe I was losing my own humanity. Maybe I should cut down, give up, lose the Aspect altogether...

Actually they weren't so small, those elvers, not pencil-sized. Unless the glass was distorting them, or the water was. They were quieter now they'd eaten all the fish: digesting, I guess, just lying at full stretch in the water. About the size of a descant recorder, they looked now, the kind we all played at school, really badly.

Oh, wait. Now they were boiling again. No more fish to boil over, so...

Oh. Now they were eating each other.

I probably shouldn't be surprised. I'd met other creatures, more rational creatures, for whom cannibalism was no kind of taboo. Some of them were human.

I'd never met anything, never heard of anything that grew as fast as these. It was hard to be sure through all the glass and the frothing water, through their churning fury, but from what I saw of writhing bodies, they looked suddenly as fat as my forearm, which –

Oh.

Okay, I'm slow sometimes. I was slow just then, at the back end of a hard day. I wanted an hour off, time to sit and chill before it all started again. I'd forgotten – or just pushed to the back of my mind – that the world doesn't work that way, to my convenience.

The Overworld certainly doesn't.

THE WHITE HORSE? Is a *rivet*. Two worlds interlock here, things come and go with no hindrance. No notice.

No delay.

Messages, other things.

Of course Oz didn't need time to arrange a reception committee. Of course there was something right at hand; there always would be, at a nexus like this.

Not elvers, not in any mortal sense. Not edible, or not to us; you really, really wouldn't want to take a bite of these things. Even if you got the chance. Mostly they'd be getting their bite in first.

I saw a mouth again. It was maybe big enough by now to engulf my head, and those teeth... Yeah. Far too many, far too long and vicious-sharp, with bits of other eel skewered on them. It's not a good look, even the other side of a reliable barrier. I'd have told her so, if she hadn't rammed her skull up hard against that glass right then.

If I hadn't seen it bulge, and heard it creak.

I WAS UP and out of there so fast, I swear I left my Aspect behind. I could feel it having to hurry, almost to chase me down, before it could clamp itself about me for whatever offensive protection it was worth.

"Come on," I growled. "Keep up..."

It is insane, of course, to talk to your talent as though it were a separate occasion from yourself. Even so.

The annexe had a separate exit, straight down into the car park. That's one reason I'd chosen to sit out there on my own, where I could keep an eye on who came and went, and what vehicles they left behind them. That, and the chance to be alone with my food and my beer and my gloomy mood.

I wasn't glooming now. Nor aching to be alone. At least my Aspect gave me something to talk to, even if I was only bawling it out.

And I might not need it to pinch a set of wheels – that was a matter of pride to me, not actually to *need* it – but it would make the job a hell of a lot easier, not to mention fast. There isn't a motor in the land that would dare fail to fire with an Aspect on the case.

It might have proved cocky about that – I did always have the feeling that the damn thing enjoyed its work – only it never got the chance to show off that night, because in fact I didn't steal a motor after all.

Because I came down the steps into the car park, and I got half a dozen strides towards the bike of my fancy – a big Harley with its engine still warm, ticking quietly to itself in the dark – when the horizon erupted.

In the dark, in a car park lined with security lights, the horizon is not actually that far away. What I was seeing was as far as I could see, which was right there, immediate, which sometimes just means *very close indeed*.

Which was those sweet delicious elvers ready now, rising up.

Who knew that eels could survive out of water? And, hell, why the hell didn't they ever tell me?

THE CAR PARK had water on two sides: the mill-race between it and the inn, and the river that the race ran into. Not that much of a river, perhaps – you could cross it with a vaulting-pole, easy – but enough. Enough to host a swarm of eel-things, at least.

They'd clogged and overflowed the mill-race, to the point where there was no water in it any more. All the water was spilled out across the car park. I was standing in it. The eels were standing in the stream-bed, rising like cobras from a basket. My feet were probably wetter than they were.

The way out of the car park, the way I'd meant to drive? Meant crossing that little bridge I'd walked over an hour ago.

The bridge with eel-heads risen on either side of it, big enough now to pluck a mortal girl off a motorbike and swallow her whole.

I might fight, mind, from the inside. Might fight my way out, even – but not if those teeth had done their work properly on the way down.

I didn't fancy making the experiment. They looked reliable, those teeth. Some of us depend on an Aspect, and count ourselves lucky; some just depend on what they're born with. As far as I could see, these things had no cause for complaint.

I suppose if they'd stayed in the water, they'd all have eaten each other until there was just the one left. The size of a wyrm, that one might have been. Maybe that's where wyrms came from, maybe they were all survival-of-the-fittest types, evolution in action, making Darwin proud.

If so, they interrupted their natural cycle to come after me. Maybe I should be proud, that they thought I was worth it. Good protein, I guess. Food with benefits. Actually I didn't think they'd get the benefit of the Aspect, though I might be wrong; and they might think the opposite, if they had the wherewithal to think at all. Right or wrong, it didn't really matter. People have eaten other people for millennia, in hopes of benefit from their strength or smarts or whatever. Mostly they've been disappointed, but it's never made any difference to the eaten.

So. I was fairly determined, actually, not to become one of the eaten. But there were still a lot of these creatures, despite all the eating each other; and they were huge, and vicious, and coming up out of the water now, squirming across the tarmac to come at me. Eating very definitely on their minds.

Eels are amphibious, I guess. Who knew?

Here they came, anyway. And here I went: back up the steps the way I'd come, to where I'd been before. There's a tradition in terror, that you run from something scary into something worse, and have to double back. And then hopefully face down what scared you first, maybe even learn a lesson from that. I'm not convinced about the lesson because really you've just levelled up, you're running from a higher grade of terror now, but even so. We cling to our traditions. This way, that way, back again.

Traditionally I suppose I should've been screaming, but... Nah. Not even to oblige the tradition.

Back into the annexe, then, which did feel kind of like hopping from one frying-pan to another. Hopefully, though, I wouldn't have to face down anything. In so far as I had one, my plan was to spend no time at all at the eelface.

Even as I came through the door, the floor reared up ahead of me, like a whale broaching. Wood splintered, slabs of glass shattered and slid across each other, and whoops.

Eelface, right there. In my face.

Do regular mortal eels of usual size look like that, is the Sargasso Sea full of cynical ill-mannered fish popping their heads up to sneer at each other? Should we rename it the Sarcastic Sea?

I don't know. I don't even know if eels are fish. I know a pair of boys who'd know that kind of thing, sans internet. Or they'd argue about it, more likely. They argue about everything.

No matter.

The eel's head was, oh, the size of me. The length of me, of my whole body, from its snout to the back of its skull. I'd still be more than a mouthful, but not much; I was fairly sure it could swallow me whole by now, if I only held still long enough. If I didn't get tangled up in its teeth.

Those teeth were the nastiest things I'd seen in a while. The length of my forearm, but wicked sharp; inward-curving, to be sure of a good grip, and don't ask me how it never punctured its own tongue;

glossy and foul both at once, the kind of colours you don't want teeth to be.

The kind of close you don't want teeth like that to be, right there as it opened wide, reaching for me. They were almost more in my face than its own.

I'd have liked to kick them straight down its throat. I had a really good view of that throat, the way it was waiting for me, gulping slowly in anticipation, grey-green and lubricated with slime. The tongue was long and leathery, lurking behind the teeth. Hunched there, quivering. Poised.


THERE MUST BE shelves of theses, shelves and shelves in academic libraries the world over, all about predators and size, how it's not always an advantage to be huge.

When they were tiny, these things could've stripped the flesh off my bones before I had a chance to shriek. Bigger, they could still have overwhelmed me while I had my hands full with just a couple. Even my Aspect couldn't have helped me, against that many that fast.

At this size, though? The thing was still opening its jaws and I was right there – in its face, yes, and wanting to kick its teeth in. As far in as I could manage it.

But. It is always, always an advantage to be smart, and measure your chances. If I paused to give it the kicking it undoubtedly deserved, its friends from the car park would be coming in behind me, and – well. One thing at a time.

This thing? I just jumped, clear over it. While it was still gearing up for a Desi-swallowing snap, I was over its head and rolling, tumbling through the doorway into the pub proper.

Not without a pang of regret, but hey. I'm philosophical. You can't always get what you want.

Sometimes, you have to play the hero.

So I dived and rolled and came up in the public bar, where people were just now figuring out that something odd was going on out there. Little old men struggling to their feet by aid of walking-stick, pulling their flat caps on firmly, you've got to be properly dressed; local young-farmer types on their feet already, staring at me and then staring past me, the way you would if there was a girl doing acrobatics out of a doorway and a giant girl-eating monster-head peering after her, peering maybe straight at you.

I said, "Get the hell out of here!"

Quite loudly, I said that. An Aspect is good for amplification.

Then I led the rush.

Out of the public bar, not out of the building, not yet. I left the front door for them. Me, I plunged into the lounge to give the same warning again. And found the landlord behind the bar, with a teenage boy just pulling a sweatshirt on over his head, over his bare torso. He eyed me from under his tangled fringe, and I felt a cold recognition.

Didn't speak to him. Spoke to the landlord instead: "Yours?" with just a jerk of the head to indicate the boy.

He nodded fractionally, knowing what he'd got.

"Congratulations." *Live with it*, was the subtext I was pretty sure he was picking up. *If you get the chance*, footnote to the subtext. "Now give me a bottle of whisky and a lighter, and see your people safe."

For a wonder, he didn't ask questions. I don't know if he had any talents himself – he looked human-normal to me, but then so did his boy now, apart maybe from those wolfish eyes – but I guess he knew that something bad was here. Hell, he kept the White Horse, and that place is a rivet. He might be mortal, but he couldn't be blind to the Overworld; he'd never have survived it.

Perhaps he didn't survive it. I haven't been back to see.

Anyway: no questions. He rolled a bottle across the bar at me, didn't ask for money. Wise man.

Wiser if he had another way out and a getaway car. Or maybe his boy and he could make the shift together and lope off under the moon to some new and preferably distant life, if he had the gift of it.

I didn't stop to ask. Just grabbed that bottle and said, "Lighter?"

"No lighters. Matches, in the other bar."

We looked at each other; we both knew that neither one of us was going back in there. Matches would be no use to me anyway, but he didn't know that.

It was the boy – in a sudden access of conscience, maybe, or to save his dad, or save the moment, or whatever random teenage impulse it actually was – who pulled a lighter from his pocket and tossed it to me.

I snatched it from the air and ran.


SOMETHING IN ME wanted to stop and fight. Something clenched around me did, at any rate. Inside, I was more ambivalent. I didn't like to run away, I didn't want to leave anybody behind me; no mortal should have to face what was rising up out of that water.

Hell, no mortal *could* face it, for more than a second or two. A moment of frozen horror, and then the teeth, the gullet, gone. That would be it, more or less.

With me in the way, between them and it? Um. They might get the time to run. Might do.

I couldn't fight the things either; I knew that, even if my Aspect didn't. Hell, I'd bounced off the wyrm, hadn't I? And these things were – well, I was guessing, but I'd guess that they were just as tough, and faster, and more vicious. And more plentiful. I wouldn't stand a chance. Teeth, gullet, gone. The only difference was – might be! – that at least I'd go down fighting.

That was probably not a particular advantage. They probably wouldn't even notice.

Besides: either I was very wrong, or else they were here for me. Directed, by some intelligence not their own. Some distant mind that was very, very pissed off with me, and didn't want to talk about it, no.

With luck, if I ran they'd leave the people alone and come after me.

Maybe I should hoot at them and throw things, to be sure they got the message

Maybe there'd be no need to do that. They'd found me easily, once the boy delivered his tip-off; they had my scent, or my psychic trace, or whatever they needed to locate me exactly. I figured they could probably follow well enough along.

Besides, the only thing I had to throw was the whisky, and I wasn't throwing that.

The front door was clear now. Everybody who was going that way must have gone already; I didn't look back to see how many hadn't made it. I could hear noises coming from the public bar, that I hoped were just the sounds of furniture and floor breaking up under the grinding passage of massive eel-bodies, as they came in pursuit of me.

Out I went, then. Found the slow and the not-too-smart milling around, seeing the road and the bridge asquirm with monsters, all blocking their most obvious getaway route. It's not only in movies that people want to run down the middle of the road, regardless of what's coming after them.

I waited long enough to yell again – "Get the hell away from here! No, *that* way, go *that* way," pointing them around the side of the building, where they could put the whole damn pub between them and the water and the eels, if they only got a bloody move on.

I didn't wait to see them do it. They were on their own now, like me, like everyone. Like me.

I hate it. It's what the world does to me, always, in the end: it leaves me on my own, and I hate it. That's not the worst of what the world does to me, maybe, but it's what I hate most. I don't do well this way, I wasn't born to be solitary. I like to look around and see someone else running with me. Arms around my waist, riding pillion.

Jordan did that. Jacey never would.

Never mind.

Neither of them was here now. Just me, and a stew of chasing eels.

I sent the fretful innocents one way, or tried to; me, I ran another.

Not down towards the water, where more eelage writhed. I'm not a total idiot.

Orthogonal to everything: I ran straight ahead, to where a hedge bordered a field of sprouting barley.

Straight at the hedge; straight through it.

Cross-country would probably be easier for the eels than it was for me, but hey. I figured pretty much whatever I did, wherever I ran, the eels would have it easy and me not. That's just the way it goes.

At least I knew where I was going, and it was this way. As the crow flies, as the girl runs when she's a daemon in a hurry with eels at her back.

PLOUGHED FIELDS ARE hard work; growing crops are harder.

Possibly not for eels.

My legs pumped, my blood surged, I told myself – quite grimly – that I could do this all night if I had to. Run and run.

For the first time, I wasn't entirely sure that was actually true, I thought even my Aspect might have a limit to its stamina, but I told it to myself anyway. And tried not to listen to the rustling, surging sounds behind me as a swarm of eels glided over a bed of crushed barley-stalks. Grinning, most likely, as they came, if you wanted to call that ready gape a grin.

I didn't look back. Head down, pick your knees up, run.

Hang on to the whisky.

\*     \*     \*

UP AND UP, and further up. It's that kind of country, where what goes up must become a down. One last hedgerow, and no more crops to kick through: now there was just coarse, tough, sheep-cropped turf beneath my feet in long rolling ridges, and I could run and run.

So I did that, I ran and ran, with *slither, slither* always at my back.

Ancient trackways ran along the ridgetops, mattering more than mortal people knew. I ignored them, if high-hurdling from one side to the other counts as ignoring. Really it's the opposite, taking very careful account of them and doing my utmost not to get entangled, not tonight, not now. Similarly, I ignored – in the sense of utmostly avoiding – the occasional striding figure glimpsed on one path or another. They might be able to help me, there was a decent chance of that. The chance that they might choose to do so? Vanishingly small. Better, always, not to get involved. Just leave them be and hurry by.

As to what I did instead...

Well. At least I had the whisky. That was something.

Might be something.

Might even be enough.


I RAN, AS we know. They followed, as we know. I didn't get away; they didn't catch me up.

I might as well not have bothered with all that running, really, except.

Except that it brought me at last to the rising slope of one more hill, where something other than a Bronze Age footpath had cut through the sward.

Been cut, that is, and more purposefully. With tools and effort, not just the passage of time and feet across geography.

Show the English a chalky hill, and they'll cut a figure into it. Then or now, no different. White giants stalk the landscape. Some of them are prehistoric, some are modern, most are Victorian. They're all sentimental to some degree.

They're not all horses, not quite. Most of them, though, yes. There's even a word for it.

Leucippotomy, since you ask.

This one? Is certainly a horse. Why else would I have run so far?

The clue's in the name. It's famous. Even the inn down the valley is named after it, and has been for centuries.

I stood there at its head – for no good reason, really, any part of it would do, if this did any good at all – and twisted the cap off the whisky bottle.

Behind me, below, came *slither, slither*. I tried to ignore it. No good reason. Concentration wasn't going to make a difference here. I suppose it maybe felt respectful, though. Or maybe I just didn't want to think how close those eels were coming, while I stood there sloshing spirits onto bone-bare chalk.

"Hey," I said. "Want to wake up? I brought you a drink..."

It's not *magic*, okay? There isn't a *spell*. You don't have to chant archaic nonsense and march around three times widdershins and sacrifice a virgin at the full of the moon.

Just as well, really. I didn't have time, the moon wasn't up and I hadn't brought a virgin. There was that boy back at the inn, and I might have felt tempted, but.

No need. He's a horse; just talk to him.

HE LIFTS HIS head and all the world is breathless still. Even the *slither, slither* has to pause, not to break the moment. Like a bubble out of time, that moment: infinitely fragile, infinitely strong.

He lifts his skull head from the earth, the dead white of bone: bone-white and dead and hollow.

He lifts his eyeless skull of a head, and looks at me.

He doesn't talk back. He's a horse. But he rises, and only his head is bone; the rest of him is art. Art made actual. A pure impression of horse, a sketch cut out of light. In the dark, he shines; in daylight, just the same. It's a different manner of light, or your eyes find him differently, or there simply aren't the words in English. Or the ideas, in any language, in anybody's head. The reality of him is... elsewhere.

He stands, and he's the size he ought to be, for me: still entirely astonishing, but astonishing in scale. On the ground he's enormous, unreachable. And then he stands up, and he's a horse. He's there. Big as a stallion should be, and he is very much a stallion: say seventeen hands or a fraction less, manageable for a tall girl. I'm tall enough.

GIRLS AND PONIES. What can I say? I'm not immune. Fay loved to ride, and Desi didn't grow out of that, she only put it aside for a while.

*Slither, slither.*

Time to pick it back up, then.

If I dared, if I was allowed.

If it was even possible. He was made of light and line, and I am... solid flesh. Very solid, with my Aspect on me. Would he, *could* he carry me?

It was his call, of course, either way, but my first move.

Right, then.

It felt suddenly worse than impertinent: lèse-majesté or something like it, an absolute trespass, doing something sacrilegious on what should be holy ground. Even so, I laid a hand on his shoulder. Just to see, really. Just to touch, to learn how he felt, to learn if he would let me.

He stood still beneath my hand, and felt just as solid as I was. Well, good.

Even so. Touching him was one thing. Mounting him? Apparently something else altogether, and something in me didn't want to do it.


I DELAYED TOO long. *Slither, slither* and here they were, relentless and appalling, surging up the slope with those dreadful mouths agape already.

I needed more time, and didn't have it.

What I did have, though, I had a bottle of whisky in my other hand. Half sloshed out in a libation, which meant half full still; and the proof of spirit used to be whether gunpowder would still ignite after it was soaked in the stuff. You can't think about spirits without flame spluttering into mind.

Flame, bottle...

Horses traditionally don't like fire, but I doubted this one would spook.

I ripped the sleeve off my shirt and stuffed it into the neck of the bottle, then tipped that upside down to soak the wick with whisky while I fished in my pocket for the kid's lighter. Okay, maybe he didn't deserve sacrificing after all. So long as the damn thing would light.

I hadn't looked, but of course it was a Zippo; Zippos are cool, now and always. I flipped back the lid, flicked the wheel for a spark, felt a touch of relief as the flame caught.

Touched flame to wick, whirled the bottle around my head to get a proper blaze going, and hurled it dramatically towards the encroaching eels.

Ah, well.

I'd have done better to drink the stuff. Turns out that regular blended whisky – yes, of course it was White Horse brand, what else? – doesn't explode like a proper Molotov cocktail at all. It barely wants to burn. I guess my mother worked harder than I knew to light the brandy on the family Christmas pud.

Improvisation is always good, in principle; you do the best you can with what's to hand. Sometimes, though? Sometimes it just doesn't work out. You can't always beat a sword with a ploughshare. In my head there was a great eruption, vivid flame and vicious glass shrapnel driving back this swarm of anxious fire-phobic eels. In reality there was a sort of splutter, a flicker, a thud. The bottle didn't even break, until one of the eels oozed right over it in its eagerness to get at me.

Okay, then. I had no time, no weapons, no choices left.

No hesitation left in me, either. Apparently.

Actually, the way it felt, my Aspect got tired of waiting for me to wise up, and did the necessary all by itself. Picked me up and flung me onto the horse's back.

That, or I vaulted there neatly and all by myself. You decide.

# CHAPTER TWELVE

ONE LITTLE MOMENT longer, the horse just stood there beneath me. Just long enough that I could entertain a universe of doubts, what would happen next; just long enough for his head to turn and his empty eye-socket to survey me, cocked at an angle that let starlight fall straight through the hollow of his skull. It was a weird night all round, but that was almost weirdest, seeing how utterly there was nothing there. Not a spark of light, not a thread of tissue, not a gesture towards human notions of how a thing might live.

"I don't know," I said, "but those things look like they might crunch your bones, even yours, on their way to me. Want to get out of here?"

There was still the chance that he might simply settle back into earth again and leave me stranded, eel-bait. I guess he had that option. Nothing that I'd brought, nothing that I knew to do could compel him. The libation was an invitation, nothing more; no kind of spell.

The Fay in me wanted to grip with my thighs and kick my heels into his flanks, grab a double handful of mane for security and ride the way she always had, in charge. My Aspect was like that in spades, urgent and imperative. I felt like I was fighting them both off at once, because there was just no way. This horse couldn't be ridden. He would condescend to carry me, or else he wouldn't. His choice.

No mane either, for Fay's reaching hands to grab at. Only that smooth solid arching line of light that marked a passage from skull to body, that I guess you could call a neck. I guess you'd have to.

It took everything I had just to sit there and watch the eels come, while he... well. Made up his mind, I guess. Though he didn't appear to have one. They were almost snapping at his fetlocks by the time he turned and trotted out of his own ground, up to the ridge above.

Suddenly he felt all horse beneath me, essence of horse, the pure thing unsullied. Whoever cut those lines in turf, they knew what they were doing. What they were shaping. The arrogance, the vanity, the nerves: all there. The heart, the courage, the grace and strength and willingness to work. I don't know, I can't imagine how the thing was done. In that moment, though, I think I knew why: for the beauty of the thing, for craft and wonder both combined. For the horse.

He was here, now, in the night and the fear and the possibility. Perhaps he had always been here, perhaps he always would be. Those were questions for another time, if I ever dared to ask them or found someone who might know. For here, for now, here and now was enough.

I didn't kick his ribs, to suggest that he might start moving. I didn't cling, I didn't yell him on. I sat like Patience on a monument, on this monumental horse. He danced away from the eels, and they followed him, us, me. Us.

I might have talked to him a little then. It's only polite, when there are two of you; it's only practical, when you really want to embed the idea that you're both in this together.

He might have listened. There were hollows in his skull, where ears might once have perked and twisted.

I did miss the opportunity of tugging his ears the way you do, the way Fay used to do. It's probably just as well, though. Lèse-majesté again: one does not tug the ears of a prehistoric symbol. Or an artwork, or possibly a folly.

Eels came, and he stood still and tall; I thought that might be folly.

One eel came ahead of all the others, and did try to take a bite of light, to gnaw his leg away.

All horse, all stallion, all temper. He lashed out with that same leg, and there was a highly satisfying crunch from the eel's head, an abrupt writhing all along its body and then a stillness.

That didn't last. Its fellows fell on it, in that same feeding-frenzy they'd shown in the mill-stream.

Well, good.

Even so, distraction is the lesser part of valour; it doesn't last. I said, "Now, maybe? While they're busy, we could maybe just get out of here?"

He thought about it. I swear, he stood and thought.

And then nodded his head – in an extremely horsey way, not like a person at all, not like he was actually answering me, don't think that – and kicked at the turf with hooves he didn't actually have, and we were away.

YOU COULD MAKE a horse of the rain on the wind, all chill and bitter motion. You could make a horse of moonlight on a millpond, bright stillness over depth. You could make a horse of stone and grass, or of ink on paper, or...

I don't know where he came from, what power guided what hands to cut the shape of him from turf on the high downs; but you couldn't make him, no. He must have been, already. Somehow, somewhere, some state of being. Essence of horse, flowing free until he poured himself into this design, until he chose to be fixed there, to sleep out the turning years until some dangerous fool comes to wake him with whispers, a splash of mannerly whisky...

Maybe. Something like that, perhaps. I really don't know. Only that – well, you couldn't make him. Not from nothing. I don't think you could even imagine him. He was beyond the reach of a human mind; hell, I was sitting on him, and I couldn't come near what he was.

Never mind. Call it magic, if that's easier. Or an expression of the collective subconscious, or an artefact of true England – the idea that underlies this grubby little nation state – or call him any damn thing you like.

Me, I call him Horse.

\* \* \*

WE RAN, HORSE and I. Well, he ran. I rode, in so far as I sat on his back and he carried me.

Maybe we didn't even need to run. Maybe he could have fought them off, all those eels, and sent them back to whatever hell they came from. Maybe. He was something older, deeper, better than them – but the good guys don't always get to win. Not just for being good. And I didn't think he'd ever been a warhorse.

Neither did he, I guess. At any rate, he seemed happy enough to run. Literally, I think. I think it was what he was made for. Like the wind is happy to blow, the rain to fall. Movement completed him; speed is what he was about. You can write a word, and then you can say it. You can cut a horse into a hillside, and then you can let him run.

I DIDN'T TURN him north; I didn't need to. The landscape tended that way, and so did he. We followed the ridge until it met a river valley, where it turned aside in confusion. Then we followed the river for a while, for a distance, but that all too clearly had its roots in the west, so we left that too. I don't know if he read my mind or if he followed his instincts or his own inscrutable whim that just happened to chime in with my needs; how would you ever tell?

Now we were working our way more literally across country, against the grain – except that it was the human infrastructure, the grain of industry that lay across our path. The land would still have eased us northward undelayed, but here was a canal that had to be leaped, and here a motorway in a cut too broad for leaping. I think there was a chain-link fence that smoked and snapped at our approach, but we held back from the traffic until a gap opened wide enough that we could canter through unremarked. When you ride a glowing implication of a horse, remarks will be made, unless you're careful. And here was a railway marshalling yard so broad we had to detour around it, and here an industrial estate where I think even Horse was feeling lost before the cloud cover relented and he could fling his head up to sight the stars and find our route again.

North, and north: he'd have galloped to the Pole Star, if he could only find good footing as he followed the Plough through starfields. Perhaps he could, perhaps I should have given him his head. Or let him take it, rather; or just let him be, just sat him and been carried into wonder.

But – well, I had a mission of my own, and time and ground were sketchy, stretchy concepts in the mind of Horse. That's pretty much where we were, I figured, in some ancient idea of England and territory, a space-time discontinuum where physics was contingent on something that you couldn't call history. It predated the coming of people: older than language, older than understanding. I almost felt like I'd committed some form of archaeology, just rousing Horse from his bed. Archaeology without spades.

Archaeology, lèse-majesté, whatever it was, I wasn't done committing it. We were coming too far, too fast. It was hard to tell exactly how we stood in relation to the world I knew – *at an angle* was the best that I could think of, as if there were one more axis where Horse stood, at right-angles to everything else – but I could still make out landmarks, though they seemed elastic and uncertain. The longer they'd been there, the more clearly they stood out. Birmingham had been only a smear of distorted light, pale and sickly and unclean, but Doncaster Cathedral was a stark clear silhouette. I'd have preferred road-signs, frankly, but you make do with what you have. When you have to.

I would have leaned forward, but I was leaning already; apparently at some point teenage Fay had reasserted herself, so that I was gripping as best I could with thighs and calves and heels, while my arms tried vainly to loop around his neck. Of course she'd tried bareback riding, but never on a horse stripped so utterly bare, naked of reins and bridle and mane too. Of course there's a thrill in speed and danger, Desi hankered for it, but – oh, yes. By this time Fay and Desi both were just holding on.

Horse wouldn't let me fall, maybe, but I wasn't willing to take the chance. Who knew where I might land, or when?

With me leaning forward that way to twine around his neck, with him being made so exactly to my scale, my mouth was right where his ear ought to be if he were a regular horse, if I wanted to say anything that he might choose to listen to.

Hell, I didn't have anything else.

I said, "Horse?"

I said, "Slow down, Horse, we're nearly there."

I said, "Please, Horse. Wouldn't want to overshoot, and have to double back."

At first, at the time, when I thought about him, it had been all about eels and getting away. The eels were far behind us now, a world away. Now it was about where we were, and where I wanted to be. Delivering a message. Pony Express.

*That's the thing about people*, I might have said into his open ear-hole. *Give us one thing, we'll always take something else. Ask for more, reach for better. We're programmed for disappointment, and we just have to keep snatching till we find it.*

Perhaps he knew it already. Perhaps he didn't care. He wanted rid of me, or he wanted to serve me, or... Who knows? He was an idea expressed as design, expressing itself in dimensions that I couldn't quite count; I sat at the perfect confluence of intellect and instinct, where –

Oh, hell. I sat on a horse, and he took me where I wanted to go. That's as much as I can say, and as much as I need to.


THE WORLD STEADIED around us as he slowed. By the time he was trotting, if you want to call it a trot, everything was fixed and focused and certain again. As certain as things get, that is, as certain as you can be in the dark in the shadow of the Overworld.

I was a little surprised to find it was still night – though there was no telling which night it was, tomorrow or yesterday or not. We might have come whenever.

Slower still, and slower. He came to a stand at last, and... simply stood. All the patience of chalk and grass, not moving beneath me, not breathing, not conspicuously alive.

He was waiting – of course, inevitably – for me. The thing was mine to do, and so I did it; I dismounted.

I slid off his back and set my feet to ground, for the first time in how long, I couldn't say. It only mattered if time were linear, if Oz could have got ahead of me. Sent his minions ahead. But he could only do that if they knew where to come, and they could only learn that by following me. I thought, I hoped.

Thinking and hoping: by and large, they were what got me by. They are what gets us by, all of us, whether we acknowledge it or not.

Thinking and hoping and good manners. I owed him thanks at least, or more than thanks. I laid my hand on his cool shoulder and tried to tell him, but I had no impression that he was listening. In the back of my mind I think I was half expecting him to lie down and absorb himself into hill and turf again, only that I had brought him somewhere alien, inhospitable, unconscionable. Never mind that he'd brought me; that wasn't how it felt.

We stood in a river valley, which might not have seemed so wrong even a thousand years ago, even five hundred, even three. Now, though? Now it was a wasteland, flat and drear. We stood on broken concrete, rotting tarmac, rubble; if he still leaned at that impossible angle, I thought it was because he was trying to lean away from everything, all at once. It was good perhaps that he didn't quite have hooves, that he wasn't quite in actual contact. I thought this land would poison him.

I remembered the Green Man when Asher took him to Hell, poison at the roots. I wanted to shout at Horse, to slap his rump and clap my hands and wave my arms and do whatever I had to, to drive him off; only I didn't think he'd go, or not for me. Not because of me. I didn't really think he'd come because of me. It was more complicated than that. Because I wanted to be here, yes, this was the place exactly – but he'd brought me for his own reasons, not for mine, and he'd stay until he was satisfied. Horses are like that, or ancient powers are, and he was both.

Well, then. There wasn't anything I could do, to or with or for Horse now. It was hard to take my eyes off him, but I was here to do the hard things, so I did.

There was the river, sluggish and foul behind torn and drooping fences, between hard high concrete banks pocked with open dribbling mouths of sewer-crock. I supposed this must once have been an industrial estate. Then it would have been post-industrial, after the businesses all closed or moved away. Now it was not even that much: just an emptiness, a blasted nothing that still oozed corruption.

Except that a mile downstream stood a gasworks, a refinery too big to move, too useful to let die. There were the great bulbous holders that rose and fell as they were full or empty; there beyond were chimneys rising out of an eely writhe of pipes and processes. Each one flared fire at its high mouth like a dragon aiming upward. I never have understood that, why it's not worthwhile to capture whatever gases they're burning off, but science is as science does, and it's nothing to do with me.

Even less to do with Horse. He looked wrong, in that flaring guttering light: as though his own shine were diminished or tainted. I did so want to tell him to go.

But I hardened my heart, as he didn't have one, and turned my back. This was what I had come for; this was where I needed to be.

I started walking over that ruined pavement, towards the distant chimneys.

He came after me.

I stopped, he stopped. I'm not even sure how I knew that. He didn't – quite – touch the ground, I wasn't sure he touched the air itself; he certainly didn't breathe the stuff, he had no use for it. He made no noise at all. How I could know without looking that he was right there at my back, shadowing my every move – well, I guess you do know when you're being tailed by one of the monuments of prehistoric England. Sight unseen, you still know it. Presence isn't only about interrupted light and atmospheric pressure-waves. Horse can eclipse the world and hush the stars in their courses.

I turned and said, "Horse." I may have said it sternly. "You don't have to come." Meaning, *Thank you, you've done your bit, go on now, go home. Go and graze somewhere clean, go and chase white mares, go sleep for a thousand years till some stray mortal wanders by with another spill of whisky, go...*

He just looked at me. Empty-headed, dumbest of blonds, mute of malice.

He didn't go.

Emphatically, he didn't go.

I sighed, and beckoned him forward with a jerk of my head. "Come on, then. Don't follow me, it's creepy."

I don't suppose anyone had ever called him creepy before, in quite that tone of voice.

I don't suppose it mattered. I don't suppose it

made the least difference in the world, not to him – but he came up and paced beside me, which made all the difference in the world to me. If a creature of unknown power and enormous impact is going to loom at you, better to have him looming in the corner of your eye, rather than in some indefinable sense you can't quite get a grip on. That's unnerving; this was just annoying, and I could scowl at him sideways and grumble as we went. Which did help, actually, because I really wasn't looking forward to what waited.

WE CROSSED THAT dreary plain, and rusting residual fencewire curled and snapped at his approach so that we could just walk straight through. I have no idea how he does that, none.

We crossed a road – empty, utterly – and came to the refinery, where the fence was bright and recent steel. Not a problem. I could have been over it in a moment even without my Aspect – which seemed to have been left behind on that wild ride, or else it was lurking, sulking, outfaced, something: not there, at any rate, not where I had had it wrapped about me the last time I thought about it, and not obviously within reach – but again, I didn't need to make the effort. He tossed his bare head at it and bolts sprang apart, metal fizzed and crumpled, it might as well have been kitchen foil for all the strength it had.

We stepped delicately through, and here we were.

Left at the gas-holders; second incinerator down. I hadn't forgotten my directions.

Here I was, at the foot of a hundred-foot chimney and not going to climb it, no.

Not needing to.

I just looked up to where its flare burned and roared against the night. And wondered vaguely about security guards, alarms, whatever – but there didn't seem to be any, so I took a breath and called out.

Called up.

Nice and simple, the way I'd called to Horse while he still lay in chalk; it seemed to be the mood of the night.

"Hey, Thom. Thomagata! Want to come down and talk to me? It's important."

Briefly, I thought he was ignoring me. Briefly, I thought he wasn't there.

Then there was a flare at the heart of the flare, a sudden focus of white fire like an oxy-fuel cutter lighting up, making the leap of flame around it look washed out, washed up, common and ineffectual.

It slipped itself free of that nimbus and came slithering down the chimney like a snake, like the snake from the heart of the sun, too vivid to look at directly. Well, too vivid for me. Horse wasn't bothered – and actually I'd seen it before, I knew what to expect. I had the skater's shades at the ready, in my jacket pocket. Sometimes it's important to be cool.

Sometimes it's important to be hot. He'd always thought so, anyway.

He'd looked small, up at the peak there: small but potent. Potent, but small. Perspective shifted, that way it does, as he came down – or else he did the shifting, taking a tip from Horse, putting himself in scale.

By the time he stood on the ground, he was my height, more or less, as he always had been. Still a fire spirit, still a lick of flame. Still dazzling.

Then he changed, dressed himself in flesh, looked to

be a man again, the way I'd mostly known him. Fire in his eyes. And hot, oh, yes. And naked, that of course. Clothes don't survive transition. Besides, he'd never think to take them with him, when he went dancing off. He was always the very definition of a free spirit.

I could have made him otherwise. The very definition of otherwise: extinguished, static, dead. Sometimes I thought he ought to be grateful.

Sometimes I thought he ought to burn me from the inside out, like he did his clothes. Sometimes, I was quite surprised he never had.

Right now, I was quite surprised to find him here where he'd said he'd be – if I were him I'd have moved on, long ago – and surprised too that he came down when I called him.

Still. Down he came, and there he stood. And looked at me, and said my name: just, "Desi."

At least it was that name that he acknowledged. It's never good when people call me Fay.

I looked him in the eye – how not? those eyes are hypnotic, like flame dancing over coals – and said, "Thom. I'm so glad you're here." Glad and more; surprised, and more. That all went without saying. At least, I didn't say it. "Listen, I'm really sorry, but I think you have to move."

"I won't be sorry." His voice had that edge of dry and bitter humour that I guess comes naturally when you've spent the last years hiding out in the burn-off of toxic gases. It also still had the knack of making me shiver from the inside out, from bones to skin. Or from deeper, from the marrow of the bone. I'd never loved him, but. Well. Hot is hot.

I said, "No, but..."

He said, "Tell me," though his eyes had shifted now to Horse. *Tell me about that,* I thought he wanted to say, only he had too much old-world courtesy. Of course he did. I'd hesitate to guess, which of the two was older. No person had ever tried to cut a shape for Thom.

I said, "Oz knows I didn't kill you." I was meant, I was sent to snuff him out, but it took me too long to understand that. By the time I did, it was too late; I couldn't do it.

*Oz, you should manage us mortals better. You should know how, you used to be one of us. Or was that just too long ago, have you forgotten how it felt? Or how to feel, have you forgotten that?*

Thom flickered briefly, as though his flesh were flame, a candle in the wind; then he steadied again and looked at me and said, "So now there's two of us."

"There always were," I said. "From the moment I lied to him – or earlier, the moment I decided to lie. The moment I decided not to do it. We were both on his kill-list after that, it's just that he didn't know it yet."

"Until now."

"Right."

"Well, then." His voice was warm by nature, when it wasn't searing hot; he said small things, and whole universes of comfort lay behind his words. He said *Well, then,* and I heard *I guess we should look after each other, then,* and never mind how close I'd come to killing him, back when he trusted me most, when I was all betrayal. Almost all. *There's strength in depth,* I heard, and *two's company,* and *we can watch each other's backs.*

And I wanted to leap onto Horse and gallop away

and pretend I was relying on myself alone; I wanted to think that I'd delivered the warning and that was enough, I'd done my bit, I was free to get the hell away from there. From him.

I wanted to betray him again, and maybe I would have done that thing, who knows? Only I was too late again, too slow again, as I always was around Thom. He slowed me down, apparently; he made it hard to think. He took my edge away. Maybe it was only comparative, because he was so quick himself, fast as a flash-fire, no slow smoulder for his fuse. He always made me feel less than I could be, and less than I ought to be. Which is maybe why I never learned to love him, because a lover really shouldn't do that to you. They ought to do the other thing, bring you up a level, make you better than you were.

I guess that made it his fault, then, that he could scorch me to the soul and never touch my heart.

Well, good.

Even so: I was here because he was here, and I owed him a duty of care. Once spare a man his life, and apparently you need to keep on looking after it, not to let your good work go to waste. Who knew?

I wanted to be full of plans, the ready one, all organised. Really, though, I'd done nothing but dash up here, fleeing eels and riding a white horse. Wasn't that enough? I'd given precious little thought to what came next after this moment, here, now.

Here, now, there seemed precious little point in worrying about it.

Here, now, here came a feather falling down.

Black feather, crow's feather. Eager to tell us something.

I think we all looked up, instinctively. Horse, fire-spirit, daemon: guilty and confessional and found.

Not that we saw anything. At least, I didn't. Still night, and all. My Aspect was a stretch away, a long stretch, and it came only reluctantly to my tug; by the time I was looking with enhanced eyes, I could find no shadow of a bird up there. What eyeless sockets saw, or fire-sight, I couldn't tell. Thom said no more than Horse did.

Even so. I think we all knew we'd been found. Stupid, perhaps, to imagine that Horse could move through England without raising a wake, without rousing every creature with any sense of what lies deep within us. Of course they knew; of course the Overworld was told.

Oz is many things, and many of them dubious, but no one has ever doubted his intelligence.

Neither his confidence. His spy had let a feather fall, and not by chance. Whether that was a Corbie up there or a simpler bird, its feather was a message. We were seen, we were known; we were watched. This was asymmetrical warfare, and we couldn't get away.

Couldn't get away and couldn't hide. Theoretically, we didn't stand a chance.

Oz might have control of the air – and of the underworld, wyrms and eels writhing up from below – but at least he didn't have bombs. His birds could follow us but nothing else, nothing worse. And if they came too close, well. Thom is quick and hot-tempered. Someone might get roasted.

I could hope.

Meanwhile, I could pull myself together. Never mind if my Aspect was laggard and sluggish, at least it was here: like an old rough security blanket to be pulled around my shoulders. Never mind the holes and the faded patches and the fraying hems, it was familiar and comfortable and right when nothing else was. I felt whole again, and strong enough to take charge if nobody else was going to.

I said, "We need to move. Thom, are you good to go, or – ?"

I think I cut myself off, before he laughed at me. I think I did.

Laughing anyway, he said, "Or what, do I need to pack some smokes? Bid farewell to my favourite fumes?"

"Well," I muttered, "you might have left some things somewhere about, just in case..."

He shook his head. Of course he did, what was I thinking? "Not me. I came as you see me; I'll leave the same way. Where are we going?"

"I don't know" – *yet* – "but, well, into the world. Where people wear clothes. Almost all the time. We'll need to do something about that. For the moment, though..."

I pulled the boy's lighter from my pocket, flicked it open, didn't spin the wheel.

Held it out, like an invitation.

I said that he's hot-tempered; I didn't say that he has the vocabulary to go with that. It's not a problem, it's a feature. We endured the blast of it, for what felt like a long time. Horse just stood there waiting; so did I.

At last he ran down. I was almost as implacable as Horse, still standing there with the lighter still held out, open, ready. When he stopped cursing, he seemed to have nothing else to say; so he shrugged, and shrugged off his human form, turning in mid-movement into an arc of flame that had just enough impulsion to dive neatly into the lighter's gape.

It flared at me, brighter, hotter than it had before. I grinned, perhaps a little savagely; mutely blessed the sullen werepup for his cool Zippo; and took prompt advantage of it, snapping the lid down hard.

No surprise, that the brass case just kept getting hotter. A simple lack of oxygen was never going to extinguish Thom. I held it in my hand, because I was gloved by Aspect and a simple core of heat was never going to trouble me, but it might set my jacket ablaze from the pocket outward. That wouldn't be good. A blazing woman riding a mythic shining horse? I'd never wanted to be written into folklore. Besides, the idea was to avoid attention, not to attract it.

I still had no idea how to do that. Not if night-flying crows were overhead. Standing here wasn't helping, though.

"Horse? Can we ride again? I don't know where, just... Somewhere else. Not here."

He'd be glad enough, I thought, to be not here. He really didn't like it here. Something in the way he stood, disdaining the ground beneath him, disdaining the very air he stood in; or you could see that entirely the other way around, that the concrete repelled him and the petrochemical fumes too. He stood utterly isolated, out of his place and time, cut off from the bones of old England. Needing soil and grass and rain, clean wind and sun and starlight, not the dull cast of smog overhead that reflected back the glare of the flares above us.

He dropped a shoulder in invitation, and I vaulted up.

He didn't have actual shoulders, but even so. Invitation and acceptance: we understood each other perfectly.

This time, I made a conscious effort to keep my Aspect with me, but no go. It just stayed behind, fell away, wasn't coming. I almost looked back, looked down, for the coat that had slipped from my shoulders. I almost called to it aloud, impatiently, like you'd call to a stubborn sulky child or a pet.

And then I did actually talk to it, because – well, I don't know why, but I said, "All right, then. You'll just have to catch up in your own sweet time. Horse, let's get moving."

Along the river, but against the flow: that should be the quickest way away from tarmac and pollution, up into the hills where these waters rose, where people didn't build so much or destroy so much, where...

Where Oz would find it easier to get at us, oh, yes. That too. Ah, well. I couldn't take Horse into town, even if he'd come; I'd feel like Lady Godiva, nakedly exposed with all my clothes on. Riding on a horse's bones, a whole new kind of bareback. Never mind that he felt all horse to me, all the horse that he needed to be. All the horse that any horse had ever been, or all of them together. I have no faith in gods, I've met too many, but he could be the source, the spirit-horse, first among equals, stripped down to the essentials.

And I could sit on him. Apparently. For now. Even with all the riders and codicils, I still couldn't quite believe that I was riding him.

Or that he'd go where I asked. Which was why I wasn't asking now, why I let him make the choices, up and up. I might be just as exposed out there, but

it was native country for him; that had to count for
something.

Didn't it?

HONESTLY, I DIDN'T know. I didn't know anything; I
didn't know what I was doing. Trying to help a friend,
bringing trouble right to him. Both.

If anything bad turned out to be my fault, I could
feel guilty about it afterwards. That was my regular
approach. Right now, I was too busy. That was also
normal; that was how the bad stuff happened. And I
did know that, and even so. You don't get to say *slow
down, guys, let me think about this* or *I'm going to be
making mistakes*. Not to the bad guys, you don't; and
often not to the good guys either.

Even assuming you're quite sure which is which.

Right now there was me and Horse, and Thom in the
lighter in my fist – and I really wasn't sure about either
of them. Horse was bigger than good or bad, older,
beyond my judgement; beyond my reach, except that
here he was between my thighs. Ambiguous, even there.
And Thom... Well. Thom had been there too. And had
reasons enough to think me bad beyond measure, except
that he didn't seem to; and he was a spark between my
fingers, and what was I going to *do*...?

For the moment, Horse at least was going to run,
and I was going to ride him. That was easy. We were
going where he took me; that was easy too.

We knew we were being spied on. Nothing we could
do about it, here and now. Easy, then.

Thom was hot in my hand. That... would probably
not be so easy later, but it was easy enough right now.

Even without my Aspect, I have asbestos fingers. He was dialling back the energy anyway, calming down, thinking things through. Not burning me. Not even trying to. I could probably put him in my pocket safely, but – nah. I didn't want to. There's attentive, and there's dismissive, and even if he couldn't tell from inside the case it did still matter. It mattered to me.

Which made it a little awkward, what came next. What had to come next.

Which was when I reached into my pocket with my other hand – trusting Horse to keep me on his back, pretty much; but he'd done well so far, and this wasn't a hellride through the undiscovered landscape of his mind, just an amble up into the hills; we'd been found already, so there was no point in hurrying, once we'd set the bad land behind us – and took out my phone.

Not my own phone, of course, that was slimed and bemired somewhere under London, but never mind. Back when we'd started dating, Jacey had never let me load his number into memory. "Don't outsource your mind, Fay. What if you lose your phone, and need to call me? It's you that needs to know my number, in your own memory. Learn it and punch it in, every damn time."

So I always did that, and I could still do it. His own mobile was lost, of course, in the same mess; his flat had been invaded and I had no idea where he'd be by now; but he's tech-savvy, is Jacey, geek from his fingertips to his machine-readable QR code tattoo, not so much linked in as plumbed in, hook line and kitchen sync. One way or another, he'd have his system up and running, he'd be online and available.

So I rang the old number, the landline to the flat. He was safe to have some kind of uplink, some virtual voicemail accessible from anywhere, that at least.

In fact, the number didn't even ring. A calm reliable-sounding robot told me that my call was being transferred; I pictured my voice being tossed across London from aerial to aerial in pursuit of my wandering man. Never mind that I hadn't actually said anything yet, I'm a simple girl and that's the way I saw it.

What I heard was a hush, a muted buzz, a couple of clicks and then a soft purring kind of ring before finally Jacey said hullo.

He sounded a little cautious, a little curious: sans his usual data, not knowing who was calling. Not of course recognising this number.

"Jay, it's me."

Nobody else had ever called him Jay. That had been a treasure once; it was a security blanket now. I'd spoiled it a little by using the same name for Jordan, but we could sort that out. Later. Too busy now.

I heard his indrawn breath; I think I heard him blink; I heard him catch one name on his tongue and use another. "Desi. What's happening?"

"Lots. Where are you?"

"At my parents' flat."

"Can they hear you?"

"No."

"Good." He had his own suite: bedroom, bathroom, lounge. He didn't need a kitchen, he didn't know how to open a tin. When he wanted to eat, he went out. It's a rich-kid thing. "So, is your own place...?"

"Trashed? Yes."

"And the cars?"

"And the cars. Everything."

"Oh, lord. I'm sorry, Jay." I didn't need to say *It's my fault,* that was evident.

"Ah, what the hell. I get to start again." He sounded the wrong kind of determined, trying to force himself through the loss and the shock of it. It was what we did, I guess. Probably what everybody does, only it comes more easily to some. Or else some just have more practice. "So where are you, and what's up?"

"I... came north." And I was still being natively cagey, but there really wasn't any point. We'd been found already. So I bit back a question, *Is this a secure line?* – of course it was, it was Jacey's line; he'd have all the security of a government agency, just for the hell of it, because he could – and instead said, "Hang on a sec."

If I tucked Thom's lighter between my two smallest fingers and my palm, I could hold that safely and the phone too, which freed my right hand to stab at keys while my legs held on to Horse. I hoped.

It seemed to work. I didn't fall, at least, and a minute later, "I've sent you the GPS. Can you get here?" *Without your cars, without your bikes* – I didn't want him to think it was his transport that had me calling him, though it was halfway true, maybe.

"I'll find a way." For a moment, he almost sounded amused. Of course he'd find a way; golden boys always do. He didn't even say *Why should I?* – apparently I was still allowed to take him for granted. "What do I need to bring with me?"

"I don't know. Just the wheels, maybe. Oz is onto us, but..." But what? *But I think we can hold out till you get here?* I had no cause to claim that, it was only a hope, and a threadbare one at that.

"Us?" he said.

"Um. Yeah." Me and the original white horse, and a fire-spirit in a Zippo. I said, "Can you hurry?" I'd offer to meet him halfway, only I didn't think Horse's ways were known to GPS. I thought we'd slide past each other like two ships in fog, just lethally out of phase.

"Sweetheart, I am hurrying. The only way I could hurry faster would be if I stopped talking to you, and started talking to someone else. Which I will do, as soon as we're done. Are we done?"

"I guess." Actually I wanted to talk him all the way here, like a traffic controller talking down a pilot – but that was Fay wishing for the comfort of his voice, and Desi couldn't afford it. Desi was busy.

Desi hung up and put her phone away and looked about her.

Was that first hint of dawn, on the horizon? It had to be, surely; not even this night could last for ever. Even so, I couldn't see much beyond that milky stain where it leaked upward into the sky. Light should be more use than that, I felt. I missed my Aspect badly; I'd grown used to it, I guess, and felt pretty much useless without it. Dependent. I didn't like that, but there wasn't much I could do. You either have night sight or you don't, and simple human, unenhanced? Simply doesn't.

Not this human, anyway. I didn't worry where we were going – Horse's eyeless sockets found his way for him, and I just went along for the ride – but I did worry what might be out there round about us, waiting to strike. We knew there was something keeping an eye out, holding a watching brief, but that was only the beginning.

My eyes were useless for the moment and Horse wasn't communicative, intent on his own purpose, just moving – it occurred to me that he only had two states, moving and not-moving, no middle ground between them; moving might be purpose enough, until he came to ground somewhere he chose not to move from – but the two of us weren't on our own any more.

Zippo lighters are cool by definition, but any fool can buy one. If you want to look anything better than a fool with a cool toy, you need to earn it. You need to *own* it.

I've never smoked – Fay never did, and Desi was too smart to start – but I can still play cool with the tools of the art. I danced that lighter between my fingers, flicked it open with my thumb, went to spin the wheel and of course didn't need to, because of course there was Thom making with his own dance, bright on the wick in the little windproof chimney. Not that he need bother about the wind. Not that any Zippo ever had burned with so bright a flame as his, as him.

Not that we needed to worry about his visible spark, when we were being tracked already.

I said, "Hey. Want to take a look around? I can't see a thing, and Horse just sees his own path."

I said *take a look around*. I meant *use your eyes, your fire eyes, your brightsight*. I could have held him up like a girl at a concert with a thousand others, swaying to the beat, waving our little flames like a prayer to whatever gods we hoped for, that they would grant whatever wish we dared.

He took off like a rocket from a bottle, like a firework shedding sparks. Like a stupid damn sprite who didn't know what was out there, who thought he was invulnerable, immortal. Safe.

I could have shrieked. I might have shrieked.

Okay, I shrieked.

What's the point in being cool, if others are idiotic?

I didn't yell his name after him into the night, I'm not that stupid. No point trying yet harder to draw down trouble, if by some fluke it hadn't noticed us yet, or hadn't hung around to watch our course.

Conversely, though, there was small point trying to hide with Thom dancing bright patterns in the dark like a firefly with jets, like a self-propelled bullet zooming hither and yon, leaving an after-image that burned behind the eyes like a signature, like a gloat.

I hadn't known he could do that. Fly, I mean, of his own volition, with nothing to ride on and nothing to burn. I wondered why anybody ever caught him – but hell, there are fly-traps, fly-paper. Cages. Skins and feathers, dead birds stuffed and displayed. Flying things get caught all the time.

We waited, Horse and I – or at least I stayed sat where I was, on his back, and he kept moving, waiting in motion – until Thom came back to us. And shifted into human form and paced beside us, hot and naked and laughing in the dawn breeze, and said, "Nothing that I can find, nobody about. Where are we?"

"Here." I thought Horse was always *here*, it was the land that changed about him. "And somebody's out there, somewhere: and now they know just exactly where here is. It's called tracer for a reason, Thom."

"I don't – oh. Yes, I do. Sorry, didn't think."

Well, no. Somewhere in the world maybe there are fire-spirits who work at a slow smoulder and aren't mercurial at all, who are soul-scorchingly thorough and think things through intensively until there's nothing left of them but ash on the carpet and a discarded slipper still with a foot inside it. Maybe there are. I've never met one, though, and Thom for sure has never been one.

"Flibbertigibbet," I said. He laughed again, and matched Horse stride for stride. I didn't offer him a ride in the lighter, and he didn't ask for it. I don't suppose he'd liked being pent up in there, and I did like to have him in the corner of my eye. *Three out of two's not bad*. Any suggestion that our army had suddenly and visibly grown larger was as spurious as the notion that he could find any safety in a Zippo, but still. A girl could fancy that she had support, as well as wheels. Heels. Hooves. Whatever.

# CHAPTER THIRTEEN

HEAT RISES. I could feel his from here, smell the scorch of him on the air like one of those space heaters that bars put outside for the benefit of smokers, keep them warm while they indulge.

Horses also rise; they have an irresistible fondness for heights. This one took us up and up, until here we were on the high moors, and the sun – which also rises – gave us long views down the valley to the smokestacks and beyond.

I guess Horse was done with moving for a while. At any rate he stopped, in an absolute kind of sense. Of course I didn't kick my heels into his ribs, or click my tongue at him, or any other impertinence; it wouldn't have made any difference if I had. This was it, we were here, and he'd stopped.

He barely gave me time to slide off, before he lay down and settled onto the turf.

Into the turf.

This was more rugged ground than he had come from, tussocks and bogs with no chalk beneath, but even so. He showed up pretty well, I thought. And wondered what they might think down the valley, if anybody actually lifted their heads to look, to see the great symbol etched on a hillside that really was not there yesterday evening. Then I wondered the opposite thing about the valley that we'd left, but actually it wasn't the same. He might not be there right now, but people would still see a design cut into a ridge. They wouldn't see the emptiness of it, meaningless in absence.

Actually, unless they were up bright and early, people in this neighbourhood wouldn't see anything either. Here came a fog, handy and right on cue, billowing up the valley like a puff of pollution from inexhaustible chimneys somewhere further, out of sight. I watched it swamp the shadowed refinery like milk clouding coffee. Even the chimney-flares blurred and disappeared, not fierce enough to cut through that dense determined blanket.

As I watched, it filled the valley from one high ridge to the other, and kept on coming. I reached out a hand for my own splendid chimney-flare, and didn't need to look around to find him. I could do that by heat alone, my open palm a detector. I could have found him in a coal mine without a torch, except that he'd probably set a coal mine ablaze just by being there.

His fingers closed over mine with the kind of impulsive contentment that I didn't know I'd missed until here it was again. Thom had always been like that, it's why he was so easy to set up and – as it turned out – so hard to let down. He wasn't like a child grabbing sweets, exactly; just uncomplicated, and prepared to take joy where he found it. Which, between Jacey and Jordan – oh, Lord, yes. Yes, *please*.

I leaned back into his solidity, and his spare arm circled my waist. I said, "We might as well get comfortable" – as my head nestled into that convenient hollow between neck and shoulder – "because I don't think we're going anywhere for a while."

Our transport had taken himself offline, and the first wisps of fog were already twining around our feet. Even with Thom at hand to burn it back, I didn't fancy blundering about in the soup of it, trying to find our way off the moor. People have died that way, and giant hounds have eaten them.

Besides, where else did we have to go? Getting here had felt urgent, all-consuming; one of the things it had apparently consumed was any thought about what came next. I wasn't quite sure even what I'd intended with the hellride, whether I was warning Thom or rescuing him. Either way, apparently I'd betrayed him where I might perfectly well have let him be.

Dawnlight is milky anyway; dawnlight through thickening fog was like sitting in creamy porridge. Cold creamy porridge, or it should have been, cold and wet both: only that I had a heat-source to engulf me, to wrap his arms and legs about me and keep the bad at bay. My Aspect was probably around somewhere, in reach, it should've caught up with us by now – but honestly I preferred Thom, for the real honest contact, skin to skin.

Which was a puzzle, now that I came to think about it, as I settled back into that all-around embrace.

It was maybe good to have something to puzzle over, given that I was at the back end of a long and exciting night, and now I had an entirely naked male as physically close to me as he could get, and we were both of us hot and a little frightened and very ready for distraction, and very accustomed to each other's bodies, and it had been a long time for him and he was always very ready, and I'd had my Aspect on and off all night and all the day before, and –

And no. Just, no. I had gone already from Jordan's bed to Jacey's; I wasn't going from Jacey's to Thom's, not overnight. I'm not that fast.

Puzzle, then. Think it through. Show your working.

"Thom?"

"Uh-huh."

"Don't do that."

"What? This?"

"Yes, that. Stop it. No, I mean it. That's not cool."

"It's not meant to be cool."

"Seriously. Don't. If you have to breathe" – and I wasn't at all convinced that he did, despite fire's traditional fondness for oxygen – "then don't do it down the back of my neck. Breathe back at the fog, blow it away."

"Spoilsport." He's a nice boy, though; he did what he was told, half-heartedly huffing at the vapour that enclosed us. That caused some serious eddies, but they didn't last. So then he rested his chin on the top of my head and tightened his grip on the rest of me, none of which I was going to complain about. Instead I cooperated, treating him like a kind of living chair while I worked my way through my puzzle, and got nowhere, and at last tried again.

"Thom?"

"Uh-huh."

"How do you *work*?"

"Huh? I don't need to work, I'm –"

He didn't have the words for what he was, so he just shrugged. Which, given how warmly intimate was our entanglement – well. *Concentrate.*

"Not that. Fool. I mean physically, scientifically, how does your body work? I had this theory about shapeshifters" – the rule of the conservation of mass, but there was really no point in throwing that at him, he'd only get confused and try to duck – "but you don't seem to fit." Like this, here and now: he was running hot but otherwise entirely human to the touch. One male body, standardly tall, standardly responsive. Standardly heavy, more to the point. But at any moment I could be toppling helplessly backwards because he was just gone, a flicker of playful light that could settle into a Zippo and add nothing to the weight of the thing but still be him entirely.

"Oh," he said. "That's because I'm not a shapeshifter."

"You're not?" A girl could get tired – *extremely* tired – of having young men tell her how wrong she was about the world, but I supposed he should know what he was talking about. Even if he knew nothing about the conservation of mass.

"Shapeshifters are mortal. I'm divine."

He felt divine, right here right now – but that wasn't relevant, and it wasn't appropriate, and I wasn't going to say it. No.

"Arrogant sod," I said instead, comfortably. And then, "You're mortal too. Why else would Oz have hired me to kill you?"

"Even gods can die," he said. "That's different."

"Is it? How?"

"We don't have a, a, a lifespan. There's no reason for it, dying, it doesn't come naturally to us."

The way he said that, it sounded like we mere mortals didn't quite make sense to him, he couldn't quite work out why we'd bother. I let my hair hide my smile, and didn't say anything until I was sure my voice wouldn't show it.

"You mean it has to be made to happen, like Oz hiring me to do it?"

"Yes. There can be accidents too, there can be self-sacrifice. Mostly we just carry on until we're stopped, one way or another."

I thought about Asher, young prince of Hell, torn apart by the Green Man far too soon; and shivered, and gave up wondering about the science of it all, if that conversation could lead us so quickly somewhere that I really didn't want to be.

Only then I couldn't think of anything else I'd rather talk about, any safe ground. In my head suddenly it all led back to this, to the two of us sitting on the cold hill's side because Oz Trumby wanted to kill us both. And I knew about me, I understood that, he was never going to be generous in the face of betrayal; but, "Tell me about Oz and you, then. Why's he so determined to snuff you out?"

"Don't you know?"

"Oz doesn't give reasons, he gives instructions." And money, and houses, and boats. And Aspects, and safety, of a sort. New identity, whole new me. I didn't stop to interrogate his motives, I just said *yes* and grabbed what I could. Looking back, I wasn't any too proud of that. Never mind that I hadn't followed through; I didn't mean to cheat him when I signed up. Put plainly, I agreed to be his whore first, and then his assassin. And then I funked it. Or flunked it, whichever.

Dancing a Zippo in your fingers may be cool, but being an assassin is probably cooler. The Woman in Black: I could've earned my colours...

Never mind. I thought I was probably happier to be here, nestled in his arms in the fog, waiting for something to happen but feeling oddly safe right now, as though some greater goddess had huffed her misty breath down to cover us, to gift me this morning.

Waiting for Thom's confession, that too. I really did want to know.

He said, "It's the same thing, really. Oz wants me dead because I said I was immortal."

"Wait, what?"

"He did what you did, he thought I was a shapeshifter. He likes shapeshifters. I did... what I do, I told him what I am. He's been wanting to kill me ever since."

"That makes no sense. I mean, it's really annoying to be corrected all the time, but..."

"But it's not a killing thing, right? But you're not Oz."

"Right. Punctured vanity, I can see that." Everyone knew you had to tread careful around the guy, and Thom just wouldn't, of course. He wouldn't know how. "But..." It still didn't seem enough. Empires can't thrive on vanity alone. Oz wouldn't have survived this long if he'd been that petty, there had to be a bigger picture. "What am I missing?"

"I worked for him," Thom said, which was my biggest surprise of the morning so far.

"You? Come on, you don't work. We've established that. You're, um, independently situated..." Sitting in a gas plume, burning waste. It was work of a sort, I supposed, though he wasn't paid for it.

"I don't have to work, no. There's always something I can burn. But I was interested, and he was interested in me, so..."

So Thom had gone for it, whatever it was. In a gadfly kind of way, I was guessing: turning up when he felt like it and doing what he fancied, which wouldn't always – or ever – be exactly what Oz asked for.

Oz would put up with that, for a while. For whatever value Thom brought, for the interest, for the kudos of having a fire-spirit in his service – and for the shapeshifting. That would be the driver. Oz's constant obsession.

It would be like rubbing his own face in his own failure: that thing he strived for that he could never achieve, the birthright he was denied. After a while, that would have grated like a microplane, sliced like a mandoline, it would have grated blood. And he would've kept Thom around regardless, just that little bit too long, as a goad to himself and his people, *this is what I want*; and at last Thom would casually, innocently have snapped the final straw. *Oh, no, I'm not a shapeshifter, I'm divine. I'm immortal.* And then, yes: then Oz would want to kill him. Because that was Oz's opposite and his other obsession, everything he truly wanted; and because nobody else gets to rub Oz's face in things, ever; and – well, just because he could. To know that he'd done it. To sneer at Thom's ashes: *Immortal, huh? How's that working out for you, eh?* Oz would enjoy that. He'd keep the ashes handy. In fact he'd probably want to work them into his ongoing eternity project, to have them on hand for, well, eternity.

He'd want to do it there and then, only that hadn't worked out for him. It's not that easy to kill a fire, all unprepared. Thom got away, or maybe left without even noticing – and Oz mulled it over, thought it through, figured it out. Found me, hired me, sent me to do his work for him.

With instructions to sweep up the ashes and deliver them back to Oz in his lair. I wasn't making that up.

So I did as I was told, what I was hired for. I swept ashes into a bucket and handed them over at Oz's, where no doubt they were now all mixed and set and immovable. I collected my payoff in keys and cash, and went my way like a successful assassin, cool and easy with herself – and Oz knew now that they weren't Thom's ashes after all, and yes. His first killing impulse might just have been vanity. Now it would be necessary repercussion, and it would fall on both of us, and he would be very serious about it.

I didn't much want to think about that, so instead I said, "What were you doing for him?" Work? Thom? I was still a little boggled about that.

No. A lot boggled.

He said, "Torchlight. He wanted an eternal flame. Well, he said he did. He wanted someone to tap into a source deep down and give him light everlasting. And who better than me, to find the source and draw it up and set it burning? That's what he said. Of course I was flattered, and it was fun, chasing down into the dark where no one's ever been, slithering through cracks between the strata, going deep. There are things down there, caves, stones... No, never mind. You can't ever see them, I can't bring them up, I can't describe them. But they are wonderful.

"And I did what he wanted, I found pockets of gas and oil, and I could have figured out ways to channel them to the surface. I was talking it through with him when he said, and I said, and like that."

"He called you a shapeshifter, and you said no, I'm divine?"

"Right, that. Something like that. And then – well, then he didn't want piped gas any more. Then he wanted me, to be his eternal flame. His *living* eternal flame. He wanted to put me in a bottle. And he tried, and I wouldn't let him. I did some damage, I guess. He didn't know, he had no idea what I can be like."

Fiery, hot-tempered, yes. It was always a surprise.

"And then I got out of there, and nothing happened, time passed, I forgot about it." That was all Thom too, shrug and move on. The opposite of grudge-bearing, the opposite of wary. "And then you came."

"Yes." I came to seduce him, which was easy; and then to inveigle my way into his house and his heart, still easy; and then to betray him and murder him, which turned out to be not easy at all. Impossible.

Instead I did the next-hardest thing, persuading him to hide up until I came to fetch him. *Until you're safe*, I said.

Which he wasn't, but I'd come anyway and here we were, on a hillside in the fog. With the world rubbed out that way, it was good for confessional, good for looking back. Good, apparently, for sinking into my own fog of nostalgia.

Thom's home was a lighthouse, and what could be more appropriate, then or now? To him, or to the rest of us?

It stood just offshore, on a lump of rock that was only an island by courtesy, at high tide, and even then you could splash across the causeway if you didn't mind getting your socks wet. No quicksand, no tidal suck, no danger. The light itself had been declared redundant long since, replaced by an automated beacon further out where the danger lay. The high blunt tower had a little house at its feet, for the keepers it used to need; Thom was in and out of there like a regular human being, dressed and everything. Shopping and everything. And if some nights there was a fierce bright beam from the lantern, well. If you owned a lighthouse and kept it in perfect working order, of course you'd want to light it up, wouldn't you? It did no harm, on land or at sea; more light is always better.

Sometimes we'd spend all night up there together, him dancing on the wick and playing games with the mirrors and lenses, me snuggled down in a nest of cushions and quilts with a good book, reading by the light of Thom.

Sometimes we'd spend all night up there together and there would never be a light at all, neither one of us would shift from the nest until dawn. Or later.

I felt nested now, my body settled into his, warm

and safe and entirely happy. Somewhere out there must be sunlight and the starting day, things to do, life and death, all the mortal world in its struggles – but not here. Here was Thom, and here was I, all bound up in this blessed fog and we were plenty for each other.

Fires sleep the night through, if you bank them up and damp them down thoroughly. Then they wake in the morning if you stir them up, shake them down and toss them something to eat. Men are generally much the same. Thom was all of that, doubled and squared. He loved to sleep, as much as he loved to dance; shaking him awake was so much effort I used my Aspect for it sometimes, just to be easy on my shoulders. Too bad the Aspect couldn't cook, I had to do that side of it myself; in human form he loved to eat, that too. Sleep was better, though, always. He'd sooner sleep than anything. Almost anything. Actually, I thought he might be asleep right now, in the fog there on the hill.

There was always one other way to wake him, that didn't involve downright violence – that was the one thing that I knew he liked better even than sleeping – but he wasn't going to get that every day. It wouldn't have been good for him, he'd have come over all smug and expectant.

Besides, I was never really in all that much hurry to rouse him. Whatever the promise of the day, whatever the promise of his body, I used to treasure that first hour more: wrapped in his heat and the quilts' softness and the day's gentle light, gazing up at the planes of glass and watching the sky beyond resolve from a milky cocktail to blue or white or storm-grey as the day chose, and thinking how I was supposed to kill him soon but I didn't have to do it now, not now, not today...

One thing about Oz, he's never in a hurry. Not for himself, and not to see any of his other projects to resolution. He's monumentally patient; happy enough to go at a geological pace, when that's what it takes. Besides, I had licence not to rush it. *Give him time, make him fall for you; make the betrayal all the sweeter, make sure he knows when it happens, that he knows what's coming and that it comes from you and from me...*

Those were my instructions, and they made my excuse. Weeks and weeks I waited, telling myself that I was only following orders; and all the while settling in to my own new identity, reassuring myself that Jacey and all his kin couldn't track Desi down, however hard they were looking for Fay.

For a while I could fool myself, it was like this fog: like swaddling for my mind, padding all my edges, dulling everything down. *If you can't see them, they can't see you. Hold on to that. And if you never move, they'll never see you. Hold on to Thom, you're being paid for this, remember...*

Actually, I thought I could see things in the fog. Just my imagination painting pictures on a blank, swirling canvas, that was all. I knew that, I wasn't foolish. Even so, it felt like I was watching my time with Thom being played out before my eyes, rather than remembering it in the privacy of my head: as though I were a clear-sighted seagull looking down through the lights of the lantern. Nothing like a crow, no, looking down on billowing white and seeing nothing through it. Oz's spies must have lost us for sure, in this charming fog. I could relax, let everything slip, indulge myself in what we'd been.

Mostly I thought that what we'd been was happy. Okay, I was meant to kill him, but I had to make him happy first, that was in my job description; and I guess it rubbed off, that happy thing. I never learned to love him, maybe, but I loved to share his company, his body and his life. He showed me how to live easy within the world, how that was possible. I wouldn't say he taught me to do the same – I still had all my secrets, grief and guilt and fear tied like knots in my heart – but just being with him was enough to loosen me up, at least a little.

Day by day, see us drifting in the fog there? Two innocents in a life-raft, afloat, cut off. Well, one innocent, and one who had been there and moved on and hoped maybe one day to move back, but in the meantime, alas, she had to kill a man. Snuff a flame.

Murder a god, apparently. I don't think anyone told me that at the time. If they did, apparently I wasn't listening, it didn't stick.

Neither did I stick to my task. At first I was inveigling my way into his heart, as ordered, the better to make the ending worse. Then I was just nestled there, frankly putting off the day; then at some point it became clear even to muddled little me that I wasn't actually going to do it.

So then we had to have the talk. You know the one: confession, apology, heartbreak. Reparation. Everyone's been there.

Not everyone's taken money to murder a god, but that's incidental. You can't weigh guilt any more than you can measure pain. We all do what's there to be done, and we all feel bad about it after.

I told Thom who had sent me, and for what; I told him to run and hide, while I pulled a snow job on Oz. While I buried Oz, indeed, in an avalanche of snow: *job done, here's the ashes, let me mix up that mortar for you now; and yes, thank you kindly, absolutely I will take my reward, for absolutely I have earned it.*

And part of that reward was his help in hiding me from the Cathars, which is maybe why he couldn't see my new knots of guilt and deception, all tangled up among the older deeper hurts. Or maybe he just wasn't looking. I was his pet then, his sexy young girl-assassin, and he loved me for it. I don't suppose it had crossed his mind that I might betray him.

He knew it now. The fog was suddenly full of fury, it seethed and boiled all about us, and where it struck it stung like whips; and we couldn't shift, we couldn't stir, we couldn't even cry out at the pain as it lashed us.

My Aspect was there but I couldn't reach for it, not even that. It was like one of those dreams where bad things are happening and you can't move. More, worse. It was like all my bones had softened in the fog and I could do nothing at all but lie there in a knot with Thom, sore and scared and suffering, waiting to suffer worse.

# CHAPTER FOURTEEN

FOG IS A seduction and a lure and a lie.

How did I ever let myself, let the two of us get snared this way?

Because I was seduced, of course. Because I was lured, because I was lied to.

Fog's *insidious*. Of itself, it is; it comes like a thief in the night. It sneaks in under your guard, it blurs your boundaries, it's inside before you know it. And then nothing is safe or certain or reliably there; and if the fog is not innocent to begin with, if it's been *sent*, then all bets are off and seduction is absolutely on the agenda.

He came striding up the hill, the fog-feller, the creature who had felled us with his fog. I would have called him a wight, I guess – though I know a couple of boys who would instantly have corrected me, *that's not a wight, that's a wraith*, or whatever. They have no *idea* how annoying that is.

Whatever he was – and *fog-feller* will do it, that's close enough – he was gaunt and long-legged and made of old, like weathered stone and twisted trees, all grey and cold and rooty. He was humming, I think, under whatever breath he had, whatever more he needed when I thought all the fog was his breath, his lungs, his purpose.

And his song, that too: the fog and the drone were both one thing, unshaped and immaterial, impossible to get a grip on. Well, I had fog in my bones now, I couldn't get a grip on anything and Thom was worse, Thom had sucked that stuff inside him and almost put his fires out. Even so, I could feel them both still working away, fog and drone together: dissolving what should have been solid and fixed, rubbing away all the distinctions between past and future, between here and now, leaving us lost in an inchoate dreamworld with nothing to cling to but terror.

It wasn't like the easy drift of an anaesthetic, not now. Not now I knew. It had been like that at first, unnoticeable, sneaking up on us as we lapsed into memory and imagination. Now it was a cold hand clamped about my heart, the only real thing there was until the fog-feller reached us and reached over and picked us up.

One hard hand each, long fingers winding around chest and shoulders like hedge-roots winding about the stones of a broken wall, except that the skin of them was rough and pebbly like dry stone for the wall, and chill like stone in a winter's dawn, and there was nothing in them that was anything like life. Except that they moved like living fingers, fast enough; and he stooped and straightened and stepped away like something cast from nightmare, fog in his eyes, and now we hung in his grip, one in each hand like dolls, like puppets, like broken things.

His cold grip on my skin matched the fear that gripped my heart. I could feel both of those, and nothing else. Where my Aspect was, I couldn't imagine. Lost in the fog. Lost for good, I supposed. We weren't getting out of this. We couldn't even twitch, either of us.

This was what I'd been supposed to do to Thom: render him helpless, let him realise that he'd been betrayed and that he was going to die now, give him plenty of time to savour that before it happened. Instead I'd chosen to confess all, give him the chance to run instead, help him find somewhere to hide up and then lie to Oz about it. And so here we were, the both of us together, facing the same fate.

The way he was stalking across the countryside, the fog-feller must be planning to take us all the way, so that Oz could actually watch us die. That wasn't like him, to be personally engaged, he mostly liked to operate from distance – but we'd made this personal, I suppose. Between us.

It didn't make much difference, anyway. We could die just as handily there as here. I did briefly wonder how it would happen – me at the fog-feller's hands, perhaps, just slowly crushed to pulp, with something more specialised reserved for Thom? – but really that didn't make much difference either. There'd be pain, and confusion, and eventually an end. Something to look forward to.

It was a pity, maybe, not to go down fighting, but not everybody gets that chance. Oz wasn't one to take risks; he'd keep us fogged until the last.

This was it, then. I wasn't exactly peaceable about it, but okay; I could live with that.

Die with it.

I didn't really have a choice.


OVER THE HILL and down onto a moorland road, with fog still billowing about us. Nobody would be reporting an unworldly creature walking in the hills; nobody would be seeing anything out of the ordinary, anything at all.

Until actually I did see something, up ahead. See it and hear it too, a single point of light and a subdued, muffled rumble.

It was just the way he carried me, this creature – maybe he was a troll, or an ogre? a fog-ogre, a fogre...? – with my head facing slackly forward; it was only by chance, but I could see what came. And my mind was clearing by the moment, washed through with fear, so that I could focus my thoughts even while my body span adrift.

That would be what Oz wanted, of course: he'd want me to know exactly what was coming, and be utterly unable to avoid it.

This, now? This was not what Oz wanted. Not what the fogre wanted, either. He stepped off the road and walked away into his fog, onto the uncharted moor.

That light must just have found his shadow, just in time. It turned to follow us, and its noise grew louder, harsher. Dropped a gear.

Motorbike. I knew that already, I'd known it from the first.

I was still trying not to hope.

He couldn't have got here this fast, could he? Could he? He didn't have a bike left to his name...

If it was him, he probably couldn't help. This fog-feller was mighty strong. I should probably hope that it wasn't him, just to keep him safe, let Oz settle for me and Thom and not add to the day's tally.

Probably.

Even so. I guess I was hoping despite myself, because however hard I tried for anxious disappointment there was really nothing in me but relief when the bike just kept on coming, when the fog-feller finally stopped trying to outpace it, when he turned almost at bay as he dropped us and stretched his arms out wide and waited for what came.

When the bike came, and the driver kicked down its stand and stepped off and shook the wind out of his hair and oh, yes, that was Jacey.

Jacey on a big white Beemer; I didn't think I'd ever seen a white one before this.

Jacey with a passenger riding pillion, which I hadn't been looking for, hadn't expected, hadn't thought to wonder about. Ought probably to regret, but I wasn't doing too well at the *sauve-qui-peut* self-sacrifice thing, it just didn't come naturally.

Actually, let's be honest, it didn't come at all.

I did contrive to feel faintly guilty about that, but mostly I was just glad that the way I'd fallen, I could still see what was happening.

Until that pillion passenger echoed Jacey, and stepped off the bike. Jacey didn't wear a helmet, but he did; and that was white too. And he took it off and ran his hand over stubble showing faintly white again, and *Oh, no, Jordan, not you too, not both of you...*

And suddenly I was all about the self-sacrifice after all, wanting to sob, wanting to scream at them, *No, go back, get back on the bike and drive away! This isn't your fight, what are you even doing here?* Which made no sense, of course, because I'd actually phoned Jacey and told him where to find us, but even so. Suddenly I didn't believe in their rescue mission, only their imminent deaths, my fault. How did they even think they were going to fight fog-feller, anyway?

Maybe they weren't thinking at all, they couldn't be thinking or they wouldn't still be standing there, staring up at him like victims only waiting for those long, long arms to reach out and club them down, if his sneaky fog didn't claim them first as it had claimed the two of us. That was the fog-feller's masterstroke, that fog. Oozing its way into the mind and body both, sapping the strength and the strength of will, marooning the soul in a body slack and helpless, with a mind all full of fancy...

It was his masterstroke, and it failed. It wasn't working at all, not on these two, not with their sinuses all full of petrol fumes and their minds abuzz with streetlights, fog couldn't touch them.

Not for the time it took Jordan to look up at the fog-feller, look straight at me, look sideways at Jacey – and do his fresh-prince-of-Hell thing, open a gateway to his father's kingdom, take us all through it there and then without any of us needing actually to twitch a muscle.

And inside of course I was still screaming *no!*, still screaming *No, don't you remember last time, Asher, have you forgotten what happened to Asher...?*

But it didn't matter, it was too late, here we were. Transposed, I guess. This wasn't the way his father had done it, subtly, shifting me little by little through some intermediate space from one world to the other so that I barely noticed the change until I was there, unequivocally in Hell. This was abrupt, all but instant, almost painful, deeply shocking. Asher had been as quick, but not so rough about it; everything Asher did, he was always cool and always smooth. And he'd done it before, of course, a thousand times. This was all new to Jordan – and of course he was still half seventeen in his heart. Which made him gauche, awkward, clumsy, urgent, all those boy-things that only mattered more the more he tried to hide them, as he did.

The human body really doesn't like swift transitions, moving too fast or too strangely, in unexpected directions. We get sick. Car-sick, air-sick, space-sick.

I got dimensionally sick, I guess. It was infuriating, when my body was so useless to me otherwise, that suddenly my head was swimming and my stomach wanted to rebel. Just when I most needed to be alert and focused, if only to keep terror at bay, to see that nothing was as bad as I imagined it.

We were in Hell, and oh, it showed. There must be other aspects to this place, but all I'd seen so far was red and dry and sour, dust and desert, and here we were again. On a hill this time – and maybe that was how transition worked: road goes to road, hill to hill? – but a long, long way from the hill we had been on before. The bike hadn't come through with us; there was just us and our face-off, in a bare bleak landscape under a hot and heavy sun. Even the light seemed red, where it fell upon us.

This was no country for fog-fellers. His fog was burning off already, moment by moment; I thought he was burning himself, never used to any sun on that skin of his, let alone a sun like this.

Something else was burning off, his cold fog in my mind. I wasn't strong yet, I couldn't move much, I couldn't help; but I found that I could lift my head, turn my head to watch him.

Watch as he blundered towards my two boys, reaching.

I still had that cold fear on my heart. I was still remembering Asher, how he brought us into Hell to fight the Green Man, how the Green Man had fought back, desperate and deadly.

How Asher died.

I thought I was going to see it all again, played out before my helpless eyes, with two boys for double the fun. I thought those long, lethal fingers would coil around their throats and choke them, break them, pull them apart.

I thought I'd be the one who had to call their parents.

Actually I was trying to do that now, right now, in a wishful-prayer sort of way. Jordan's dad was master here; shouldn't he know what was happening, shouldn't he come? He'd found me easily enough before, surely he could find his own boy when it was needful, surely he couldn't lose both sons the same damn way?

Or there was Thom, of course; a creature of fire should do well in Hell. I looked for him, and was relieved to see him moving, that at least – but he was barely moving more than I was, and less in control. He flickered between flesh and flame, a mortal figure and then a fiery one and back to flesh again. I didn't think that was wilful on his part. I thought he'd forgotten quite what he was, this or that. So much for being both, either one at whim, the way I'd always loved him; so much for being any help at all, here and now.

So I turned back to the fog-feller and the boys, expecting to see disaster, ruin, horror acted out in front of me.

And did, I saw exactly that.

*Oh, Jay...*

He wasn't even angry, that was the thing. I'd seen him every way he came, I thought – but not like this. Not clinical. I couldn't even call it cruel, there wasn't passion enough for that; and this was Hell, so nobody could call it cold. But...

Well. It was like the same thing in reverse, what the Green Man did to Asher acted out the other way around. By his brother, and without any of the frantic urgency of that dreadful other death.

I guess the fog-feller was doomed, from the moment he found himself in Hell. Doomed like his fog, baking from the inside out. His only hope would have been to kill Jordan quickly and hope to land us back where we'd started, on a fog-friendly moor. It had worked before for others, so...

Nah. The fog-feller was doomed. Whether he hoped or not, whether he was just lashing out in a final futile gesture, whatever might be happening in whatever fog-filled cavity made his mind. Jordan had died once this week already, more or less; he wasn't about to do it again for the fog-feller's convenience, or for his salvation. Or at all.

Which I ought to be glad about, even as that fist of fear unclenched itself about my heart. *I'm okay, he's okay* – I should have been rejoicing. But, not like this. Not at this. Not to see him methodically take that wight apart, limb by limb.

He didn't have to do that, the thing was dead already, near as dammit. Crisping. That wasn't fog that came filtering out of his mouth and eyes, not now, no. That was smoke. He might be trying to reach the boys, trying to threaten them, trying to kill – but he didn't stand a chance. He was moving in slow motion, barely able to keep his feet; nothing in that long lean body worked right any more. I could almost hear his joints crunching like charcoal as they grated bone on bone.

Actually, no, scrub that 'almost.' My Aspect came back, I felt it, like an apologetic dog cringing against me; I could move just enough to shrug it on, more from instinct than decision. Then I really could hear the fog-feller's bones shattering inside him as he crept forward, as he kept on creeping forward, the poor fool.

Jordan could just have stood and watched, he didn't have to go to meet the guy.

He didn't have to seize one helpless arm and wrench it from its socket like an old limb dead on a tree, toss it aside like refuse.

He didn't have to ignore the fog-feller's whistle of agony and reach to do the same thing to the other arm, and...

I didn't have to watch. I didn't want to; he reminded me too much of me when I was playing Desi in his sight, just to make it so absolutely clear to us both that she was not Fay. Hunting vampires and slaying dryads and naiads and whatever else came our way, building myself up as the ruthless efficient killer without a qualm.

I like qualm. It was one of the things that drew me to Jordan so much against my better judgement, that he had qualms galore. My Aspect helps me to hide them or override them, but actually so do I.

I looked aside then for reassurance, for a glimpse of Thom, the best living evidence that I really wasn't a cold assassin. He still didn't look good – fog-sodden fire is never going to thrive, if it can keep itself alive at all – but he was doing better, at least. Holding himself together, not flickering now from one state of being to the other. Drawing strength, I suspected, from the same Hellish qualities that had destroyed the fog-feller, that ancient dryness and the inherent heat.

As I watched, he drew himself slowly up to sit hugging his knees, with his head hanging down between them.

Well, hell. If he could manage that much...

I pushed myself to my feet, or let my Aspect pull me; that was more how it felt, at least. Actually I thought the thing was feeling guilty, over-eager to help now that there was nothing much to do.

Nothing except this one astonishingly hard thing, to stand and walk over rocky ground towards two boys. One of whom Fay had loved, deeply and simply and disastrously; both of whom Desi had slept with; one of whom... Well. It was complicated.

My Aspect kept me vertical, at least, it was that much use to me. I felt rocky on my own account, amazingly shaky in my legs. Chilled and numb still from the fog-feller's touch, but it was more than that. In Hell, but it was more than that. Unsure of everything suddenly, from the Aspect that was holding me up to the alien ground beneath my feet to my own place and purpose in the world, but it was more than that.

Walking towards the two people I had spent so much time running away from, and with good reason. Yes, that would pretty much cover it.

I wasn't worried about Jacey any more, but Jordan – well.

I walked among the ruins of the fog-feller, strewn limbs still leaking smoke. His head lay some distance off, blessedly not facing in my direction, and I didn't think I could even recognise the boy who had done that, even though I supposed – I had to suppose – that he'd done it for me.

Maybe he'd done it for Jacey, to build a friendship, to have an adventure together. Something exciting but not too risky, a first tentative step back into the Overworld, a way to say *Hey, look: prince of Hell, here I am, and see what I can do...*

And, incidentally, *Hello, Desi. Here I am.*

Maybe I'd like to believe that. Some of it, all of it. Something.

As it was – well. Hard, just to walk towards him. Harder when I had to keep looking down, not to step into the detritus of his victory, not to feel bones crunching underfoot inside their leathery skin. I'd far sooner have kept my eyes on him, just to prove that I could.

Prove it to myself, mostly. I didn't suppose that he'd care.

Damn, I did hate being rescued.

I thought about that, those last few steps – and then I said it aloud.

"Damn," I said, "I do hate being rescued. But thank you."

Keep it light, keep it easy. Be graceful, and ironically sincere. I could do that.

Stand eye to eye with Jordan, I could do that too. The scar on his throat was livid in that red light, trying to drag my eyes down, but I resisted.

I resisted some. Might have glanced at it, down and back, just the once. Damn.

I turned to Jacey, to give him equal time, not to let him feel cut out or Jordan special: "Thanks from both of us. Thom may not be up to saying it for himself, not for a while yet, but I think he'll be okay. Which he wouldn't, neither of us would, if you hadn't turned up just then. How did you...?"

He smiled, in that tired tight way that boys do when they're really secretly pleased with themselves and are trying to be cool about it, trying not to whoop and high-five and bounce about like kids, but it's a real struggle with all that adrenalin still piping around their system and the endorphins mixed into the cocktail and the heady smell of petrol in the air and a girl to impress and, and, and.

He said, "Oh, we were zooming in on the coordinates you gave me, only then we saw this patch of fog moving cross-country and there was no way that was natural, and it was coming from where you must have been, so we took a detour to check it out."

"Well," I said, "I'm really glad you did; but how...?"

Tired-and-exhilarated must be a good state for telepathy; my voice trailed out into hand-waving and bewilderment, but again he understood, and answered the question I couldn't finish. "I just called Jordan, straight off. I knew he had his new bike" – well, of course he did: prodigal son freshly reunited with his parents after so long lost, they'd be slaying fatted calves left and right – "and I figured he'd want to play." Meaning *race to the rescue*, but yes. Never mind how complicated his motives, of course he'd do this. And most likely he didn't still want to kill me, I thought Jacey had probably been quite careful to check on that. I could relax, then. Though it wasn't noticeably happening. "Turns out," Jacey went on, "you can cover a lot of ground very quickly, on a bike that does a ton without thinking about it. When there are two of you to spell each other, and you don't much care what the rules say."

Two golden boys, of course they didn't. They wouldn't have been in touching distance of the speed limit, all the way up from London; if motorway traffic got bad, no doubt they'd raced up the hard shoulder. If any police had spotted them, well. One quick check on the bike's registration, and that would be enough. *Let them go, don't get involved, don't risk it.*

Sometimes it's good to be prince.

I guess.

They were looking good on it, anyway, both of them: the wind of the journey still in their eyes, in their heads. Tangled in Jacey's hair. Not in Jordan's: that bare white frosting on his scalp wasn't enough to hold anything, though it was plenty enough to declare him to those who knew. What he was, where he came from, what he meant.

I supposed he'd grow it out now, wear it in some kind of aggressive declarative quiff: *Here I am!* I regretted that, as much as I regretted everything lost in him, the boy he'd been: shy and avoidant and the opposite of cocky, putting himself down, never recognising his own bright quality.

No longer that, but still. Looking good, oh, yes. He'd always been pretty, delicate, almost dainty for a boy; he used to make me feel protective and clumsy both at once, like some hulking bodyguard with sausage fingers and a musclebound frame. Which is a neat trick if you can do it, and he could.

No longer that, either. The scar on his throat might snare the eye, but something else would hold it: he looked powerful suddenly, a lion in his kingdom, a prince come into his own. He was cocky now, but there was more than that; he was cocky with a reason.

Also I thought maybe he was strutting a little for my benefit, bantam cock showing all his feathers.

I did hope that wasn't why he'd... done what he'd done to the fog-feller, to impress me with how much he had changed. Or to repay me, perhaps, for all those times I'd been so emphatically Desi.

I did rather fear that it was, one or the other or a complicated mixture of the two – but a girl could still hope.

I looked him in the eye and said, "Well, then. At least this time it worked."

His turn to be telepathic, like the old women of the Graiae sharing their one eye between them, which is not a thing you want to see if you can avoid it. Really not.

He said, "Yes, this time." Just that. His voice still held that new huskiness; I supposed it always would. For a moment there his eyes were all old Jordan, the boy I knew, who had seen his brother die in a place just like this, in a manoeuvre just the same. The Green Man had been no fog-feller, to be felled so brutally fast; he'd fought back the only way he could, and fast enough to save his life. For that day, at least. Now of course he was hunted more aggressively even than I had been, and would be until they caught him.

This new Jordan, I thought, might join the hunt.

Might lead the hunt, rather. He was probably still not much of a joiner. But there would be no one more anxious to see Asher's death avenged, and no one better able to achieve it. A burning hunger and a cold rage together had to be good for something.

I didn't think they'd be good for him, but that was another matter, and I had no right to raise it. Not any more. Circumstances change so fast; it takes nimble footwork just to keep up, and your heart lags behind even in the best of times, which these most emphatically were not.

Still. There were four of us here, me and three men who mattered to me, one way or another – or all the same way, if you wanted to be crudely reductionist, which I didn't, thanks all the same – and we were all of us still alive and likely to stay that way, I thought. For a while, at least. At least none of us was trying to kill any of the others any more.

I thought, I hoped.

I thought I'd better check.

I said, "Thanks, Jordan. Truly."

He shrugged – a little bitterly, perhaps? – and said, "You used to call me Jay."

Which was exactly the reaction I was hoping for, working for, that pang of regret in him, the sense of something lost. Whether he was old Jordan reviving or new Jordan reconsidering, this boy had left his blazing anger behind him. Or slaked it, maybe, with the slaughter of the fog-feller, but I thought he'd moved on. Gracelessly, perhaps, but none the less. He might have gone from the hunted to the hunter; at least he wasn't hunting me.

I ignored all the subtexts he was slapping in my face, and just said, "Yes," and glanced at Jacey. *I used to call him Jay too, so let's not get ourselves confused, shall we?*

The telepathy was still running hot in both of them. They twitched in unison, which let me feel a little bit smug, as well as a little bit heartsore; and then – because even Desi can be kind, while Fay was always soft all through – I turned my back on them both, and went to Thom.

Who was just picking himself up, a little warily, still a little uncertain of his shape. Well, I could help there. I took the lighter from my pocket and flicked it open.

"You want to?"

"Yes," he said, meaning *Yes!* – "but I ought to, you know, thank the guys."

"They enjoyed it," I said, hoping that that really wasn't true; I wanted them to have been too anxious to enjoy the wild testosterone-stoked run up here – some chance! – and especially not to have enjoyed the encounter with the fog-feller, whose fallout was all about us. However well that fell out for us, it was really quite important that in retrospect they didn't feel good about it. Jordan especially.

But they were allowed to pretend for a little longer, and they were certainly allowed to be appreciated. So I let Thom go and left them strictly alone for a minute to do their male thing together, harsh laughs and shoulder-slapping and jokes about Thom's nakedness, which he might have managed to overlook, but they couldn't possibly, oh, no.

I just waited, patient as a monument, the lighter in my hand; and when he'd done the polite for long enough, Thom came back to me. He shifted form in a moment, balancing briefly, gratefully, bright and burning on the Zippo's wick before I snapped it shut.

And held it – him – in my hand, hot and reassuring as I turned back to the boys where they stood waiting. Maybe I'd think of them as willing patient rescuers, maybe I could do that; it would surely be easier than anything else, everything else that they were.

Had been.

Were.

I said, "Guys, I love you both, and I'm really grateful because we really needed you and you came, and we'd be dead if you hadn't" – which was all obvious but needed saying none the less, willing patient rescuers need to hear these things – "only we're not done yet." Obviously we weren't done. Oz was still in his lair and still in a killing temper, and now there were four of us he'd be coming for; which actually wasn't what I meant at all. "Or rather I am, I'm done for a bit." Even my Aspect was barely holding me up against the lingering feel of fog in my bones, the chill of it in my blood that all the heat of Hell couldn't quite bake out, the woozy unbalance in my head. I couldn't fold myself into a flame and tuck myself away in a handy brass case and slurp petrol till I felt better, but, "I need somewhere to lie down" – *alone for once* – "and something to eat when I get up again, and there are three ways I can think to make that happen, but they all start the same way, us getting out of here and back to the bike."

Jacey looked at Jordan; Jordan looked at me. And nodded, and didn't noticeably do anything else, but there was a queasy kind of jolt in the world around us and we were back on the moor and the bike was right there and I did manage not to throw up but that was absolutely as much as I could manage.

Jacey did better, shaking his head, bringing his hand up to his nose, saying, "Brother, you really need to practise that. Alone. I think I'm bleeding."

Jordan's lips quirked, but he didn't say anything. Didn't look away from me.

I said thanks, and then I said, "Okay. One bike, three of us. Three ways to go. One, I just take the bike and leave the two of you to sort yourselves." *And don't think I haven't thought about it. Don't think for a moment that I don't want to. I love you both, and I'm helluva grateful, and right now I'd be delighted to drive off and leave the pair of you in the middle of this suddenly sunlit moor.* They didn't react, so I smiled for them, a little dizzily, and went on. "Only I don't think that's a very good idea, because I'm really not feeling on top of things right now, or I would probably have done it by now. So two, Jacey drives me" – *me and Thom*, but let's not complicate anything more than it is complicated already – "and Jordan makes his own way." *Jordan can go to Hell*, in other words, and I was fairly sure he'd have ways to get around when he was there. If nothing else, he could always call his dad. And like Jacey said, he could use the practice, going to and fro. Which I very carefully didn't say. I just held his eye and didn't stop talking. "Or three, we all three of us" – *all four of us* – "squash onto that lovely big bike, which I'm fairly sure is all manner of illegal as well as uncomfortable as well as unsafe, and whichever of you is the better driver" – *that would be Jacey*, but I didn't say that either – "takes us slowly and carefully and I don't care where, just so long as it is somewhere else than here and there is a bed. Because that's what I need, and I need it now."

*Be patient, be willing. Rescue me again. Please?*

# CHAPTER FIFTEEN

SOMETIMES, BOYS CAN still surprise me.

Looking back, actually thinking it through, I could hardly have said anything worse: anything better designed to stir up old memories and new rivalries, challenge their young-men's egos and set them at each other's throats.

And yet, and yet. Sometimes, even when everything else is going spectacularly badly, when the whole clumsy edifice of your life is crashing down around you and all your worst mistakes are rising up right there in your face to damn you – even then, something can just go right.

It was right that I went to Jacey when I needed him, and right that I called him when I did. It was right that he went to Jordan, that the two of them came up like the cavalry to rescue me. Afterwards I could have just gone off, me and Thom, it was terribly tempting, but I was right not to do that. The boys could have fought over me like dogs for a bone; it was absolutely right that they didn't.

Patiently, willingly, they steered me towards the bike. If they spoke aloud at all, I don't remember it. I don't usually like being manhandled – without a positive invitation, at least – but right then I was grateful. I just wanted to give myself over to someone else for a change, to be rescued, yes: and they'd been elected, and they rose admirably to the task.

Jacey picked up the crash-hat and clamped it firmly over my head. It was still warm. It probably smelled of Jordan, or at least of whatever costly body-wash he'd used that morning – princes of Hell don't sweat, but they do absolutely pamper themselves – only the dust and the heat and the fog and the aftershock and the exhaustion were all coming between me and my regular awareness of the world. I could hardly stand, I was just a puppet tied to my Aspect's apron-strings; I couldn't smell a thing.

I missed it, but only in that distant, distancing way: how you're aware that things are missing when you're almost utterly gone yourself. Jacey swung his leg over the bike and settled in with no discussion. I looked at Jordan, not knowing what came next, right out of the loop telepathy-wise; they must've switched to a different frequency, no girls allowed.

He cocked his head on one side, said "You're not going to manage by yourself, are you?" – and lifted me astride the bike, casual and easy, as if I were a little kid.

Time was – until just a couple of days ago, actually – I could've taken Jordan with one hand tied behind my back and no Aspect anywhere in reach. I still had to look down to find him, I still outweighed him in a purely mortal way, the physical matter of us. Everything else had changed radically. He'd passed a landmark, and come into his own; we were standing in his place of power. And to be fair, I couldn't have resisted a strand of wet spaghetti just then; and to be fair, it wouldn't have made a blind bit of difference if I'd been revving as hard and hot as that bike, he could still have picked me up and done whatever he liked with me.

That felt weird, or would have done if I'd been up to feeling anything. As it was, I stored it away to feel weird about later. For now I just let it happen, the way sleeping people let the world carry on without them.

Jordan almost had to settle my arms around Jacey's waist for me, almost. Did say "Hold on tight," as if I were an even littler kid than before.

I still didn't know what was happening, if we were leaving Jordan or not; only then he swung aboard behind me, and reached over to slap Jacey's shoulder in that traditional off-you-go gesture. Well, I guess it was his bike; he was still captain, Jacey was just the pilot.

Jordan's a scrawny little thing, and even so three of us was a squash. I was the meat in a male sandwich, squeezed between one boy and another, and I didn't mind a bit. Given that one had hunted me for years and the other had threatened to kill me such a little time before, I felt bizarrely safe. Even once we started bumping slowly over moorland in search of a road that might lead anywhere, even then. They felt rock-solid, pillars of reassurance, just absolutely right.

Thom was a warm spot still clenched in my hand, and that was right too.

I didn't really need my Aspect any more, but I kept it on anyway, if only because I was too tired to be bothered to do the other thing.

Far too tired to figure out if that was right or not.

FINDING YOUR WAY'S not so hard in daylight when there's no fog. Jacey brought us down onto a road, which might or might not have been the same road he'd found us on when he was fog-hunting. Then he opened up the throttle, the bike grunted in response, and suddenly the world was unreeling on either side of us.

If we'd had more room, I honestly don't know if I'd have leaned forward onto Jacey's shoulder or backward onto Jordan's. As it was, not a problem; I didn't have space to lean either way. Instead, I just closed my eyes against the dizzy and waited out the time.

Unkind people might say I fell asleep, or passed out. If the boys were that unkind, at least they did it silently, telepathically. At least, that's what I'm claiming. I was alert all the way, say I, and they didn't say a word.

When I opened my eyes, though, I did find Jordan's arms reached around me to grip Jacey's jacket, making bars on either side of me to stop me toppling sideways. Like a little, little kid in a crib.

I hadn't noticed him do that. Last I'd been aware, he was holding on behind him and touching me as little as he could manage.

It wasn't him that roused me, though, it was the

bike's engine slowing to a tickover, dying altogether. We were there, I guessed. If I wanted to know where there was, I did have to open my eyes.

So I did that, and never mind how heavy my eyelids felt, or how hard it was to focus.

Took me a second, even then; but this irresistible bubble rose like gas in my throat, and I almost choked on it before it broke into a hard, painful giggle.

"Seriously, guys?"

"It's this or keep driving," Jordan said in my ear, dry and cool and not trying to hide his own amusement. "No real hotel for fifty miles, at a guess. And it'll probably be better than it looks, unless it's a hell of a lot worse. Trust me, I've stayed in a lot of these. One way or the other, it'll be something to remember."

Jacey didn't say anything, but his body did. His body said he wanted to keep driving, another fifty miles, another hundred, however far it took. And that he wasn't going to say so, because it was my call and he wasn't sure I was up for it, so.

He was right, too. I was absolutely not up for another fifty, or another five. Five yards looked a long way, from the kerb to the door. I hugged him for his courage, remembering the last place I'd seen him sleep, his dad's suite in the Savoy; and then I totally failed to self-sacrifice, because I really couldn't do it.

I half-squeezed, half-oozed out from between them, stumbled up the crazy paving between the straggly roses and the pond with the fishing gnome, and rang the bell before either one of them could change their snarky superior minds.

\* \* \*

WHICH IS HOW we came to be staying at the Jollie Roger guest house, which was about as far a cry as you could get from the Savoy and still be on the same planet, never mind in the same country.

"Roger was my husband, dearie. Such a merry man he was. So I thought, when I had to take paying guests after he was taken, I'd name the business after him; and then, well, things just took off from there. You know how people are..."

"I do, Mrs Jolliffe." People give you things. If you give them half an excuse, the vaguest imaginable hint, that dooms you for every Christmas, every birthday yet to come. Animals are easy, of course: if you collect elephants or hedgehogs or cats, you never need to buy a single elephant, hedgehog or cat, once people know it. Or teapots, or thimbles, or...

Or you give your guest house the least hint of a theme, and there you have it. Or you will do, in a slow accumulation. If I'd known more, I might have known that every rose in the garden had a piratical name; if I'd been paying the least attention anyway, knowing nothing, I should still have noticed that the gnome by the pond had an eye-patch. And a skull-and-crossbones hanging from his fishing rod.

Once inside, even I couldn't miss it, even in my current state. Another Jolly Roger hung over the hallway mirror; the stairway was decorated with fishing nets and glass floats; scrimshaw work was everywhere.

I'd asked for two rooms: "One for me and one for the boys. No, no luggage, this was all... unexpected, we've been up all night and no one's fit to drive..."

She didn't bat an eyelid, our buccaneering widow.

Perhaps she should have done. I got the Edward Teach room, and the boys got Henry Morgan – and after a minute they were tapping plaintively at my door, "Desi? Will you swap? You've got the twin beds, and we got the double..."

She must have misunderstood the way I said "boys." But by then I was halfway out of my clothes, halfway into one of those charming twin beds. "Go away," I said. "The other one's for Thom, if he wants it." If I let him out. "You'll just have to share."


MY SUSPICION IS that they just didn't go to bed, then or later. I didn't care. Golden boys aren't like us mere mortals. Besides, they hadn't been fog-bound and adrift. Me, I shed my clothes where I stood, thought briefly – very briefly – about a shower, had second thoughts and crawled into bed.

Wondered if I ought to release Thom, if only to ask him whether he'd rather stay in flame form or try the other bed – or join the boys, whatever they were up to – but he'd keep, I thought. Or else he'd find his own way out. He was a free spirit; brass lids do not a prison make, nor cotton wicks a cage.

Last thing, I remembered – just – to shrug my Aspect off. Otherwise it's like waking up with your contact lenses in, if you still have the old-fashioned kind, the way Fay used to: briefly confusing and abidingly uncomfortable and you really wouldn't want to do it on a daily basis. Better not to do it at all.

Also it's like having a cat in your bed, which is like paying Danegeld. Let it happen once, and that's that: Aspect expects.

So. Off with the Aspect, let it puddle on the floor where it'll be handy, not that I'll need it. I'm going to sleep. If I dream, I'll fix my dreams without it; dreams give you superpowers without benefit of actual, y'know, superpowers. If Oz sends the Corbies to tap at my window, or another fog-feller to ooze beneath the door – well. They can do as they like, slay me in my sleep, I won't care. I'll be asleep.

SOMETIMES I LOVE sleep for the company, for the way you doze and rouse and nuzzle in and feel them wake and doze again and never forget that you're not alone tonight, skin against your skin and breath in your hair, someone else's heat and smell and presence. The weight of their body, the weight of their gaze, the weight of their voice as they talk in their sleep.

Sometimes I love it for the dreaming, that sense of stepping through a curtain and finding adventure. Old friends in new places, haunts and discoveries, surreal shifts that never clash with your knowledge of the dreaming world. When you're a daemon, your sense of the surreal can be challenging – I have seen men turn to stone, birds turn to men, worse things – and even so. Dreaming never lets you down.

Sometimes, though? Sometimes I love it just for the thing itself, for the being asleep. Being somewhere else, downtime. Switched off. Gone.

SOMEONE SWITCHED ME off. Time passed. I didn't notice.

\*    \*    \*

YOU SLEEP ON trickle-charge, and sooner or later you have power enough to autostart.

Almost always, it's too soon. Which is odd, because you haven't noticed the time passing, you've no idea how long it was, you've been off and now you're on again, that's all. It's a flicker of unexperience, a discontinuity, you can't measure it. Even so. Chances are, you want more off. You want to go back to that nothingness, you want to be gone again.

I woke, warm and settled, and even rolling over was too much effort, so I didn't. For a while I just lay there in this heavy slack envelope that was my body. Maybe I breathed, come to think of it. Once in a while.

Eventually I opened my eyes, if only for the anticipated pleasure of closing them again and sleeping more. I puzzled for a little while over the strangeness of the room, before I remembered where I was. Where we were. *Who* 'we' were, given that I was alone in a single bed and the other one was empty.

Jacey, Jordan, Thom. Old boyfriend, old boyfriend and, um, well. Someone else I used to sleep with. Call him a boyfriend and have done, let's keep things simple.

*If it's not complicated, it's not worth it.* Who said that? Never mind. They're an idiot, whoever.

Oz was out there somewhere, wanting me dead and Thom too. Probably all of us, by now. That was a complication, unless it actually made things easier. For sure it took priority. So long as we were fighting to stay alive, perhaps we wouldn't need to fight each other.

If I just stayed in bed, maybe I wouldn't need to fight anyone.

I hadn't bothered with drawing the curtains – no mere daylight was going to disturb me – and the sunbeams nosing in looked almost as lazy as I was, dust-heavy and angled low, almost ready to lie flat and give up altogether. Shadows were already gathering in the corners of the room, which meant I'd slept all day, which meant...

Oh, hell. I hadn't slept enough, but even so. It really was time to be up and doing, or at least to check on what the boys were up to. If I left them longer, who knew what trouble they'd have got me into?

So I did it, I dragged myself out of bed, one weary leg at a time. A short stagger to the en-suite and a quick – a very quick – cold shower, which wasn't as effective as advertised but did at least hurry me up.

Then I scrambled damply and reluctantly into the same old clothes and made my way down to the guest lounge.

Where, blessedly, I found the boys sharing a sofa, hunched over a smartphone. That must be Jordan's: another new toy, much more swish than what he'd used before.

"We were just arguing the toss," Jacey said, "which one of us came up to wake you."

"Yeah? Who lost?"

"He did," Jordan said. "That's why we were arguing."

I curled my lip at him in a silent snarl, and slumped into a chair. Of course the seafaring trend saturated the room, from the books on the shelf – *Treasure Island* and *Moby-Dick* and Hornblower and O'Brian and *My Granny Is A Pirate* – to the prints on the wall to the knick-knacks on every spare surface.

The prints were repro etchings, sailing ships in their prime; the knick-knacks were everything, sea-shells and lighthouses and crab claws all in pottery or glass, each one on its own individual crochet mat. My room was just the same. I'd noticed finally, after I showered, how even the spare toilet-roll lived under a woollen cosy. It would all be insufferably twee, if there wasn't that piratical theme running through the house; my loo-roll cosy was in the shape of a barrel of rum.

"Yo ho," I said cheerlessly. "So what are we going to do?"

They eyed me sideways, as if they'd both been depending on me to tell them. Perhaps they had.

"Um," Jacey said, "we thought we'd find a pub, get something to eat."

"Good plan," I said, "I'm starving. Just so long as you're not expecting me to come up with something brilliant over the scampi and chips, because I'm telling you, I've got nothing. Talking of which, I don't suppose either of you thought to bring a change of clothes?"

Two mute shakes of the head, glances that were even more sideways than before.

"Not for me," I said, with an excess of patience, "for Thom. Never mind. If you haven't, you haven't. He'll just have to sit the night out in the Zippo."

"You could ask Mrs J if she's still got any of her husband's things," Jacey said. Malevolently, I thought.

I scowled at him and said, "Did you find a pub, then?"

"Down the road, yes. Walking distance. If you're up for walking?" He was suddenly doubtful, looking at the state of me.

"If the alternative is that one of us – one of you – has to drive, and then moan all night because he can't be drinking, sure. I'm up for a walk."

The boys looked at each other, as if waiting for the other to volunteer – but they were doing the telepathy thing again, and they weren't thinking about driving. I picked up the backscatter, just enough to understand them. And sat up straight, and would have thumped myself in the head for effect except that it was just too much effort, and said instead, "I'm sorry. I'm being a bitch, aren't I?"

"No, no," Jacey said hastily, unconvincingly, meaning *yes, yes,* "you're just logie, that's all. You've had a bloody awful time of it, even before we started tossing you to Hell and back, and you need food. Food and beer. We'll take you. I'll drive if you like, I don't mind driving. And I promise not to moan."

"I'll drive," Jordan said. "And drink. It's not a worry." I was just about to say tartly that he might be immune to the police but it would worry me, and no way was I riding pillion behind him if he'd been on the beer because I knew what a lightweight he was when it came to alcohol – but then he went on, "It can't get near my bloodstream. I don't have blood any more, remember? I don't even know if I can get drunk."

"Asher used to have a good try at it," I said. And then hated myself, of course, for picking at a wound so fresh.

Jordan didn't blink. Maybe he didn't need to any more, maybe closing his eyes had become something voluntary, something he should learn to do for society's sake. He said, "Yes, but did he ever get there?"

"Fair point," I said, stubbornly not backing off in the face of that stare. If I'd put one foot in it, I might as well add the other. "Maybe he was just drunk on company, having a good time without benefit of alcohol. Drinking for the hell of it, because he liked the taste or couldn't dump the habit. I don't know. Let's go and find out, shall we? Let's walk," I added, up on my feet to give a good example. "Walking's good, when you feel this crappy." You don't actually have to look at each other, when you're walking along together. Sometimes that makes it easier to talk.

"Gets the blood moving," Jacey agreed. "Those of us who still have any," with a glance at Jordan: half to goad him, I thought, half to see if he'd giggle.

He didn't react at all, except to say, "I'll ask Mrs J for a front-door key," and quietly disappear.

In his absence, I said, "Jay" – which was totally taking advantage, and I don't apologise for it; I had to use whatever tiny advantage I could scrape up, caught between these two – "how's he doing? Seriously? What's he been like?" He'd seen his brother die and his girl betray him; he'd been bled dry by his parents and reborn as something close to a god, after clinging frantically for so long to his determined humanity; no blame to him if he'd turned suddenly psychotic, though he didn't seem to have done that. Instead he'd come racing north on a rescue mission, for me. Which was the opposite of betrayal, and I really didn't understand it.

Jacey shrugged. "I don't know what he was like before. He's been avoiding us, remember? For longer than I like to think about. He's not much like his brother, he's very quiet; but you would be, wouldn't you? After all of that?"

Brother, girl, parents. Hell. Oh, yes. Even I'd be quiet for a while.

I was going to say, "So how about you, then, how are you doing?" Because he was being fairly quiet himself and he had his own shocks to process, even if they weren't quite as traumatic – only then Jordan came back into the room.

Giggling in a kind of frantic silence, doubling over, hugging himself, almost gagging himself in a desperate effort to contain the noise that was trying to overflow him.

I guess we both just stared at him for a moment there. He looked like a teenager, utterly swept up, out of all control. Then I remembered that he actually was a teenager, in a complicated kind of way; and then I came over all grown-up and responsible. Mostly because Jacey was just standing there staring uselessly, starting to giggle himself just at the unexpectedness of it all.

I grabbed Jordan's shoulders – he was warm under his T-shirt, almost hot, almost Thom-hot: just like Asher used to be, of course – and steered him to the sofa, pushed him down into it, said, "Do I have to hold your head between your knees?" in my best growly voice.

He shook his head, mutely, piteously; and then grabbed a cushion and buried his face in it to muffle the laughter that was so obviously going to come regardless.

Which was at least slightly more grown-up than the other thing, the laddish thing, which would be to sprawl on his back and bellow regardless. I gazed down on him with a kind of exasperated affection – and then surprised myself, at least, by dropping to my knees and putting my arm back around his shoulders, cradling him as best I could in that mutual awkwardness, murmuring private nonsense at him until dry gulping laughter ebbed into snorts and gasps, until finally he lifted his face from the cushion and I could be stern again, just what he needed.

"What in the world was that about, Jay?" Fair dos, one each. I owed him that.

I wasn't going to get back into the habit of it, though, no. Not with either of them. I was going to stand resolutely outside the habit. Old habits die hard, maybe, but this one was doomed.

His eyes were always his best feature, or at least first among equals. The lazy way is to call them hazel, because sometimes they're the golden-brown of a hazelnut and sometimes the green of the leaves of the hazel; they vary with the light or with his mood or with the moment. Just then, this unexpectedly close, I could see both green and brown, and a kind of smoky heat that perhaps I was imagining or just carrying over from memories of Hell, and a bright fierce spark of delight that was new and better to see than the fear he used to carry. Never mind that it was inhuman. A mortal human's eyes would have been wet from all that extremity of laughter, but not his. Not now.

Either he knew that something was missing, or else it was the other thing: his new superior Overworld self didn't at all understand what had just happened, how he could seem so weak. Either way, there was a twist of bewilderment to his face, just for a moment.

Until he opened his mouth to explain, and was suddenly whooping; and stopped, and swallowed drily, and tried again.

"Johnny Depp," he said, in a kind of strangulated voicelessness, the best he could yet manage.

Our turn to look bewildered. "Try slapping him," Jacey suggested. "It won't make any difference to him, but you'll feel so much better."

I grinned, and lifted my hand threateningly. His came up to catch my wrist, breathtakingly fast and rock-solid. Even with my Aspect on I couldn't have shifted a millimetre against that grip, even before the extra finger curled deliberately into place alongside his more regular ones. That finger had been special even when he seemed not to be at all special himself, when he was trying so hard to be and stay a normal boy, that one crucial day short of his eighteenth. Now it was like his hair, worn blatantly, a badge of difference and more, a mark of strength. It was like limestone shifting into granite; I couldn't have moved before, but I couldn't imagine anyone, anything moving against this.

Those eyes sparked brighter, and he managed a smile that was nothing to do with hysterics.

I wanted to patronise him absolutely in response, call him a good clever boy and ruffle his soft velvet head.

Actually, this close again, I *really* wanted to ruffle his soft velvet head. But wiser counsels prevailed; if he thought I was patronising him, he might just crush my wrist because he could. If he thought something else – well, I had no clue what he might do, but I didn't think it would end well for me or any of us.

Better not to let him think anything at all. I said again, "What, then? Jordan?"

"Johnny Depp," he said again, seeming cold stone sober, eye to eye. And then, "She's got a, a, shop window dummy, a mannequin, in the corner of her sitting-room. An Auton. Only I think she must have got it from a cinema, from a *Pirates of the Caribbean* display. It's Johnny Depp got up as Jack Sparrow. The whole damn thing. Costume, wig, the lot. Oh, God..."

And he was off again, releasing me because he needed to wave his hand in a wordless apology as the laughter stole him away.

Jacey and I looked at each other, pointedly. He said, "Maybe we should drive after all? We could keep him pinned between us, hold him up..." *The way we did you* went unmentioned, implicitly there.

I shook my head. "The walk will do him good. He'll be all right once we get him moving. Briskly. You take one arm, I'll take the other. Frogmarch him if we have to. Let's just get him out of here before Mrs J comes to see what's up."

Inwardly, I was kind of glad, twice over. If Jordan could still fold up like this, then maybe the boy I'd known wasn't lost entirely; and conversely, the boy I'd known would never have dared let himself fold up like this. If the new Jordan could be this free, that was nothing but advance.

Either way, it had to be a good thing.

Didn't it?

I WOULDN'T HAVE thought, but Jacey checked that Jordan had the front-door key that we'd sent him for;

and promptly took charge of it himself, not trusting this cackling idiot to look after anything so crucial. Then we took an elbow each and steered him out, swiftly and silently, like rescuing a drunk kid from a party before the grown-ups got wind.

Quick-march in the fresh air, and sure enough, Jordan sobered quickly. I wasn't quite sorry. Not quite.

"Seriously," he said. "When we get back – or, no, leave it till the morning, but you both need to find an excuse. When we're handing the room-keys back, just get in there. You need to see it. Johnny Depp in the corner of the room. Really, she ought to have a parrot. I don't know why she doesn't have a parrot..."

"I don't know why you don't shut up," Jacey grumbled. "We've got bigger things to worry about than one old girl's obsession."

"Well, not so much," I said. "One really old guy's obsession, that's not so different."

"Except that one of them will kill us all, and the other one will only kill one of us from laughing at it, except that actually I might just kill him anyway even if he stops laughing, just for the instant gratification and the retrospective justice of it."

"You might try." Jordan's eyes glimmered in the dusk. The boy I'd known had spent his life running from that inheritance, that power: not afraid, just not wanting it, rejecting it and all that it implied. The boy he'd become, this boy seemed to revel in it. As his brother had, as Jacey did. It would be hard, I suppose, not to do that, one way or another. Jacey took it for granted, his birthright, he'd never known anything else and never seen the world another way. Jordan was – of course! – more complicated, and more abrupt. However much you didn't want a thing, I guess it's hard not to welcome it when strength comes surging through your body and the future opens up, limitless and free, while you're still young.

Before the boys could get into something laddish that would either exclude me altogether or else leave me feeling even more morose, I said, "You know, I haven't the first idea where we are."

That's what comes of keeping your eyes closed while someone else does the driving. They spoke in unison to tell me, but I wasn't much better off: a village that I'd never heard of, on the fringes of a town I barely had. Okay.

I cast a glance up at the glooming sky. "What do you reckon the odds are that Oz knows, though? Where we are?"

"I wouldn't bet against it," Jacey said. Jordan didn't have the betting habit, or not yet; he just grunted agreement.

"Yeah," I said. "That's what I thought, too. If he can follow Horse, I'm sure he could follow fogfeller, or his spies could." I cast a suspicious eye at pigeons on a roof-ridge, starlings on a wire, the sudden shadow of a seagull dropping onto a streetlamp. I didn't trust that one at all. I might not know where we were, but I had a vague sense how far the sea should be. And my head was full of pirates: were-pirates, now. Of course they'd transform into seabirds. Maybe it wasn't a seagull at all, maybe it was an albatross. How would I know?

I shivered and reached out before I thought, tucked an arm through a boy's each side of me. Which I couldn't have done if they hadn't already been walking that way. I don't know if it was consciously protective or arrogant or accident or what, but in that unthinking moment I was nothing but grateful. My body was still heavy and laggard, and the last thing I wanted was a fight, because the next-to-last thing I wanted was to reach out for my Aspect. I wanted food and beer and maybe a bit of future planning. If that came with some awkward talking and a bit of attitude-adjustment, so be it. Awkward I could deal with, even if my notion of dealing came down to *Please, can we not talk about that now?*

I reached, I tucked; both boys reacted. A moment's stiffness that I felt beneath my fingers like a sort of choreographed mutual stumble, a glance at each other – which would've been over my head except that Jordan's shorter than I am, so he had to peer around me, so I knew – and then they locked step and fixed bayonets and marched steadily towards the sound of gunfire.

Well, no, but they both stared straight ahead and walked forward and I swear they both grew hotter under my hands as all the blood rushed to their skins. Well, all of Jacey's, and whatever it is that Jordan has instead of blood these days and never mind that he was hot already, I still say he got hotter. The same way that he was quiet already and grew quieter. Apparently someone who isn't saying anything can still lapse into silence, deeper and more private than before.

I sighed internally, and kept a stubborn grip of both their arms, though I felt suddenly like a magnet with its poles the wrong way round, being repelled from both sides equally. *Please*, their bodies were saying, *can we not do this now?*

Too bad. I had them both and I wasn't letting go. Apart from anything else, I might just grind to a halt in the middle of the street there. Equipoised between pub and bed, sans oomph to make it either way.

I thought about it for another dozen steps and then decided to say so, more or less, since the telepathy obviously wasn't working any more, me-to-them.

"Another time," I said, "I'll send the two of you off together on your own, and you can do the male bonding thing over the pool table or whatever, and eat crisps and talk about me as much as you want to, and I don't even care where that leads. Right now, I'm sorry but you have to carry me along with you. I need this. *This*." With a little tug at each elbow, to be sure that they understood. "I need you, the pair of you. Are we clear?"

Jordan grunted again; Jacey patted my hand, in a gesture that might have been infuriatingly patronising another time but right now was just fine, thanks. I didn't mind being patronised, when I was leaning half my weight on him.

"Good," I said. "Right now, the other thing I need is beer. We'd better be going in the right direction, or you two are in such trouble..."


PUBS COME IN many guises. Some are foul. Actually more and more of them are foul, which is like a measure of how everything is getting worse, which is like a measure of how I'm getting older. I hate that. Soon I'll have to have a lawn and everything.

Pubs on the margins, neither city nor country, caught between the suburbs and the industrial estates? Often the worst. All too often. TV screens on every wall, corporate muzak, microwaved food, no decent beer. Children. Everything I hate in a public house.

Maybe Jacey has an app on his phone to lead him away from all of that. Maybe he has native tracker skills. When we lived together, I was too young to know what was good, and too much in love to notice.

Which is a universal story, I guess, and no surprise that it ended badly. Now we were grown-ups, and trying to rebuild; it would do him no harm in the world, that he steered us to a pub like this.

From the outside, you'd never have known. It looked like a shoebox, broad and flat. My heart sank. It was probably no older than I was, and that's never a recommendation. A good pub is like a good wine, it needs time to settle and then more time to mature. Also it needs angles, shadows. Dust.

Call me old-fashioned, and get off my lawn. That's how I feel.

So we walked into this dull brick building, and it just goes to show. What you see isn't always what you get.

It looked just as dull inside, more like a church hall than a pub: chipped formica tables and lino floor, strip lighting. I was half ready to turn around and walk straight out again, except that my bones ached with a still-foggy chill and I wanted to sit down.

The boys were being telepathic again. Jacey took charge of my unresisting self, propelling me towards a corner table, while Jordan headed for the bar.

"Unprepossessing, isn't it? But you know how this goes, in all the best stories: you can't judge a book by its cover, every frog is a prince, the best things come in plain wrappers. Besides, there will be beer, and there will be food. Hang on to that thought, and trust me."

I glowered at him across the table and trusted him not at all, until Jordan came over with three pints balanced between his two hands. There's a skill to that, when your hands are small; partly it's practice, partly it's confidence. He used to bite his lip and watch his footing. Now he didn't even watch his hands. I bit my own lip instead, and missed my old young Jay in all his tentative potential. And couldn't regret him – it had been my choice, after all, to do this, to move him on, to give him back, and I still thought that was right – but even so. I missed him on my own account, and wasn't sure what I had now. Whether I even had a friend.

"Okay," he said in his unrecognisable new voice, laying down the glasses and lining them up, "I didn't know who'd want what, so there's a mild and a bitter and an IPA."

"They have *mild?*" I may have been gaping.

"Sweetheart. You're in the north now. People still drink real drinks up here. Besides, this place is in the Good Beer Guide." Jacey was smug; of course he had an app. Unless he just had a good instinct and a sharp eye for the decals on a pub door.

Either way. Jordan went to slide a glass towards me, but he was too slow; I already had my hand around it.

Tall straight glass, black, black liquor with a tawny head, oh, my.

Mild doesn't mean weak. Mildly hopped is what it means, and young and sweet and malty. These days they tend to be quite light on the alcohol, but they don't have to be.

This one wasn't.

I sipped, and sighed, and sipped again. I guess the boys sorted themselves out, with drinks and chairs and so forth; I wasn't paying attention.

When I looked up, when I spoke, it was for a cause. "I don't suppose this place is in the Good Food Guide too, by any chance?"

"As a matter of fact," said a voice behind me, "yes, we are."

If I'd had my Aspect on, I'd have known she was there, never mind the distractions of my glass. But then, if I'd had my Aspect on, I wouldn't have been enjoying the beer so much, I'd have been too aware of all the world around me. Swings and roundabouts.

And she was a nice lady bringing menus, because Jordan had thought to ask for them; and I don't know if he'd asked for these too but she left us nibbles in pretty white bowls, to sustain us while we considered our options. There were crisps and roasted cashews and –

Holy cow.

Pork scratchings. *Home-made* pork scratchings. Strips of rind rubbed with sea-salt and aromatic herbs, roasted until the rind puffs out like popcorn into a crisp lacy honeycomb with a blanket of dense juicy fat beneath: like the crackling on a Sunday dinner only better, and you don't have to bother with all that extra stuff on your plate, the meat and vegetables and so forth.

I didn't grab the bowl and tug it to my side of the table, that would have been unmannerly. I didn't even growl when the boys reached out automatic hands to help themselves. I don't think I did. I must have made some kind of noise, or glowered, or something. Jacey gave me an amused glance, took a bare single scratching and nudged the rest in my direction; Jordan went back to the bar, to negotiate for more.

Usually, I'm actually quite good about sharing. Usually. That night, not so much. I did get better, once it was obvious that we weren't going to run short. And that Jordan would be paying. I was entirely happy to dine out on his dollar. On his family's dollar, that is, now he was a poor little rich kid again.

An hour later I was happy inside as well as out. There hadn't been a whole lot of talking: just more beer and more crunchy salty goodness until eventually even I was craving solid food to follow; and then there was slow-roasted pork belly with mash and greens, and steak-and-kidney pudding, and proper fish and chips. And poaching from each other's plates, and fencing each other off with cutlery, and more beer, and I suppose in the end we had to start being serious but I didn't really want to. Hell, I'd even got the twitch of a smile out of Jordan, when we'd both been fighting over the last trace of his tartare sauce. Which was home-made too, and the best I'd ever tasted, which was why I stole his last chip to dunk in it.

"Told you this'd be a good pub," Jacey said, leaning back to watch us with a self-satisfied leer.

"This is not a good pub," I said, "this is a great pub. Some pubs are born great: the old coaching inns, f'rexample, or those taverns built into the mediaeval city walls. Some achieve greatness; you know the way a perfectly ordinary pub becomes the place that everyone goes, because it has the best jukebox in town or the best food for twenty miles or whatever.

And some have greatness thrust upon them. Like this place. Which has everything against it, including an almost total lack of customers" – we were still the only people in, bar two old men on bar-stools – "and yet. Great beer, great food. No atmosphere, but hey. If it had everything, we'd never get in the –"

I stumbled then, because I made the mistake of looking at my audience in mid-oration.

"Well, what?" I snarled.

"Oh, nothing." Jacey was positively smirking now, resoundingly pleased with himself. "It's just nice to see you feeling better. Have another pint and carry on."

*You haven't changed*, he was really saying. *Despite the name, and the Aspect, and the years and the experience. You were always like this, holding forth about something or other as soon as you got some beer inside you...*

I scowled at him, and turned to Jordan in hopes of a more sensible response. Nostalgia was the last game I wanted to play just now. I couldn't be Fay for one boy and Desi for the other, I couldn't chop and change inside myself, uncertain from one moment to the next who I was or who I ought to be. Who I ought to be with.

Inside my pocket, my hand was suddenly fidgeting with the Zippo. One flick, and I could have a third alternative. Thom was the easy choice, utterly uncomplicated.

Oh, and utterly naked, that too. And utterly heedless of it, but even so. Better not...

Not that either of these boys was actually making me an offer, mind. Jacey was preoccupied with his own smarts and our shared memories; Jordan had apparently been listening to me all too carefully, hearing what I didn't mean to say. I hate when that happens.

"Some are born great," he quoted back at me. "Some achieve greatness. Some have greatness thrust upon them. It's like a summary of the Overworld, isn't it? With immortality to substitute for greatness."

And there we were, back in the moment. Back in the story. *Damn you, Jordan.*

"Damn you, Jordan," Jacey said. "Lighten up, will you?"

"No," I said. "No, he's right. We need to talk about this. It. Him. Oz is still out there – hell, we all know exactly where he is – and vice versa, that too. He knows where we are. And he... thinks he has an interest."

"In seeing us dead." Jordan was being laconic, apparently, as well as direct. Maybe that was the beer. He wasn't used to it, after all. Hadn't been. Now, who knew?

"Yeah, that. So I guess we have two choices. We can run him to earth, or we can run away." *Again*, but that didn't need saying.

"No point in running," Jacey said, "if he knows where we are. If he can just follow us. That's not really running, is it? That's leading him directly to us, whenever he cares to come. Like waving a flag and saying 'Okay, we're going over here now...'"

"What are you suggesting, that we should take the fight to Oz? Beard him in his den, just walk in and have it out with him, face to face?" *Do exactly what he wants*, I was saying actually, *give ourselves over to him in his place of power?*

Put it like that, of course it wasn't an option. That's why I put it like that.

I had some experience of running; Jordan had a whole lot more. A hell of a lot. I looked to him for sober rational good sense, to set against Jacey's folly.

"Yeah," he said, his eyes smoking. "That. Oz Trumby? I'm not running from fucking Oz Trumby."

For all his long denial, he still had all the arrogance of the born immortal, prince of Hell. *Some are born great* – it was a truth settled into his bones. Now at last he had the power to support that, and of course he wanted to use it.

I guess when the worm turns, it turns all the way. I thought about saying that, just to make him angry, make him storm out if I could – only then he'd get on the bike and storm all the way to Oz's and die stupidly, uselessly, alone. And then his parents would have lost both their children, and it'd be my fault both times, and...

No. I didn't say a thing, I just waited for Jacey to realise what idiots they both were, and calm everything down, and –

"Okay, good," Jacey said. "You and me, we are the big battalions, right? If we go in together, we're going in strength. Desi's got her Aspect, sure, that'll look after her – because you do know she's not going to stay behind, right? – but we'll take the rough stuff. No offence, sweetheart, but, well. I guess you achieved greatness, on this new scale of Jay's, but..."

How did I ever come to be involved with two such extraordinary morons? Simultaneously? What did I do to deserve this? Give me Thom any day, over these two. One might be regarded as unfortunate, but two...

I took a breath, and hit them hard below the belt.

"Have you forgotten the Green Man? *Both* of you? There was only one of him. And you were there, Jacey, and so was Asher, and so was I." *And so was Jordan, but he was still seventeen then, he didn't count. He was the trophy we were fighting for.* "Immortal doesn't mean what you think it means, if you think it means you can stomp lesser beings and not die. Ash died, remember? And Oz may not be immortal-born, but he's strong like anything, and, and *established*" – it was the best way I could think of saying that: they knew what I meant – "and he'll have half an army in there with him. You won't stand a chance, if you just go bulling in there on your we're-so-superior high horses. They'll tear you apart."

I said that last deliberately, so that they'd remember what had happened to Ash in all too much horrid detail, as I was. I don't think the male imagination works right, so they wouldn't be seeing their own selves torn apart that same way, as I was, but even so.

One of them shrugged; one of them scowled. Neither of them raised an argument. Both of them hated me, I guess, a little, for being right.

Jordan went back to the bar for more beer. It was easier to watch his back view than to meet Jacey's eyes, so I did the easy thing. I'm like that.

Besides, he does look good from the back. From the front too, actually, but I've always liked my boys neat and slim and callipygian, I've always admired the curve of a young man's back.

I don't believe I sighed, I'm not that gauche. I haven't sighed over a boy since I was an adolescent.

Jacey said, "You used to do that with me."

"What?" I don't believe I blushed; I haven't blushed over a boy since etc. I may have snatched my eyes back to the table. I may have looked stupidly caught-in-the-act. Whatever.

"Follow me all the way, without shifting a muscle from where you were."

"I was just..." I stopped, took a breath, met him eye to eye; said, "I'd be doing it with you now, if it was you up there fetching the beer." *And Jordan sitting with me here, in an awkward silence...*

"I don't think you would."

"Jacey –" I realised that I had no idea, none, where that sentence was heading – *Jacey, you and Fay were long ago, and she's not here any – ? Jacey, you're still the only – ? Jacey, Jordan and I were never – ? Jacey, come here – ?* so I stopped that one too. Instead, I turned my gaze stubbornly back to Jordan and made light of everything, said, "You know, it's only been a couple of days, but I swear he's moving differently."

"Well, he's not trying to hide any more. He used to want to disappear, every step he took. You could see it in him. That's if you could see him at all; he was pretty good at disappearing."

"Until I found him," I said. Was that a boast, or a confession? I wasn't sure. "It's more than that, though. He's got that sudden infusion of Overworld cockiness, he wants to strut because he doesn't know what else to do with himself; but all those years of self-effacing are still in him, they're built in deeper than muscle-memory, call it bone-memory, and – well, look. The rush of confidence gets mixed in with the discretion, and it's coming out as grace.

He moves like he's on a catwalk suddenly. I know girls who'd kill for that walk."

And then he turned with his hands full of glasses, and it was an absolute expression of balance, and I knew exactly how that felt because I felt exactly that way when I had my Aspect on, when I couldn't make an awkward move if my life depended on it, and –

Oh.

Oh, *yes.*

That, and Johnny Depp.

Just like dominoes falling over, pieces dropping into place, clickety-click and rat-a-tat.

*Now* I had a plan.

Now I just had to sell it. To Jacey and to Jordan, and I wasn't sure which would be the harder sell, only that both of them were going to fight it from start to finish.

Jordan brought beer, distributed beer, sat down.

I said, "Remember *Return of the Jedi?*"

Jacey would have scowled, but he was scowling already because I'd watched Jordan all the way back and I expect my face was a giveaway. It was Jordan who said, "Those bloody teddy-bears?"

"Ewoks."

"Whatever."

"Yes, but the good bit, the first twenty minutes."

"Leia goes into Jabba's lair in disguise to rescue Han –"

"– And gets caught, yes, that. And then Luke comes in alone and all heroic to rescue everybody."

"Okay, yes. What about it?"

"Darmok and Jalad at Tanagra," I said, changing the metaphor abruptly.

It only took them a moment to come back in unison, "Temba, his arms wide."

I love geeky boys; they make hard things easy.

Sometimes.

So then there was some hard arguing, because they didn't like it at all once they understood what the metaphor was. What I was using it for, which was just to bully them into doing what I wanted.

And then the pub shut and we had to go back, so we did that; and once we were across Mrs J's threshold I kissed both boys indiscriminately – because there had been quite a lot of beer, all told – and went to bed, leaving them no doubt to argue more between themselves.

And in the morning, well. We went our separate ways.

*Ride a cock horse to Banbury Cross*
*To see a fine lady upon a white horse.*

I'd thought I understood that. I thought I'd done it all already.

I was wrong.

# CHAPTER SIXTEEN

First to leave was Jordan, slipping out of the back door and the garden gate in the early morning, in the dawnlight. He went sneakily while Mrs J was laying tables for breakfast in the front room, for all the world as though he was hoping to avoid attention.

Before he left I kissed him, just because. My mouth still held a taste-memory from last night, and I wanted to check it. And yes, it was quite a lot like kissing Asher used to be; and no, it was nothing like kissing Jordan just a week ago. He tasted of desert places now, and his breath was a hot dry wind. He made me think of barberries, sweet and tart all together. Also, wine full of tannin: that sour leather mouth-puckering thing that young claret does, but you want to keep drinking it anyway.

I didn't keep kissing him. He was on a mission, and besides. Jacey was right there, and Jordan was

– well, not reluctant exactly, but nothing more than cooperative. Two days ago, he'd wanted to kill me. Half-wanted, maybe. Neither one of us had forgotten that.

So I kissed him out of curiosity, and then I let him go. He ducked off down the garden path, suddenly oddly awkward for a prince of Hell; we hung back watching through the window.

Birds rose up from a hawthorn hedge as he passed the gate, a crowd of them, a cloud. Then we couldn't see him any longer, not through Mrs J's net curtains. Jacey said, "Upstairs, quick," so we doubled back up just as she called us to table.

"Two minutes!" we cried, pelting on up to the boys' room, where they had a better view of the back lane.

A view of Jordan, for a precious couple of seconds: that white head unmistakable between the green and brown of the hedgerow and the grey of the road. Until there was a ripple in the air like the sudden heat-haze when a racecar engine starts, and then suddenly no boy.

"I've never seen that done before," Jacey said, "I've only ever been a part of it."

"Me neither. Me too." I'd wished plenty of people to go to Hell – out loud, quite often – but I'd never actually seen it happen.

And barely had time to process it before Jacey was pressing a damp towel into my hands and gesturing me back into the corner of the room. His towel, or Jordan's? I couldn't tell; I didn't even know if princes of Hell needed to shower. I was sure they didn't sweat. But then I rarely sweated myself these days, I mostly let my Aspect do the work, and I did still take showers all the time.

Jacey had a towel too, so either he'd showered twice or used two towels or else Jordan did too wash. Thinking back, I remembered that Asher used to, need or not, so that was probably definitive. Jordan wouldn't want me to say so, but Ash had pretty much defined the path his elder brother followed.

The air shimmered, right there in the room, between us and the rumpled double bed. There was a blast of scorching wind, and out of nothing, there was Jordan. Looking utterly nonchalant, hands in pockets, as though it was no work at all to shift from one world to another so precisely, to put himself exactly in this room that was upstairs and a hundred metres away from where he'd left.

You'd never know that he'd been counting every step from the moment he left. He played cool for all it was worth, until he chanced to look down and see the smoke rising about his feet, where he'd imported a little Hell-dust onto the carpet.

He yelped then, and danced out of the way. I grinned savagely, and joined Jacey in beating out the flames.

Well, let's not exaggerate. Just a few smoulder-spots: nothing that Mrs J would even notice, among the violent paisley patterns of her flooring.

"One down," Jacey said, "two to go. Desi, are you sure...?"

We'd been through this. We'd been through all the alternatives, over and over, and this was still the only plan that worked. "I'm sure," I said. "Get going, both of you. Jordan, you'll want this."

Blessedly, we both wore T-shirt and jeans as standard uniform. His were as new, as crisply black as mine, and as travel-worn and grubby; we didn't need to swap anything but jackets. He took my smart denim, I took his disreputable leather. Even he doesn't know how long he's had it, or where he picked it up. It had survived the streets with him; now he was making it survive the Overworld.

Right now, it was having to survive me. I have better shoulders, so it came closer to being tight; but it wouldn't hurt the thing to fit itself around a proper body for a while, before it went back to hanging shapeless over his scrawny frame.

He was wearing mine the same way, the way he always did, flapping open; I frowned at him and zipped it neatly up to his chin. While I was there, I rescued my phone from the pocket and replaced it with his own.

"Anything else?" I asked.

"Nothing I need," he said.

I nodded. "Me neither. Let's go, then."

So we trooped downstairs, where Mrs J scolded us for letting the toast get cold while she laid heaped plates before us, a full pirate's breakfast. Apparently pirates like bacon and eggs and black pudding and sausages and beans for breakfast, with toast and marmalade and pints of coffee and, "Are you sure you don't want porridge, anyone? Or kippers? It's no trouble."

We were sure, yes. Plates were wiped clean, but we were stuffed.

"Time to hit the road, then. Mrs J? Can we...?"

We'd conscripted her into this part of the plot, just because none of us fancied stealing from her. We'd had to lie, of course, but you get used to that. Jordan had concocted a sweet story about how I was on the run from a smothering relationship, a boy who loved me all too much. We knew he was lying in wait on the main road, because a friend had phoned to warn us; so the boys were going to act as decoys and lead him one way, while I scarpered in the opposite direction.

In pursuit of which, please, Mrs J...? *Dear* Mrs J...? You'll get it back, honest, but could we just borrow...?

We could; we did. She disappeared into her own quarters, and came back with Johnny Depp's piratical locks, the long dark wild wig her dummy wore beneath its hat.

We stripped out the beads and ribbons plaited into it, and – well, it still didn't look much like my own hair, but it was long and dark and that would do. Close enough to pass, if it passed at high speed on a motorcycle.

So that went on Jordan's head, and his vivid white crash-hat followed, just the same get-up that I'd worn yesterday. Once I'd sighed and zipped my jacket up again on his stubbornly scruffy self.

"Go on, then," I said. "And be careful, yes? No heroics. I hate dead heroes."

"And you," Jacey said. "You're taking more risks than we are. You're being *stupid*."

Which was true, but I was doing it anyway, and we were all resigned to that.

The boys went out of the front door then, while Mrs J and I watched from the window. Mostly, I was watching watchers. I quite enjoyed seeing Jordan playing me, sitting pillion on his bike as Jacey drove it away, but the rising birds held my attention. Three of us, and one had left already; here went two more; I hoped that birds could count. I hoped there might be a Corbie or a weregull among them, to do the counting better.

I had quite a number of hopes for the day, and precious few certainties. Only that it was down to me now, to be as sneaky as I could. I was on my own, which isn't really my best side; Jordan prefers it, but he's had the practice. Me, I like companions. So long as they do what they're told. Sidekicks, I guess. Subordinates.

Getting the boys there – well, that had been hard. Underling wasn't a natural role for either of them. Even now, I wasn't sure that they were quite persuaded.

Still: they'd gone, with a flock of birds to follow them.

Two down, one to go.

"Now, dear?"

"Please, Mrs J." *Before one of those sharp-eyed birds figures it out, or the boys do something stupid, or...*

If we were lucky, there was no one left to watch the house now. If birds could count. We couldn't count on that.

But Mrs J had a garage that adjoined her house, with a connecting door from the utility room; and for a wonder, she's one of those people who actually use their garage to park their car. So we went through together, and I did the movie thing of lying in the footwell behind the front seats, all covered over with the classic tartan blanket. Then she pottered about, raising the garage door and driving the car out onto the street and getting out to close the door down again, and being very obviously a single woman setting off alone.

I don't know if any bright-eyed birds were actually watching, or thinking in any way about what they saw, or reporting back to anyone. But we did it all as though they were, and then she drove to town and found a quiet alley to unload me, and made sure I had cash enough, and saw me around the corner to the bus station.


AND THEN I caught a bus.

One bus, and another, and one more; and then a walk in welcome sunshine, following tourist signs to Hawker's Hole.

I wasn't the only one. There were holidaying families and couples in clinches, solitary hikers and teenagers in gangs, all mooching in a slow parade through village streets and then up a country lane. Here was a pub – of course! – with a car park. Through the car park, and here was a path across a field full of cows, and a stile with a booth beyond. In the booth was a woman selling tickets, two pounds a time and kids half price. The teenagers weren't buying, not at any price; perhaps they'd try to sneak in another way, but I thought most likely they'd head back to the pub to try their chances, as soon as they thought their relevant grown-ups weren't watching.

*Good luck with that*, I thought, quite genuinely. Been there, done that. Adolescence is all about change, transition, trying to release your inner butterfly; alcohol is the magic potion that can make it happen sooner, brighter. Every kid knows that.

They couldn't all find themselves gifted with an Aspect, but they could all imagine it, work for it. Drink for it.

Talking of which: I paid my two pounds, trudged up the path, reached for my Aspect as I went.

Was glad to feel it settle across my shoulders, safe and reliable and there at my beck and call, not a hint of reluctance or over-reaction or independence of mind. Of course not, it didn't have a mind. But I'd almost grown used to having it bolshie or enthusiastic or absent, adolescent, unpredictable, the worst thing in a weapon. It was nothing but relief to face none of that, now of all times, coming home.

Its home, that is. In so far as a gift, a talent, a strength can have a home. A point of origin, at least. A source. I was bringing it back to the source.

With, um. Very different intentions than when we left.

Up the path, and here was the dark mouth of the cave, Hawker's Hole its own self; and here was its guardian, and here were all the people who had come up before me, gathered about. Emphatically not going in. It really isn't that kind of cave.

Wikipedia lists it as a petrifying well. Which is oddly appropriate, if only they knew. Perhaps they did; perhaps someone's being clever. Someone who knows Oz Trumby all too well.

Anyway. All along the upper lip of the cavemouth, there's a constant drip of water. If you want to step through into the cave proper, it's like walking through a cold brief shower. Only you have to duck, because there's a rope hung just below that lip, and all along the rope...

Well. There's a guardian, a man who's always there; he might be husband to the woman in the booth. She takes your money, he takes your precious things. Your toys, your teddy bears. Your baby's bootees. Your wedding veil. Anything that will soak up moisture. Love letters in a packet tied with ribbon. The hair you cut off in a plait when you were twenty-one.

He takes them and he hangs them from the rope, on their own individual string. Soon enough, they're sodden; but by that time you've gone, because what's the point of hanging around, what's the attraction? There's nothing to see here but dripping things.

Except that perhaps you come back in a year, a few years; and perhaps your offering is still up there, still petrifying. Hardening, whitening, turning to slow stone on its stiffening string.

If it's gone all the way, then it's gone. Once they're done, he takes them down to make room for the next. I don't know what he does with the stony things. Maybe he just collects them, in some hidden storage-cave. Maybe he gives them away, maybe he sells them far from here. Maybe he eats them, maybe he's a lithophage. Who can say?

I wasn't there to stand with the tourists paying homage, or the bored and scornful adolescents, or the tearful children realising what they'd lost. I wasn't there to make a sacrifice on any dripping altar, either. Unless I sacrificed myself. I might do that.

I might be mad, to come here.

Still. Here I was, all unannounced and hopefully unexpected. When you send people to fetch someone, and they don't come – well. You send again, maybe, and more persuasively, but you don't expect your quarry to turn up anyway, dangerously, independently. You don't expect your quarry to come hunting you.

When you think they're driving down to the other end of the country, you really don't.

Shouldn't.

I hoped.

THE PATH GOES on, past the dripping cavemouth and the busy little man. Sometimes kids run up that way, but they usually stop at the hedge, whether or not they can read the sign that says *Private – No Public Right of Way*.

The sign hangs on a gate of solid wood, like a door in a frame in the living hedge. It's all very Narnia. There's even a doorknob, and a keyhole.

If anyone had the key, that would be Oz; but one thing for sure, Oz wasn't trekking up and down to open it. Nor sending a minion. He liked his minions to come and go, any hour, day or night. The gate is never locked.

Turn the knob, open the gate, step through.

From the outside, the public side of this high hedge, it looks as though what it hedges against, what it's holding back, is open moor. That isn't true, exactly. There is a rising slope of bare rough ground, but this whole hillside is actually enclosed; where there isn't a hedge of maximum spiny unfriendliness, there's an impassable ditch. Unless you can fly, this gate is the only way through, or at least the only wise way. Even if you don't know what lurks in Oz's hedgerows and ditchways – does the phrase "were-leech" mean nothing to you? – the wisdom is easy to see.

It is possible to be both wise and foolish, both at once. Actually, it's commonplace.

I, even I, with my Aspect on and everything, I didn't try to leap a ditch or force my way through any hedge.

I, even I, knowing exactly what I knew about Oz and his cohorts, even knowing the absolute certainty that someone would be on watch, even if they weren't expecting me?

I opened the gate, and stepped through.


I WAS RIGHT, they weren't expecting me. If they were, there'd have been a bigger welcoming committee, more alert.

One bored wolf? Not a problem.

I've always fancied a wolfskin rug. Something to shock my vegetarian friends. Maybe I'd pick it up on the way out. Hell, if she hadn't wanted to contribute to my decor, she shouldn't have died in costume.

Sometimes, I was sure my Aspect got into my thinking. Fay had never been that coldly ruthless. Hell, Fay had been halfway vegetarian herself. Desi thought salads were animal fodder. And then she wanted to eat the animal.

Even Desi left the wolf for later, though: hung on that thorny hedge to bleed out.

The hillside rose surprisingly sharply, this side of the hedge. You couldn't see from the other side, but the hedge was planted right at its foot, just where a map-maker would have painted a contour line if they were working in 1:1 scale, direct equivalence, charting the actual landscape.

There was a well-trodden path from the gate around that rise, to where the same hands had set another solid wooden frame.

This time, the frame was in the face of the hill itself. Which somehow made all the difference, because you really couldn't call it a gate this time. That was a door. If it were only a round door, it would be a hobbit-hole, and that means comfort. Tragically, it was stubbornly oblong, and that means... Well. Oz. Nothing to do with comfort.

It was an unguarded door now, or I hoped so. He might have some little scuttling thing watching it from inside the keyhole, but there was really nothing I could do about...

Okay. I did crouch down and peer through.

Only quickly, and there was nothing to see: just a lit tunnel, an emptiness, a come-this-way-if-you-dare.

I did dare. I had to. I was the day's surprise.

Softly, then, and with my Aspect clamped about me like a second skin, I turned the handle on the hillside door, and pushed it slowly open.

Still nothing. The lights were foggy and romantic, storm-lanterns set in niches, wicks aflame in cautious chimneys, fire contained and safe. The tunnel was a passage sloping down, to the heart of the hill. Nothing moved, except the light and me.

I closed the door behind me, just in case. I'd have locked it, if I'd only had the key.


I'D BEEN THIS way before, but not alone and not trying to sneak. At every step I expected hidden doors to open, guards to step out. Fearsome guards, naturally. Or maybe they wouldn't bother with doors, maybe they'd just manifest from the walls, rock and earth compounded together into invulnerable creatures of terrible strength. Or they'd just watch me, strange eyes of dust lurking deep in every fissure; or...

I didn't skulk, then. It's hard to sneak without skulking, but I walked steadily down the centre of the passage, absolutely as far as I could come from hugging the walls. I was afraid the walls might hug me back, hands suddenly reaching out to snatch at me. I'd hate that.

So, yeah. Straight down the middle, open and honest, an invasion of one. Just call me Luke. Jedi powers and all.

Well, some of them. Even if they were only borrowed. I snuggled closer into my Aspect, and wished I could have sent it in ahead. Or instead, that would've been good...

Here was the curve in the passage, I remembered this, and the steps that led down to Oz's chamber. It was oddly quiet down there: no buzz of voices, so that I could hear the drip-drip of water quite distinctly. Hey, maybe he was sleeping? I remembered it as a bustle of activity, the heart of an empire, continuously beating; but I supposed he must have downtime, even he.

If he did, he was sleeping with the lights on – but only a few. There was a glow coming up, rather than a blaze. I remembered it as brighter than that.

Increasingly hopeful, then, I took those steps at a calm and steady pace. Down and around, and here was the chamber I remembered, a great vaulted cave where the walls ran with moisture and the stone shone in the light and the floor was always puddled like spilt milk.

And people had been coming and going before, splashing through the puddles, barefoot and reverent; but not now. Now only every other lamp was lit, and I hadn't realised there was so much open floor, or so many blackly gaping mouths around the walls, unlit passageways that might be leading anywhere.

Actually, of course, they all led here. They might be coming from anywhere, deeper in the hill, but here was what mattered.

Here was Oz.

The floor was only smooth and roughly level around the edges of the chamber. Towards the centre, it started to rise: first in ripples, like sand after the tide has drawn back, broken up by rivulets of water and all those standing puddles. Then it was more like abandoned sandcastles, heaps and softly rounded mounds of solid stone, some with an occasional drip still falling from high above to show how they happened, how centuries of water laid them down and built them up.

They're hard to notice, though, unless you're looking down deliberately, trying to avoid the real feature of this place. I guess a lot of people would do that. People here not by choice, people who've been fetched in to face reprimand or cold stone fury. You'd watch your feet, and see all the shining detail of that textured floor, only because you didn't dare raise your eyes to meet the master here.

Half of those rising mounds are dry now, because most of the falling water has been rechannelled. Workers must have clung to the ceiling, one way or another, high above that dreadful drop, constructing painstaking pipework, all so that Oz can have his steady unrelenting shower.

Those low rises are just outliers, hesitations before the main event, rocky reefs around a sudden island.

There's an upthrust, an irregular promontory of stone; and at its height, where the constant deluge batters down, that's where you look for Oz. Where people have looked year after year, for centuries.

Oz who was born human, and didn't want to die.

Oz who had found his own strange path to immortality: a path you didn't walk, a place to hunker down while time marched by and missed you.

No one knows quite how long Oz has been sitting there, in the keeping of his own petrifying well. Long enough that his skin has sealed itself into the walls of stone that have built up around him, so that only his head shows now, bald and sleek and running milky-wet. He sits a hard seat; he is his own throne.

What skin still shows is pallid past believing. Even the pupils of his eyes have bleached, a blue so washed-out they're hard to distinguish from the ancient ivory of the whites around. His gaze is perhaps the least human thing about him, except for the wish that set him there and the will that kept

him there, his determination to transform. Not to be
human at all.

I guess he got his wish. Normal mortality has
leached out of him like colour, as the minerals and
salts and I don't know what have leached in. The
borders between magic and science, between the
mortal world and the Overworld, are never clear;
they're smudged for all of us. For Oz Trumby,
they're positively smeared.

Those dreadful eyes of his were closed, and I
thought that was a blessing. Short-lived, because I
did need to wake him up, but a blessing nonetheless.
It gave me time to draw a breath, to look around,
to settle my nerves a little, be ready to play the cool
collected daemon for all that I was worth.

Then his eyes sprang open, and – well, no. Not
worth very much after all, my daemon act.

His mouth opened and his great fat pale tongue slid
out across his lips, just as mine did the exact same
mirror thing. Except that only one of us was doing
it deliberately; for the other it was purely instinctive,
as she found herself suddenly dry-mouthed and
trembling.

That was embarrassing, the trembling. I hated
embarrassing myself in front of him; which was
about all I had, that hatred, to stop me ducking my
head and staring at the floor as so many unfortunates
must have done before me. You could call it pride,
you could call it self-contempt, but whatever it is it
kept my chin up and my eyes fixed on his.

I didn't have enough left – courage, breath,
anything – actually to speak. I met his gaze, and that
was as much as I could manage.

He ought to be gross and leprous, a kind of calcified Jabba the Hutt, but really he's not. If he eats at all, I don't know what he eats; I'm guessing he pretty much gets his nutrition by osmosis, from the waters that run constantly over his scalp and skin and the stony growth that encloses him. Minerals, salts, whatever. Whatever he needs, clearly, but not much in excess. His face is lean; the rest of him is hidden.

Lean and hungry, yes, that too. When he smiles, you can't help but see his teeth. And think perhaps how good they must be, how strong, all that calcium; and wonder what he wants them for, how he uses them. Apart from the smiling, which he does deliberately often, just to be sure you've noticed.

He smiled. "Desdaemona. My prodigal child. You've been a long time gone."

I nodded, and wondered what would happen if I hammered with both fists on his rocky crust, if I could break through to whatever there was left of flesh within. Somehow, I doubted it. My Aspect didn't blink at brick walls, but this was different.

Besides, I'd have had trouble breaking a stick of spaghetti just then. Aspect or no Aspect. Oz can do that to you, just by looking.

Besides, he didn't seem at all surprised to see me. I'd been kind of counting on surprise, just to give me a brief edge, buy me a little time to do something. Say something. Something.

He said, "I am disappointed in you, Desdaemona."

I was disappointed in myself. I wanted to be kicking him to rubble; apparently I couldn't move at all.

He said, "I showed you kindness, I gave you gifts; I asked that you do a thing in return, not a hard thing, and you cheated me. You took everything I offered, and did nothing to earn or deserve it. Worse, you lied. You deceived me."

"Yes." I did indeed, all of that; there was absolutely no point in denying it. And at least I'd managed that single simple word.

"Yes. And now you are back, and not I think to visit. Not in a kind way. Have you come to lie to me again?"

"No, Oz." Confession is good for the soul, I guess; words came more easily, now that I'd got myself started. "I came to ask a favour."

"Ah, more? Still more, that I should do for you?"

"Yes. You should leave me alone. Me and mine, the people that I care for. You should promise me that. Call off the dogs, the birds. Everyone." And then I looked around and said, "Where *is* everyone?" and he giggled, and then I knew. "You were expecting me, weren't you?"

"Of course. Did you think you could surprise me? I knew you were coming; I always know where you are. I have followed your progress with, ah, an *intimate* care."

I thought his people had found me too easily, found me and found me. As though I carried a bug, a tracer; but Oz wouldn't use technology that way. I said, "How?"

He said, "What I gifted you." He didn't mean the house, or the boat, or the bankload of cash. I hunched more deeply into my Aspect, and wanted to wrap my arms around it, *mine!* "What you carry," he said, "even when you don't wear it; I could not lose track of that."

What, was it a trap as well as a weapon, as well as a defence? Yes, of course it was. I should have known. Today was a trap too, there were shadows moving in every tunnel mouth, Oz's people coming out all around me, but that didn't matter if I'd been betrayed already.

Just for information, because I like to know things, I said, "How not?" Probably I should have wondered more and sooner, how it was that Oz had Aspects in his gift; he wasn't an immortal, he only strained that way.

He said, "You wear the soulskin of a demon. We harvested it particularly for you – and of course we kept the demon close. He always knows where his skin is."

Oz has a repertoire of gestures that his face can make, all the movement that's left to him. They are brief, and clear, and precise.

I already knew that he wasn't speaking in metaphors, that's not his way. When he nodded – to my right and behind me – of course I had to turn, I had to see what suffering I'd caused, was causing, right this minute as I hugged my Aspect to me.

*Mine!*


I DON'T KNOW exactly what a demon is, but Jordan must. They inhabit Hell, I think. They're true immortals, I do know that. Oz must hate them, for that alone: a free and powerful creature that need not fear death, it's everything he wants and cannot have.

This one... looked like a fish out of water, stranded, hurting. Gasping.

Worse, it really did look skinned. Raw. Revealed.

One of Oz's thugs – some changeable creature currently in human form, shaped as a man – held it by the neck. He didn't need to. His grip hurt it, I thought, and it wasn't going anywhere.

Did I think that Oz looked hungry?

This thing was *starving*, and I was what it starved for. What I had, rather, wrapped all around me: its psyche-self, its soulskin. It should have been able to hurl that goon right across the room, tear Oz's people all apart, rip him from his stony shell and gut him utterly to find precisely how far the petrification reached inside him. Instead it could do nothing but stare, stare at me and hunger.

Hunger hopelessly: even if I gave it up, I didn't think the demon could inhabit its own skin again, any more than a cow could dress itself in cowhide.

Of course Oz had always known just where to find me. That stare would find me out if I was half a world away. Find me and hate me, hunger and despair.

I wanted to shrug the Aspect off, I wanted to give it back if I only could; but I seemed to be holding to it closer than ever, hugging it tighter and turning away from the demon's agony, turning my back.

Turning back to Oz.

Saying, "So. Will you let me be? Me and mine, all of us? Just wipe the slate clean, leave us alone, forget you ever had anything to do with me?"

"The slate," he said regretfully, "is very... busy. There is much written on it. Debts and promises and lies." He probably remembered when slates were the tools of use in inns and eating-houses; he certainly must remember when they were the tools in school. I wondered if anyone had ever shown him a computer, or a mobile phone.

I said, "Nevertheless."

He said, "Because you ask it? No reason else?"

"Yes," I said. "Exactly that. Because I ask it. Will you?"

He did seem to think about it for a moment, but I suppose he was only playing. Then he said, "No. No, I will not." Then he made another of those expressive gestures, to bring a couple of his goons up where they could grab me. If they did, I supposed I'd have to fight them. If I could, if the Aspect would work for me in here, where I'd first received it, with its poor source looking on. Likely it wouldn't. Oz was looking smug, as if he had a total handle on the day.

Before the thugs could reach me, though, I pulled the Zippo regretfully from my pocket and flipped the lid.

I really hadn't wanted to do this. Oz saved my life, when I was young and needy; it was a hard favour to forget.

But now he wanted that life back, and more, and I wasn't having that. He wasn't getting it.

Thom danced into life on the lighter's wick.

Oz's eyes brightened, with more than the sudden reflected dazzle of Thom's flame.

"Oh, you've brought him to me! You want to bargain, with what you should have given me before!"

"Well," I said, "no, actually. What do you think I am?"

And I turned with all the grace that I could muster in my pilfered Aspect – *surprised you that time, Oz, didn't I?* – and I tossed that good solid tossable lighter neatly towards the goon holding the demon who had given me so much and so unwillingly.

This was all I could give it in return: little enough, and briefly unkind, but I thought in the end – in the swift end – it might be grateful.

The goon was startled, but swift; he reached his free hand out to catch the lighter, the way you do when someone throws something in an easy lob.

Of course he wasn't thinking. It was a lighter; it was alight.

He might have burned himself anyway, only it was alight with Thom, which is a whole different seething flammable kettle of fish-oil.

Perhaps the goon was smart enough to catch a flaring lighter and not burn his fingers doing it. For sure he thought he was, he didn't snatch his hand back in all the time he had to think about it.

What he didn't think, he didn't think *that's a living flame, that is: that makes its own choices, and it's hotter than Hell...*

Thom skipped from the lighter's wick to the goon's thumb, a moment before the man could make his catch.

And then ran in a course of flame all up one arm and across the shoulders and down the other arm, leaving everything burning as he went, hoodie and hair and flesh and all. And lighted on the demon, and engulfed him.

Whatever they are, I guess demons carry something of Hell in their DNA. For sure, they are more flammable than mortal flesh. It went up like a torch. Immortal creatures die too, eventually, not always too soon; this was there and gone and ashes in a moment, a kinder touch than ever I had hoped for.

And Thom still hadn't stopped moving, though he didn't go after any more of Oz's people. They were panicking, anticipating, some of them running already, back into whatever damp cave they had come from.

I didn't think that would help, in the long run. Immediately, though, Thom danced to the nearest wall, and folded himself small, and vanished into a crack too fine to see unless you had eyes of flame and a shifting sense of scale.

Then I turned back to Oz and told him the rest of it, in case he hadn't worked it out yet. Or maybe I was really telling his people, those who were still hanging around, oozing out of shadow again now that the immediate threat had disappeared.

"Thom's not pleased with you," I said. "So now he's doing what you asked him to before: he's going down deep, to find fuel. Gas or oil if he can, but if not it doesn't matter. This is coal country; he'll find veins and veins of it, too fine for men to work. Not too fine for him, no. Not at all. D'you know, there are fields not far from here where the ground leaks smoke night and day, because the coal seam below is on fire? They can burn for decades, centuries maybe. Really, really slowly, because it's wet and there's not much air, they're like fires banked up for the night, just keeping themselves in. Smouldering away.

"Thom needs a place to be," I said, "and this will do him fine. Once he's got it burning nicely. It'll be too hot for all your friends, Oz, can you imagine? Smoky, too. This place will be like a chimney, drawing all the smoke together, puffing it out of your little doorway up top. Everyone's going to leave you, Oz. Everyone but Thom.

"Can you imagine?

"I don't actually know what'll happen to you. I don't know if Thom is flaming furious with you, or smoking, smoulderingly angry. Maybe he'll use you as a wick, in a sort of not-at-all-spontaneous human combustion. Maybe he'll burn you out of that shell and just leave the hollow shape of you behind, like those people at Pompeii.

"Or maybe not. Maybe he'll leave you to sit there in the heat and the smoke of it. You could live a long, long time that way, Oz. That's what you wanted, isn't it...?"

Oz was showing his teeth again, but he wasn't smiling now.

His eyes were frantic, darting about from wall to wall, from niche to shadowed niche, realising just how trapped he was. Trying perhaps to guess where Thom was, how deep down; where he might show himself when he rose again; what he might have done already. What he might choose to do next.

Still, Oz has always been about the detail. Even in his terror, he didn't forget what was important.

That's why the teeth, because he was snarling at his henchmen.

"Kill her," he said, to whoever was left, whoever hadn't run already.

I didn't bother to look around, to see who it might be. I felt hands closing on me.

On Jordan's jacket, rather, which I was wearing open, unzipped, the way he did, although it was cool down in the cave there and not cool at all to look so scruffy.

A thug grabbed for me, and I shrugged the jacket off and left it with him.

And shrugged my Aspect off and left that too, at last, a breath of sweet relief; and ran, like anyone with any sense was running.

Just me, just a fit healthy normal girl with no enhancements, running pell-mell and helter-skelter as fast as I could up the stairs and up the long passage towards the door and the world outside.

And getting there, chased but uncaught, unmolested; and pulling the door open just immaculately in time to surprise Jacey and Jordan, there on the threshold, two golden boys, princes of the Overworld come to rescue me, just exactly too late to do it.

# CHAPTER SEVENTEEN

LATER, WE SAT perched side by side, all three of us on the big white bike where it was parked up in a layby. Squeezed between them, I kicked my heels against the Beemer's flank and sipped brick-red layby tea bought from a van. The boys were eating something unimaginable, warm and greasy and pressed between the halves of a flabby white bun. Drive-by dining. Each of them had offered me a bite, but that was ritual, not real; they were only teasing. They knew how revolting it was. They must do, they were eating it.

Besides, I was mad at them. Not in the mood to let them feed me. Or tease me, either. Not yet. Not till I'd done with scolding them.

"You were supposed to be leading Oz's spies *away*, you morons!"

"We did that," Jacey said, scowling at a drip of red sauce on his jacket, scooping it up on his finger, sucking it off. "For half the morning, for a hundred miles we did that. We figured that was far enough."

"So then you just turned round and headed for the caves, and drew everybody's attention to exactly where you shouldn't?"

"By that time we figured you'd be in and out. Or in, at any rate. Needing help, maybe. So we came back, a bit quicker than we'd gone."

"Less wind resistance, once I'd dumped that bloody wig."

"Oh, Jay, you didn't? You'd better buy Mrs J another one. God knows where you'll find one, though..."

"Make him go back and find this one," Jacey said maliciously. "Teach him to go tossing things into hedgerows."

"*Any*way," I said determinedly, dragging us back to what mattered, which was me scolding them till they were sheepish, "you just brought all the trouble back with you. Or you could've done. What if the Corbies had been following you? You'd have led them straight to me."

"We did try to call you," Jacey said, "but we figured you probably didn't have a signal, all that underground."

"Or maybe I'd turned my phone off, sweetheart, not to let it give me away when I was sneaking in and idiot boys started phoning..."

"Oh. Yeah. There would be that."

"It was an idiot plan anyway, mind," Jordan said. "It's not exactly sneaking, if you go right up to him and have a confrontation."

"Worked, though, didn't it?"

"Only because we arrived just in time to save you

from those musclebound hulks pounding up behind you."

"I could've –"

"No, you couldn't," Jacey said. "Not without your Aspect."

And that was true, of course, and something to get used to.

"Will it, y'know, just die now? Now that the demon...?"

"I don't know. I don't want it back, though. Even with hulks on my tail and you not around. That's why I left it, I just couldn't..." Simply the thought of it made me shudder, now. Now that I knew what it was, where it had come from, what the price had been. The boys felt that, I guess; they both leaned in a little, nicely sharing the duty, holding me tighter without either one of them needing to risk a positive statement, a claim, an arm around me. That might look territorial, and they were treading so cautiously around the margins, it was really rather sweet.

"Of course not," Jacey said. "You wouldn't want that. We can do it better, anyway. Whatever you want, but clean. From the top. From my dad. Or from Jay's." Ducking territoriality again, or maybe remembering just too late how very much I didn't like his father.

"Both," Jordan said. "Why not? The best of everything."

"No," I said. Slowly, because it was a big decision; flatly, finally, because it was my decision and I discovered that I'd made it. They would treat me like a minor royal, load me down with honours that I hadn't earned, the best of everything. Power, immortality, more money than I could ever spend. They were offering me the world, more worlds than one – and I shook my head at them and said no, and it was really hard to do that, but it was still the right thing to do. I'd loved being a daemon, right until the end there, but...

"No," I said. "I don't want superpowers, I want just to be a girl again. Nothing extra. I want to be human, I want to live in the same world that regular people do. Now I'm not running away and I don't have to hide any more. I want to get strong in the gym, stay fit in the pool. I want to defend myself the old-fashioned way, martial arts. Maybe I'll take up cage-fighting. I want to be able to scare the pair of you stupid."

Jordan gave me his twitchy, anticipatory smile; Jacey said, "It won't be easy, just being a regular girl. While you're still spending your time with us, I mean." There was no *if* in there, no option of a doubt. "A foot in each camp, you could get torn in two."

I wasn't entirely sure that he meant it quite the way he said it, as if he was talking about the mortal and the Overworld and nothing else. Nor was he sure, I think, once he'd heard himself.

I guess we were all listening, all hearing the same thing. All very aware of the three of us, sitting here in complicated company. It was Jordan who said, "So what do we call you, then? Now? You were Fay before" – *when you were with Jacey*, he was saying – "and Desi when you were a daemon." *When you were with me.* "So what now?"

He wanted another decision, a declaration. This way or that, or maybe the other.

"Idiot boy," I said fondly. *I'm not answering that.* "We'll work something out." This way, that way. Maybe the other.